Children of
Covenant

Children of Covenant

Fred Howard

ISBN: 1540894800
ISBN 13: 9781540894809
Library of Congress Control Number: 2016920565
CreateSpace Independent Publishing Platform
North Charleston, South Carolina

For My Grandchildren
With the hope that their generation will live in a more peaceful world.

Part I

When Abram was ninety-nine years old, the Lord appeared to Abram, and said to him, "I am God Almighty; walk before me, and be blameless. And I will make my covenant between me and you, and will make you exceedingly numerous." (Genesis 17:1–2 [NRSV])

Chapter 1

May 4, 2016

I smael Hagarson could not believe what he was hearing.

"So what you're saying is they won't sell the property to *us*!" he said, with more anger in his voice than he meant to display.

"That's not what I'm saying at all, Mr. Hagarson," Sonny Harden calmly replied. "Mr. Street has decided not to sell to anyone. He's thinking that he may reopen the store. He needs something to do with his time. So, he's taking it off the market." The words slid out of Harden's mouth smoothly and evenly as if they had been rehearsed for days.

Ismael was representing the local Islamic community in their attempt to buy Street's property for the masjid they hoped to build. *Masjid* is the Arabic word for mosque. Mr. Street's department store had been empty and on the market for over two years, and they had made him a generous offer, well above the appraised value of the property. Ismael expected there to be obstacles in building a masjid in a small town in the Deep South. But acquiring property was not one of them. Street's old store, which they sought to buy and renovate, was run-down and on the south side of town.

The town, August Valley, had seen steady growth since the middle of the twentieth century. But that growth was almost exclusively toward the university and the air-force base, both located north of the downtown area. The south side of town languished, and vacant storefronts were more the rule than the exception. Anyone who owned them had little prospect of selling or renting. However, despite this less-than-desirable factor, the location had many advantages for the Islamic community. It was about as close to a central location as they could either afford or hope to obtain, given the community's ambivalence to the idea of a mosque in their town. Also, as it was formerly a department store, there was ample parking. Parking for a congregation requires plenty of land—quite expensive close to city center. And the building, with a few minor modifications, would serve their needs well.

Muslim communities have learned through experience the many obstacles they may face in getting through the permitting process and other local governmental red tape. Many mosque projects have been delayed or scrapped entirely by obstructionist city and county commissions that used inadequate parking as a convenient and politically expedient way to deny them a permit.

"But that old store has been for sale for two years," Ismael countered, trying to regain control of his emotions. "Strange that he should change his mind now that he's finally gotten a good offer."

"Now, Mr. Hagarson, you have to know how Mr. Street is," replied Sonny, relaxing as he began to feel that control of the conversation was now his. "He never wanted to give up that business. When I showed him your offer, I guess the reality hit him that he's about to give up his dream of reopening one day."

"Bullshit!" Ismael exploded. "He has no intention of reopening." Seething as he spoke, Ismael had no intention of backing down now. "His buddies on the city council got to him. They don't want a mosque anywhere near this town, and this is the best strategy they could come up with to stop it."

Ismael's outburst threw Sonny off balance—though Ismael's anger was not entirely unexpected. "You're taking this all wrong," Harden said. "What I'm telling you comes from Mr. Street and no one else. The Muslim community has been a presence in our city for many years, and we've always gotten along just fine, haven't we?"

Sonny's conciliatory words did little to assuage Ismael's growing anger. While it was true that the Islamic community had been meeting for several years in a small house in a run-down neighborhood near downtown, the general feeling among the Muslims was that they were barely tolerated. In no way did they feel that they had "always gotten along fine" in the community at large. Though they did get along well with immediate neighbors at their present location, city officials had acted rather coldly toward them in any business they tried to transact in August Valley.

"We've gotten along, as long as we stayed in our place, where we weren't too visible," Ismael replied. Once again he was trying to regain his composure. "Few people even know we're around in that little house of ours. But if we were down here on Main Street, visible from First Baptist and First Methodist Church, then the town would have to deal with the reality of our presence."

Harden sought to regain his equilibrium. "I assure you that has nothing to do with this situation or with Mr. Street's decision," he said in as matter-of-fact a voice as he could muster. "Besides, as I'm sure you know, real-estate law forbids any kind of discrimination on the basis of religion or ethnicity. Our firm would never be a part of discrimination of any kind."

Ismael, having his retort at the ready, responded, "This situation has discrimination written all over it."

"That would be difficult if not impossible to prove," Harden replied. "I'm certain the Muslim community wouldn't want to endanger its goodwill in August Valley by pressing the matter. And I'm sure if we work together, we can find another suitable location for your mosque."

"Suitable? Suitable to the city council or to us?" Ismael sarcastically replied. "How far out of town would it have to be to be 'suitable'?"

"Now, now, Ismael. Is it okay if I call you Ismael? We want to work with you in every way we can. I'm speaking for Real Estate Associates, of course. I can in no way speak for the City of August Valley."

"Then you admit that the city had a part in discouraging this sale."

"No, no. That's not what I mean. I just meant that we have several other properties that would meet both your community's needs and the city's zoning requirements."

"Ah, yes, the zoning requirements. That's what scared the city council and made them twist Street's arm not to sell. They knew they would have a hard time finding a way to stop our project with some nitpicking zoning clause. With churches all around us, it would just make it too hard for them to deny us the zoning permits. So, they somehow convinced Street not to sell so they could prevent the project up front. What is it you Southerners call it? 'Good ol' boy politics'?" Ismael, ethnically and religiously Muslim, was born and raised in August Valley and had a firm grasp of Southern language and culture.

"This is no conspiracy against the Muslims," Harden told Ismael. "I'm afraid you're a bit paranoid, my friend. And you're vastly overestimating the power and reach of the city council. Let's look at this from a purely practical standpoint. The council knows how much Muslims contribute to the city's economic base. We get a third of our taxable revenue from tourists, and just about every motel on our stretch of the interstate is run by a Muslim family. The Muslim community is valuable to us. Why would we possibly want to antagonize them?"

"That stereotype of my people offends us very much." Ismael's tone shifted momentarily from anger to hurt. "My family is one of those families you speak of. For many Muslim immigrant families like mine, running a motel is the only work they can get. It's honorable work, and it's work we can do without compromising the principles of Islam."

"I meant no offense," Harden replied rather unapologetically. "We also have many Muslim doctors in town and college professors, like you. Brilliant people and well-respected professionals."

"Well-respected people who have no decent place to meet and pray," Ismael responded in a mellower but still rather cool tone. "Look, Mr. Harden, August Valley is not ground zero. We're not trying to build our mosque in a place that might be offensive to the people of this town. This isn't New York City. My people are decent, hardworking citizens who just want the same things everyone else wants. Earn a living wage, raise our families, be with our friends, worship God. Why won't this town allow us to do that?"

"No one has any intention of stopping your people from doing that," Harden declared, wondering how the phrase "your people" would sit with Ismael. Harden was astute enough to know that the phrase was a potential PC bomb; however, Ismael had just cleared the way for Harden to use it when he referred to the Muslims as "my people."

"I don't know what else to say," Harden declared, wishing he'd never gotten involved in this deal. There was no upside for him now. No commission, no satisfied buyer or seller. Only the knowledge in his heart of hearts that, though he'd done everything right according to the law, Ismael's suspicions were on target. The city simply didn't want a mosque intruding on its genteel, homogeneous Southern landscape.

Though multicultural change is inevitable in a town with a modern university and a military base, for the typical small town in the South, that's just a concession in the mind. A highly visible mosque at the center of town would mean conceding, finally and materially, that their cultural and religious landscape as they knew it was forever gone with the wind. And the city simply wasn't ready. So, consciously or unconsciously, it was resisting with every means at its disposal.

"Mr. Street's decision is final, I'm afraid." Harden just wanted to go home. He felt unclean and wanted to take a shower.

"I won't accept that," Ismael replied, with defiance still in his voice. "I'm going to talk to Street myself."

"I don't think it'll do any good," Harden said, relieved that—at least emotionally—Ismael was taking him out of the loop.

"Allah will see that justice is done." And with that, Ismael stormed out of Harden's office.

Stepping out of Harden's office into the street, Ismael wondered how he could distance himself from all that had just occurred. The sun was setting when he'd first arrived for his meeting with the realtor, and now it was completely dark. The streets of August Valley were busy with locals patronizing the city's many downtown restaurants and watering holes. Though the streetlights were now on and provided more than ample light, they did little to dispel the darkness in his mood. The town seemed more menacing than ever.

Though it was two blocks away from Harden's office, Ismael's car was in front of Street's store. He'd parked there on purpose, in anticipation that he'd be able to gain access to the inside after his meeting with Harden. For weeks now, plans had been taking shape in his imagination for the floor plan and design features of the masjid, and what parts of the existing structure would remain, and what parts would need renovation. He was anxious to survey the inside of the property again. That is, until Harden's news changed everything.

As he walked up Main Street toward his car, trying to sort through his anger—trying to sort out toward whom he needed to direct it and why—Ismael saw a light on in Street's store. Once he got directly in the front of the store, he could make out the figure of someone moving about in the back office.

Chapter 2

May 5, 2016

" he word *Islam* means submission," Ismael told the group of students gathered around his desk the next morning. This particular group of graduate students had stayed after class to question him further about his religion. The class was currently studying the political situation in the Middle East, and the issue of religion's impact on the region's conflicts had come up in the class discussion. One student asked him specifically about Islam and its unique role in Middle East tensions, since it is both a religion and a political philosophy.

Ismael taught political science and, like the conscientious professor he was, stuck to the subject he was paid to teach during class time. But today, as Ismael gave objective academic answers to the students' questions, some of the students wanted to prod their professor further. So Ismael invited those interested in exploring this issue further to stay after class. A few were curious enough to accept his offer and take advantage of a chance to quiz a congenial Muslim about his religion.

"But submission to what?" Ismael continued. "To God, of course. Allah. *Allah* is simply the Arabic word for God. But what does it mean to submit to God? People have so many different ideas about God. Who says what God says? For the Muslim, it's the words of the Quran, revealed to the Prophet

Muhammad as a direct recitation from God to him during his periodic retreats into a cave over a period of twenty-three years beginning in AD 609."

"I tried to read the Quran," one of the students said. "In English, of course. It talks about Moses and Abraham and Jesus just like the Bible does."

"The Prophet considered the Jews and Christians of his day to be 'People of the Book' and entitled to respect," Ismael said. "Muslims see the Quran as a continuation of the Old and New Testaments, not a replacement for them. The Quran assumes its readers are familiar with the Bible stories and its cast of characters. Just like much of the Christian New Testament would make no sense without knowledge of the stories and culture of the Old Testament, so it is with the Quran. Adam, Noah, Abraham, and Moses are all referred to in the Quran, and we Muslims hold them in high regard. The Quran talks a great deal about Jesus and considers him a great prophet. The scriptures of the Jews and the Christians are meant to be read alongside the Quran as parts of a whole. Think of it as humanity's developing understanding of the nature of God and our relationship to him."

"But the Quran doesn't read like the Bible does," the same student said. "As I said, I tried to read it, but I didn't finish. I just couldn't follow it."

"That's frequently said by people of other religions who try to read the Quran," Ismael explained. "The reason is that the Quran is not so much a story but more like a collection of sayings. It assumes you know the stories in the Bible, but it doesn't focus on the stories themselves. Instead it focuses on interpreting the stories, exploring their spiritual and moral significance."

Another student said, "Muslims call Muhammad 'the Prophet.' So, does that make him like Isaiah, Jeremiah, and Ezekiel?"

"That's right," Ismael said. "All those prophets you mentioned are revered by Muslims as well, because their writings are part of the Umm al-Kitab, the sacred scriptures. The Umm al-Kitab is considered a continuous story that begins with the Old Testament, extends through the Gospels, and ends with the Quran. The Prophet Muhammad is considered to be 'the Seal of the Prophets,' because his message, the Quran, is seen as the final revelation in this sequence of scriptures.

"So, that's why Muslims think their religion is the most true?" another student said, expressing his statement as a question.

Ismael was pleased at the inquisitiveness of these students. He was also glad that they felt comfortable enough with him to converse freely and ask such questions.

"Don't people from all religions think their tradition is the best one, the one that is the most true?" Ismael smiled as he said this. "Take Hinduism for instance. It is the oldest of all the great religions. It's like the grandfather of all religions since it has the longest heritage. Buddhists might think of themselves as superior also, because their religion is about surrender of the ego. They are unique because they claim no God. They've avoided a lot of the hefty baggage associated with that word, 'God,' and the idea of a special tribal deity. Jews make no bones about their specialness. They say they are God's chosen people. Christianity claims special dibs on its brand of truth, because they claim Jesus is uniquely divine. Islam became no less prejudiced than any other religion about the unique superiority of its truth. Our religion developed in an Arab population hungry for its own special message, and history obliged us by giving us one."

Ismael didn't say it, but personally he sometimes wondered to what extent Islam's brand of exceptionalism, with Muhammad as the Seal of the Prophets, forever closed out the possibility of further revelation and shut out all hope of interfaith dialogue and understanding. In Ismael's experience the Muslim community was only beginning the hard work of asking itself that question.

"But, Professor, don't terrorists use the Quran to justify their war on our country?" another student asked. "I heard an interview with one on TV who said the Quran told him to fight the jihad, the holy war. Fight those who fight you on the path of Allah."

"I won't deny that some extremists, just a tiny fraction of people claiming to be Muslim, interpret the Quran in such a way," Ismael said, his countenance becoming serious. "But if you search the Bible, you can find plenty of scriptures there that can also be interpreted hatefully. The Quran's message, just like the Bible, is basically one of peace. A well-known passage in the Quran says, 'Whoever kills a human being, it is as if he has killed all mankind.' That pretty clearly promotes peace and condemns any act of terror."

Ismael knew he wasn't being completely truthful with that last remark. The verse he was referencing actually said, "Whoever kills a human being, *except as punishment for murder or other villainy in the land*, it is as if he has killed all mankind." Terrorists gave themselves wide latitude in what they considered "villainy in the land." Any of the United States' meddling in the Middle East qualified as such, in their opinion.

Ismael faced a dilemma familiar to many Muslims living in Western society. He tried to live in two worlds. To inhabit the Muslim community as a true follower and yet at the same time completely be a part of the Western world's ideal where everything could be an object of scrutiny—even one's religious faith. He liked to think of himself as a "prog," a progressive Muslim. The term "progressive Muslim" is not an oxymoron, regardless of the monolithic view of Islam held by many conservative groups. Islam is a diverse religion, composed not only of different denominations (for example, Sunni and Shia) but also of adherents with widely differing capacities to reflect and think critically about what it means to be Muslim.

Recent developments did give Ismael hope that reform was underway in Islam. For the first time in history, it seemed the stage was set for reform in Islam to finally happen. Why? Well, for the first four hundred years or so—that is, up until the advent of the Internet—interpreting the Quran, the Sunnah (lessons from the life stories of Muhammad), and the hadith (the sayings of Muhammad) was pretty much completely entrusted to the scholars and clerics of the Islamic community. Religious authority resided with these institutions, and they guarded the tradition, and their power within it, fiercely. The cyber revolution was beginning to change all that. Young Muslims today were much more likely to seek religious or spiritual advice from sources available through the Internet or social media. As a result, educated Muslims were less and less afraid to ask critical questions and speak openly about matters of religion. A tradition whose members had for so long been mired in fear was finally approaching escape velocity.

Since 9/11 Ismael, like many Muslims, had rededicated himself to Islam. One's faith is never dearer than when one senses that it may be lost or "hijacked" by some extremist minority. Initially, after that horrific event, he had tried to walk away from Islam. But at his core, he ultimately realized being Muslim was who he was. He wouldn't let the fringe element define Islam for him; he found a new determination to define the faith for himself.

Further, Ismael had long ago admitted to himself that his loyalty to Islam was inextricably enmeshed with his loyalty to his mother. His mother came to America in 1971 as a refugee from the Pakistani civil war. She had no money. However, she was fairly fluent in English and soon was able to find work in the motel industry as so many displaced Asians did at that time, becoming a part of the "Patel motel" phenomenon. The motel industry is a natural fit for Muslims. It's the family living together, working together, creating their own self-sufficient community.

His mother was pregnant with him when she came to America. His father had been a casualty of the war, Ismael learned as he grew up. He was raised by a single mom, working long hours at motels, staffing the reception desk, cleaning rooms, and doing laundry. She worked hard, lived frugally, and was eventually able to take a managerial position in the lodging industry. This was fine for her, but Ismael's mother wanted better for her son. She wanted him to get an education and become a professional. She encouraged him through all his years of school and did everything she could to make sure Ismael was able to attend college when the time came.

His mother was fiercely dedicated to the Islamic faith. The reason for that ferocity was a bit of a mystery to him. She came from a family that was at best only nominally Muslim. Yet she attended the masjid faithfully once one was finally organized in August Valley.

Ismael remained restless that evening, still ruminating on his unpleasant meeting with Harden. Sleep eluded him for hours as he went over and over the events of the day. When slumber finally overcame him, it was fitful and disturbed by alternating dreams.

In one dream, he was a child again, and his father was alive and living with him. He was helping his father collect wood to build a fire. While in the dream, he couldn't make any sense of what he was doing, because he saw no food to be cooked. When he asked his father about the purpose of the fire, his father would only answer him in riddles.

His other dreams were haunted by his encounter with Street in the back of his store and their odd, inexplicable conversation. What was Street going to do? Was there any significance to Street's nervous fidgeting with that length of rope as they had talked?

Chapter 3

May 2, 2016 (Three days earlier)

Ike Benheart had no idea what Lee Street wanted to talk to him about. Street had called the Unitarian church's office last week and asked Ike, the minister, to call him back. When Ike returned the call, Street volunteered no information. He just wanted to meet with Ike at his office as soon as possible.

Street was part of a prominent family in August Valley. He was one of four siblings—three brothers and a sister—who shared in the inheritance of Street Inc., a large enterprise started by their father. Patterson Street Sr. had started this forest-products company to capitalize on the family's vast landholdings in and around August Valley. Each of the brothers was involved in the various business ventures. Lee concentrated on commercial real estate and, until two years ago, operated a large department store downtown. The Streets were also quite active in local politics.

Lee was the only one of Patterson Street Sr.'s four children without children. He'd never been married, at least to Ike's knowledge.

But what made Lee's call especially odd was the fact that Street had never darkened the door of the Unitarian church where Ike was the minister. The Streets were members of First Baptist. Having grown up in that same church as the preacher's kid of its minister, Ike knew the Streets' commitment to that church was strong and their religious affiliation unwavering. It wasn't likely Street was coming to consult Ike about a religious matter. Street's only special request when he called was that they meet in the evening. Ike simply passed that off as signifying nothing but Street's busy schedule.

Street appeared nervous and unsure of himself as Ike invited him into his office and offered him a chair. Ike sat in the other chair positioned in front of his desk angled to partially face Street's. Street had brought with him a notebook and a Bible. Ike was immediately curious. And a little wary. *What a fearful little man,* Ike said to himself as he took full stock of his visitor.

"Thank you for agreeing to meet with me, Ike," Street began. "I understand your church welcomes gay people. I'm trying to get a handle on that. Our church recently did a study on the Bible and homosexuality, and I'm trying to sort this thing out for myself. Our pastor taught the class, and he made his theology quite clear on this matter. But obviously other ministers see things differently. I was hoping you could explain your theology and help me understand how you arrive at your interpretation of some of the Bible's teachings on this issue."

Lee Street must be a closet gay! Ike couldn't help but think to himself.

Ike responded, "It's interesting to me that you would question your pastor's teaching on this matter. In my experience, most people just aren't curious enough to do that. They simply accept whatever their minister and their religious community teaches them. So, I'm wondering what's happened to stir up your doubts."

"You're quite insightful, Ike," Street replied. "I have a nephew who's gay. Gordon's son. He lives in Atlanta. I worry about him. I'm worried about his soul. Sometimes he seems so depressed. I worry that he might do something drastic. I often ask myself if he's going to hell for this." Street fidgeted and broke eye contact with Ike as he related this information.

"Is that what you learned in this class?" Ike asked.

"We learned that homosexuality is an abomination in the sight of God."

"Leviticus, chapter eight, verse twenty-two," Ike answered. "You shall not lie with a male as with a woman. It is an abomination."

"Yes," Street replied, turning his Bible to the passage. "You know your Bible well, Ike."

"Being one of the few churches in the South that welcomes gay people, I keep a few scriptural references at the ready whenever I'm questioned," Ike explained. "Did your class spend any time talking about the situation of the Hebrew people when this part of Leviticus was written? What their historical and cultural context was?"

"Not really. Leviticus was written when the Hebrews were in captivity, wasn't it?" Street said.

"Yes, that's right. This passage is part of what's known as the 'holiness code' of the book of Leviticus, which was written by the Jewish religious leaders during the Babylonian Exile. The holiness code was a behavioral covenant, a sort of survival pact, meant to give the Jews in exile a distinct identity and to see themselves as a separate people from their captors. Their leaders knew that, unless they set the people apart and gave them a sense of separateness and national pride, they would quickly be assimilated into the Babylonian culture and disappear forever from history."

Continuing, Ike said, "Leviticus eighteen twenty-two is a favorite of those who choose to condemn homosexuality. It's short and to the point. Those who would make their feelings clear on where they stand on homosexuality seem to especially like that word *abomination*. The point is made so well and so concisely that it's plastered on billboards up and down the interstate by church groups partial to the not-so-subtle message contained in this passage and in the companion passage in Leviticus chapter twenty, which prescribes the death penalty for such an act."

Street read this passage also. "That's quite interesting, Ike. But the message here is pretty clear. Homosexuality is a sin punishable by death." There seemed to be resignation in his voice as he said this.

"Right," Ike agreed. "But if you accept that verdict, then you must also accept the verdict that children who talk back to their parents must also put to death."

"What?" Street responded incredulously.

"As you see there, the same holiness code in Leviticus twenty that prescribes death for homosexuality also condemns other offences such as cursing one's parents with the same harshness and imposes the same penalty for that offence. It's right there in an earlier verse in Leviticus twenty. 'All who curse father or mother shall be put to death.' I have to wonder whether people who get so incensed about homosexuality would want their children punished in the same way the first time they were caught sassing their parents? Seems just a bit ruthless to me."

"Okay, I'll agree with you on that," Street conceded. "But what about other places where the Bible mentions homosexuality? Like Sodom and Gomorrah."

"I believe that story is in Genesis chapter nineteen," Ike said.

Street turned to Genesis.

"This story tells about two angels who appear in Sodom as ordinary men traveling through the city," Ike related. "It seems that rumors have gotten back to God about how wicked the city is, and God sends these angels to check it out. The two men arrive in Sodom late, and it appears they won't be offered hospitality by anyone. In this lawless society, this leaves them at the mercy of these thugs and sexual predators. Abraham's nephew Lot, knowing how dangerous it is for these strangers to be left on the streets at night, offers them hospitality and takes them home with him just before sundown. Lot's actions spoiled the plans of the gangs that watched the strangers come into town and were eagerly anticipating a night of sporting sex. They threaten to break into Lot's house unless he surrenders his two guests to the mob. The two strangers make like angels and intervene to save Lot, his wife, and two daughters. Then God rains fire and brimstone down on the whole city and destroys it."

"That's a good summary of the story, Ike," Street says. "Our pastor said the fire and brimstone was meant to show us God's wrath toward homosexual desire."

"Yeah, sure, like that's the only thing that got God riled up in this story. Never mind that Sodom is completely ruled by these thugs that are free to break into someone's house and gang-rape guests at will. Surely that wouldn't have anything to do with God's wrath, would it? God was only offended because all this lustful activity was directed toward members of the same sex. Please, Lee. Give me a break."

"I hear what you're saying, Ike. But still, that's what our pastor says, and that's the way people in our church believe. That God condemns homosexuality."

The fear in Street's eyes, momentarily displaced during their conversation, had returned to his countenance with a vengeance.

As Ike suspected, Street's problem wasn't intellectual. It was emotional. It wasn't what the Bible said. His problem was what his minister said it said. He'd been "raised right," which meant he had become the sort of person one became when raised by God-fearing, regular churchgoing Bible-belt parents. Being raised right, he'd been taught from an early age to put great store in every word of the religious authority of his community. The minister being the highest authority.

Lee no doubt imagined God as a stern, brooding father figure standing eternally behind the universe, keeping it under constant surveillance. God's love was conditional—dependent on our willingness and our efforts to keep his commandments. And ignorance of these commandments, these laws, was no excuse. God might be merciful, but we shouldn't count on it. Better to know what God wanted from us and do our utmost to keep our performance up to standard. Was homosexuality a sin? Interpreted narrowly and uncritically, the Bible seemed to say that it was, though Lee also seemed to know the passages could be refuted. Otherwise he wouldn't have come to Ike for a second opinion.

For moral clarity, most people need an authoritative religious voice. Street's minister had no doubt offered this class to settle the matter once and for all for the sake of his flock. If Street wished to remain a part of the community, he would have to accept the prevailing view that homosexuality was a sin—an abomination to God.

Such a prevailing view places homosexual Christians in a catch-22 situation. They have nowhere to go with their true self. They can deny themselves and their sexual identity, admit their homosexual desire as sin, and confess. Or they can live in the hell that this narrow understanding of Christianity creates for their true nature.

Confession, according to the Christian spiritual paradigm, functions to unburden the sinner. The penitent admits the transgression before God to a priest or minister and is thereby relieved of the heavy weight of guilt. The sinner has laid down the sin and, if truly contrite and accepting of absolution, never has to shoulder its heaviness again. The minister acts as an arbiter for God, and the act of confession often carries a greater gravitas when done in the presence of one of God's intermediaries, a priest or minister. According to this spiritual physics, the mass of sin is not displaced; it disappears altogether, miraculously vanishing forever from the cosmos.

God might be forgiving if someone repented of an abomination. But if homosexuality is the true nature of the person, his or her true identity, then "confession" would amount to no more than a denial of true self. To "confess" one's genuine personhood as a "sin" requires such a soul-torturing repression. Yet, according to the literalist, fundamental paradigm of Christianity, if someone acknowledges homosexuality as sin yet continued living such a lifestyle, then that person is hopelessly mired in sin and beyond God's mercy. That person certainly couldn't be a Christian. That person is condemned forever.

Like many Christians caught up in literal-minded communities, if Street were to come out as gay, he faced the bleak prospect of being both cast out of his church community, hell on earth, and cast out of heaven in the afterlife. Presuming he was indeed gay as Ike suspected.

And now Ike was more convinced than ever that this was the case.

Chapter 4

Ike grew up very close to his mother's sister's son, Steve. Close, that is, both geographically and emotionally. They lived at opposite ends of the same street in August Valley. Hardly a day went by that they weren't playing together or spending time at each other's house. Born within a month of each other, they were more like twin brothers than cousins.

Though Ike said he always looked up to Steve, looking back now he realized what he really felt was envy. Steve was talented and smart and had a flair for art. He loved to draw and paint, and there was evidence of his gift everywhere. The walls in his room, his high-school notebooks, even scrap lumber his father left lying around in the garage were ample canvases for him to reveal the uniqueness of the way he saw the world around him. It was almost like a compulsion. If he was near a pencil or a crayon, and there was a flat surface around, he was going to be sketching something.

The August Valley of those years was no different than any other small town. There were no secrets. You might tell someone something and swear him or her to secrecy, but once one person knew, everyone knew. The grapevine was more dependable than the local newspaper, and certainly faster in its delivery. Also, typical of small towns in the South, its values were steadfastly conservative. Particularly when it came to sexuality. Homosexuality was denounced, privately as a matter of course and publicly from the church pulpits of most every denomination. Particularly from the pulpits of the Baptists.

So, when Steve decided to come out to his family at the age of seventeen, his condemnation was pretty much a given. He started to be shunned by his church family. No one spoke to him unless they had to, yet everyone seemed comfortable talking about him behind his back. They said Steve was "confused" (the euphemism of choice) about his sexual orientation, a figure of speech which was actually quite ironic. Steve was anything but confused. He was certain about his feelings toward members of both sexes. Otherwise he never would have had the courage to come out, risking the love and acceptance of his family and community.

After overcoming the shock of the news, Steve's family decided to hate the sin and love the sinner, accepting him in private while disapproving of his professed behavior in public. He endured the taunting and teasing of his friends and most of his relatives as long as he could. Within a few weeks, he could stand it no more and left town.

Rumor had it that he went to Savannah and found a gay community there. He phoned his mother occasionally, but no one else at home ever heard from him. He was absent for over a year. Then, unannounced, he showed back up.

It was Thanksgiving Day. His mom always cooked a big spread, and everyone in the extended family was there. Ike could never forget that day—try as he might. It had chiseled itself into his memory.

Steve arrived before the holiday dinner, surprising everyone, including his mom. He seemed genuinely glad to be home, and glad to see everyone. It was like old times. His family was so delighted to have him home, and everyone was having such a good time that thoughts of what brought about his exile seemed to be forgotten, at least for a day. Forgotten, that is, by everyone but Steve.

After dinner, as everyone was breaking away from the table and going off to watch the ball game or put away the food, Steve excused himself and went outside to his father's pickup truck. He reached in the gun rack, took out the shotgun, got a shell out of the glove compartment, loaded it, put the barrel of the gun into his mouth, and pulled the trigger. He would no longer have to endure his inner turmoil.

Days later, an uncle of Ike and Steve's would explain it to the family in this way. "It was the gay community Steve took up with. They were the ones that incited Steve to do this."

What a convenient explanation for Steve's uncle and for the entire family, church, and community. That explanation absolved them of all blame for what Steve had done. The guilt and shame that his family and friends had heaped upon Steve had nothing to do with his suicide, in his uncle's tidy accounting.

His church family came up with a similar satisfactory explanation. Satan had had a hand in it, they said, and when the reins of your life are given over to evil, terrible things befall you. Ike was incensed by how easy it was for all of them to find a way to tell the story to absolve themselves and make each other feel better.

However, Ike came up with his own explanation. When Steve left home and made his way to Savannah, he found a place where he was accepted for who he was. But even though he began to find himself while living in the more supportive environment of the city, he could not escape the voices from his past that continually spoke to him of sin and shame. To silence those voices, Steve found it necessary to go back home and perform one more act.

The ties of family and faith are strong, and his community got a graphic demonstration of just how powerful these ties can be. By his act, Steve placed his body and the blame squarely at the feet of those responsible for this tragedy. His church had condemned him to this fate. His family may have loved him and welcomed him, but they had done nothing to intervene and protect him when the community inflicted guilt and shame on him for his homosexuality. No family or friends stood in solidarity with him. Isolated and alone, he saw no option but to take his own life.

To say that Ike took Steve's death hard would not begin to capture his sadness, frustration, and anger. He was completely devastated. The loss left a hole in the pattern of his life, a hole that he had trouble filling. Previously an outstanding student, his grades began to suffer. He alternated from sullen to angry, with no in between. He turned to alcohol for relief. His teachers noticed the change, but no one intervened. Close to graduation, Ike was allowed to coast through the remainder of the year mostly based on the merits of his previous academic excellence.

In the wake of Steve's suicide, Ike made a decision that changed the course of his life. To honor Steve, he resolved that for the rest of his life, he would stand up for the dignity and the rights of gay people no matter what it cost him. While this decision wasn't the one that led him into ministry—he had long ago decided to follow in his father's footsteps—it did play a significant part in what kind of ministry he would have. He could think of no better way to advocate for people like Steve than to reform the church and its stand on homosexuality.

Long gone were the days when Ike would allow himself to suffer a conversation like the one he had just endured with Lee Street. Homosexuality had long ceased to be a debatable issue for him, and he usually refused to listen to the biblical arguments of conservative Christians against gays. For Ike, listening to such arguments would be just as absurd as listening to someone argue the case for the slavery of African Americans, the subjugation of women, or any of the many other oppressive points of view that have been advanced in the past by using scripture to deny full humanity and equal rights to certain groups of people. Sifting through the Bible to find ways to condemn people is a hateful enterprise, and, from the day he was first ordained, Ike vowed to resist the proponents of this view with all the resources at his disposal.

Ike had answered Street's questions only because Street came across as sincere in his intentions and listened as if he was honestly seeking answers. Though it pained Ike to listen to the usual litany of biblical quotations Street's minister had fed him to justify fear and hatred of homosexual people, he heard Street out. *Obviously, the guy was questioning his minister's views*, Ike thought. Otherwise he wouldn't have approached Ike. Ike listened and answered Street honestly, hopeful that Street might be open and receptive to a more inclusive view on the subject and able to transcend the onerous verdict of his church community. Hopeful, that is, but certainly not optimistic.

Chapter 5

May 6, 2016

Ismael drove onto campus that morning still trying to dispel the dark mood that had engulfed him from his meeting with Harden evening before last. As he pulled up to the building on campus where his office was, he noticed several squad cars in the parking lot. This was rather curious. He found a parking place with some difficulty, stuffed some exam papers he'd been grading into his briefcase, and headed into his office. When he got there, three officers, including the sheriff, were waiting outside the door. The sheriff asked Ismael to step inside.

Once inside, the deputy closed the door.

"Are you Ismael Hagarson?" the sheriff asked.

"Yes, I am."

"You're under arrest, Mr. Hagarson."

Stunned, Ismael could only think to ask, "On what charge?"

The sheriff answered, "For the murder of Lee Street."

Chapter 6

"What? This is ridiculous," Ismael muttered to the sheriff as the deputy placed the handcuffs on him. He felt all the color drain from his face. "I'm a peaceful man."

"You'll get a chance to tell your side of the story, Mr. Hagarson. But right now, you will need to accompany me," the sheriff replied matter-of-factly.

"Lee Street is dead? What happened?" The sheriff made no comment but just repeated to Ismael that he would get a chance to tell his side of the story. Then the deputy read Ismael his Miranda rights. The officers then escorted him out of his office and the building. By this time a crowd had gathered around the building to see what the commotion was about. Ismael had to suffer the indignity of a perp walk in front of his colleagues and many of his students.

Ismael tried to remain calm. He did a mental review of what he knew about the night in question. He rode to the police station in silence. His head was spinning from the shock of all this. Street was dead. Here he was accused of murdering him. What could have happened after his odd encounter with Street two nights ago? He knew he had best keep silent until he had a chance to talk with an attorney. He knew being a Muslim placed him at a disadvantage in American society and, by extension, in the American legal system. He'd better not make any wrong moves. How much deeper his regret was now that he'd shown anger that night. *Harden must have reported my display of temper to the police. Why else would they think I'm the one that killed Street?*

Chapter 7

May 7, 2016

Ike stared in disbelief at the headline on his iPad as he drank his morning coffee. "University Professor Under Arrest for Murder." The day before he had learned of Lee Street's death, but details were sketchy, and reports were conflicting. This article was the first Ike had heard about Ismael Hagarson being suspected of the murder.

The whole situation seemed surreal. *What in the world is going on?* Ike puzzled to himself. Obviously, Street was dead. But what circumstances would have implicated Ismael Hagarson, a Muslim?

Whatever the circumstances were, one thing was certain. August Valley's little corner of the world was now changed forever.

"Honey, what's wrong?" Becky, Ike's wife, asked, noticing her husband's look of intensity and concern as he gazed at the news. "Some disturbing news this morning?"

"They've arrested a professor at the college for murdering Lee Street," Ike replied.

"What? What's his name? What possible motive could he have had for killing Street?"

"Whoa. One question at a time. His name is Ismael Hagarson. He's Muslim and teaches political science. The article doesn't give much information as far as motive," Ike said, "except to say that Hagarson was negotiating to buy Street's store so that the Muslims could build a mosque there. Apparently, Street refused to sell it to them."

"So they're saying this guy Hagarson murdered him over that?" Becky asked.

"No, of course the article doesn't say that. It just gives the facts as they are known."

"Street's been trying to sell that place for years," Becky said. "Amazon put Street out of business. Independent department stores are dinosaurs in this economy. If the Muslims wanted to buy it, I'd have thought Street would jump at the chance to unload that property."

"Well, I know the city council wouldn't be too thrilled about the prospect of a mosque right there in downtown August Valley," Ike suggested.

"I'm sure they didn't like the idea," Becky was quick to retort. "Lots of people in this town would have problems with it. Like those kooks at that anti-Muslim rally at the courthouse last week. That got a lot of people's attention. There are some really scary people in this town," Becky emphasized this last remark, watching her husband's response. The Muslims weren't the only targets of prejudice and bigotry in this town. The Unitarian Church had received its own share of threats over the last few years because it supported gay rights.

"Those types try to scare others because they're scared themselves," Ike replied, his voice breaking as his anger surfaced. "They're afraid of anything new. They're afraid because they see the world is changing, and it scares the living hell out of them. They don't want to have to give up their feelings of superiority."

"Well, they scare me. There's no telling what they're capable of doing—to this Ismael Hagarson or to you," Becky stated, her voice full of emotion.

"You know I'm always careful." Ike got up from his chair and embraced his wife, trying to reassure her. "But you also know that I'll never live my life in fear."

"When I walked in the kitchen," Becky said, "you had this concerned look on your face. I remember that look from college. It's that same countenance you had when you got so passionate about the Student Interfaith Ministry. You're not thinking of getting involved in this case because you think this professor is being targeted because of his religion, are you?"

Ike didn't say anything to his wife, but he was torn.

Should he say anything about the conversation he had had with Street two nights before his death? So many thoughts were stirring in his head. If this Muslim killed Street, perhaps it was a hate crime, and the Muslim did it because he knew what Ike suspected—that Street was gay. But what if there was a possibility that Street committed suicide? Shouldn't that be obvious to the police? Did Ike really want to present evidence that might help the Muslim's case? Time had not changed Ike's ambivalence toward Islam.

There aren't many Muslims in the United States, less than 1 percent of the population. The percentage is only a fraction of that tiny percentage in most places in the South. That, combined with the relatively sequestered life that most Muslims choose to live, means that someone living in this area of the country can easily live out his or her life and rarely if ever have any contact with the Muslim community. Ike didn't have to worry too much about his feelings toward Islam. He didn't expect any Muslims to attend the church. There were hardly ever any interfaith events in the community of August Valley. For the most part, Muslims were barely even perceptible. So likely he wouldn't have to worry about addressing the prevailing anti-Muslim sentiment imbedded in Western society in general and in the South in particular. Nor would he likely ever have to deal with his own negative feelings about Muhammad and his disdain for the violence Islam seemed to foment.

Maybe he should wait until more details about Street's death emerged. Specifically, how he died and whether or not suicide was even a possibility. If it wasn't even possible, then there was no need for Ike to say anything. That would be a relief—not having to give testimony that might aid a Muslim. But if the Muslim was innocent and he said nothing, Ike wouldn't be able to live with himself. No, he knew he was likely going to have to say something—to somebody—because it was the right thing to do. Damn. Integrity. Sometimes a costly trait to hold as part of one's self-image.

Being born and raised in August Valley gave Ike the perspective of an intimate insider. Knowing local politics the way he did, Ike had every reason to suspect that the city council would have done everything in its power—whether ethical or not—to prevent the mosque from going forward. Ike had seen the rights of minority groups trampled on before in his hometown. The cleverness of local politicians in using technicalities to deny people their First Amendment rights knew no bounds. Fear and bias aren't valid reasons for failing to permit a mosque, but some obscure zoning regulation or land use clause could easily be invoked. Ike had good reason to wonder if something like that had happened to get this Muslim riled.

Ike also had the insider's edge in understanding the religious climate of his hometown. His father, Abe, had been the pastor of First Baptist Church of August Valley—the same church Street attended. As the preacher's kid, Ike's parents had regularly deposited him in Sunday school from day one so he would be given the finest upbringing in the conservative Christian doctrines of unreflective biblical literalism. He marveled once again at how far his journey of faith had taken him since those formative years.

He smiled wryly as he remembered studying the Hebrew patriarchs during those Sunday-school years. God had promised Abraham that he would be the father of a multitude of nations. However, when Sarah was unable to conceive, she gave her slave girl Hagar to Abraham, and Hagar bore him a son, Ismael. Years later Sarah finally became pregnant and had Isaac. Sarah didn't want Ismael sharing her son's inheritance, so she demanded that Abraham cast out Hagar and Ismael. According to legend, Isaac's progeny became the Jewish people, and Ismael's descendants became the Arabs. In that Sunday-school teacher's view, this story explained why Jews and, by extension, Christians, do not get along with Arabs and, by extension, Muslims.

Easy explanations have a way of perpetuating themselves, Ike thought, especially when they neatly resolve some of the capriciousness of history and make the world as given to us into an intellectually tidy package. Explanations satisfy and thereby suppress whatever impulse we may have toward critical thinking. The sibling rivalry of Isaac and Ismael is a powerful allegory that functions well in explaining centuries of religious and ethnic strife. But just because it seems to work as explanation doesn't mean that there aren't other ways to look at the story.

The story of Isaac and Ismael had begun to haunt Ike, especially since 9/11. Isaac and Ismael were brothers. Maybe only half brothers, but definitely close blood relations. Why didn't the world place emphasis on this aspect of the story, the brotherhood of Jews and Arabs? Instead, the world chose to focus on the dysfunction of Isaac and Ismael's parents. How tragic, Ike mused, that all the millennia of bitterness and hatred between the Semitic people started, according to legend, because of a family squabble.

The irony of the present situation suddenly hit Ike. If Ismael Hagarson had been denied the property to build the mosque as the newspaper suggested, the mythic story was once more repeating itself. Ismael had, to a certain way of thinking, been cast out again.

Chapter 8

Ismael had a visitor to his jail cell. Someone he had never met, a fellow identi-fied to him by the guard as Rev. Ike Benheart. Ismael had no idea what the reason for his visit was, but he assumed that because he was a minister and came from a liberal church, he was there to make some gesture of pastoral support.

The guard ushered in a tall, clean-cut, neatly dressed, pleasant forty-some-thing man. Ismael did not recognize the face—but he knew the name.

"Professor Hagarson. My name is Ike Benheart. I've come here because I have some information that may help your case."

"Come in, Rev. Benheart. Please, have a seat. Can't offer you much in the way of hospitality. This is all rather embarrassing for me," Ismael said as he gestures to the chair and moves to sit down on his cot. He pauses a moment to compose himself and assess his visitor before proceeding. "I hope it's true, that you have some information to clear all this up. Because I know nothing about Mr. Street's death. But the police think I did it, and nothing has come to light so far to change their minds."

"I had a conversation with Lee Street two days before he died," Ike informed Ismael. "I have reason to believe that he might've been suicidal," I didn't report it at the time, because he just seemed nervous and maybe a little depressed. I just didn't think of suicide at the time. Who does? But when I heard he was dead, well, then the thought he might've killed himself immediately came to me. But I don't know the circumstances. Or even whether suicide is a possible explanation. Why don't you tell me what you know, and then I'll let you in on what I know."

"I'm not sure if I should," Ismael said. "I don't think I'm supposed to talk to anybody until I check with my attorney."

"Who's your attorney?" Ike asked.

"Jim Harbuck," Ismael replied.

"Good man."

"Yes, I hope so. I've only met with him once. Right now, he's doing some investigating and filing the papers to try to get me released on bond. But he told me for now I'd be safer in here. There's people in this town that don't like Muslims."

It's pretty easy to understand why, Ike thought to himself. Like so many people in the Western world, he had problems understanding Islam as well.

Like many ministers in his faith tradition, Ike had studied Islam rather extensively during his seminary years. Then, when in training, it had not been uncommon for him to cross paths with Muslims in the process of doing interfaith work. But, despite his best efforts to grasp this sister religion, he'd come away from the struggle with a sense of defeat. Ike wanted to say to Ismael, "Can you understand why people might feel that way? Just look at the headlines on most any given week."

Instead, Ike said, "Being Muslim must put you in some rather difficult situations. Particularly this one."

"Well, I'll admit we Muslims have something of a PR problem," Ismael responded, "With all the extremist nut jobs grabbing headlines these days. But these anti-Muslim wackos are pretty extreme too. There's been hate crimes against us in other towns, and some of these around here seem capable of violence as well."

"How's your family handling all this?" Ike asked. "You have family?"

"Yes, a wife and a son. Her name's Eisha. She's pretty devastated. It's been tough for her, enduring the isolation and suspicion that's cast our way because we're Muslim. Now this. She just wants to hide, or leave. But she can't hide, and she won't leave because, like a good Muslim wife, she's going to be loyal to her husband."

"Any other family?" Ike asked.

"Not in the area, but Eisha's sister came from Michigan to be with her."

"How about you? How are you holding up?" Ike continued, fully in pastoral-care mode now.

"I'm scared," Ismael confessed, his lower lip beginning to quiver. Then, taking a deep breath as if to jump in and rescue himself from emotionally drowning, he added, "Circumstantially, I know it looks pretty bad for me. But I didn't do it. I'd never harm anyone. I'm a man of peace. Just ask anyone who knows me."

"I believe you," Ike said, which wasn't exactly a lie. He didn't know what to believe, except that, based on his conversation with Street, suicide was certainly a possibility. "And I'm here to try to help your case. That is, if what I know can be of any benefit."

"What is it you know?" Ismael prodded.

"I had a long conversation with Street on the Monday night before his death on Wednesday," Ike said. "He was…how should I say it…not in a good place. Emotionally. Spiritually. I have reason to think he was depressed. Have they told you how he died?"

"Harbuck told me," Ismael recounted. "He'd been hung. They found him in his store, hanging from a rafter. Hands tied behind his back with a zip-tie."

"Could it have been a suicide?" Ike asked.

"That's one of Harbuck's theories," Ismael said. "He's checking it out. It's pretty hard, though, to tie your own hands behind your back."

"Hard, but not impossible," Ike said. "Any signs of a struggle?" Seeing how large a man Ismael was, he realized the Muslim would have had no difficulty in subduing Street.

Ismael could tell from Ike's stream of thought that he was a person who grasped things quickly and examined all possibilities. Ismael was beginning to like this Rev. Benheart. "Harbuck said the pictures in the police report showed an overturned chair and a broken display case. These could be signs of a struggle. Could also have been caused by the victim thrashing about as he choked to death."

"Maybe he left a suicide note," Ike speculated. "Have they searched for that?"

"The police did a thorough check of his office in the store when they investigated the scene," Ismael answered. "No note was found. Harbuck requested a warrant to search his home. Haven't heard about that yet. If Street wrote one, he didn't leave it out in the open."

"Okay, but...I'm still fuzzy on why you are the prime suspect," Ike suggested, changing the subject. "The paper said you were negotiating some kind of real-estate deal with Street. So what? Why should that make you a suspect?"

Ismael studied Ike thoroughly and thoughtfully. *Should I trust this guy? I've got to trust someone.* After a long pause, he began.

"I'd never had a conversation with Lee Street. At least I hadn't until that night. We—the Islamic community—has been trying to buy his store and renovate it so that we can have meeting space. But we've done all our negotiations with the real-estate agent." Then Ismael recounted the conversation he had had with Sonny Harden that evening and how he'd lost his temper. "I left the real-estate office angry. It appeared to me they were discriminating against us just because we're Muslim. I told Harden I wanted to talk to Street myself. Then I went to my car, which I'd parked on the street in front of Street's store. I saw a light on. I tried the front door. Locked. So I went around back, and the door was open. Knocked and went in. Mr. Street was in his office there just inside the door. He acted as if he didn't hear me, because he didn't get up. I didn't want to startle him, so I said, 'Mr. Street, could I talk to you?' He acted as if in a trace or something. Or maybe he was just drunk. There was an open whiskey bottle on his desk - nearly empty. He never looked at me. Just said, 'Now is not a good time. Come back later.' He was fiddling with something on his desk. Thinking back on it, it might have been a rope, but I'm not sure. It was dark and...it was all just so weird. The way he was acting. As badly as I wanted to talk, seeing him like that, I just lost heart. So I left. That's it. That's all I know—until the police show up at my office yesterday with a warrant for my arrest."

Ike listened thoughtfully. After a pause, he said, "So you got angry in front of Harden—and that's the sole basis of their case against you?"

"That, and the fact that I was seen going into the store that night. Oh, and one more little detail. I'm Muslim. And in this country—in this town—that's probable cause."

"Muslims are human too, aren't they?" Ike retorted. "Or did I miss something in my world-religions class?"

"All too human, I'm afraid," Ismael confessed.

"Sounds like you had every right to be angry," Ike found himself saying. "Your suspicions about the powers that be discriminating against you are probably spot-on. Though probably difficult to prove. I know this town. Born and raised here. They'd stoop to most anything to prevent a mosque from being built in this town."

"Well, it's beside the point now," Ismael replied. "The mosque is now the least of my concerns. I've got a murder rap hanging over me. Shouldn't have let my anger show. Huge mistake."

"Unfortunate, but just circumstantial. Unless...say, you didn't threaten to cut off Harden's head or anything. Or did you?" Ike said, unsure as to whether Ismael would see the humor in this, or just consider it in bad taste.

"Cute, Rev. Benheart," Ismael responded. "Too bad I didn't have a knife handy, or I might have."

"Call me Ike. Well, talk about PR problems; now, if you had said that to Harden, it would definitely have created one," Ike quipped. "Seriously, what does the Quran tell Muslims to do when they get angry? The Bible says Christians are supposed to turn the other cheek."

"Okay, Ike. And please call me Ismael. The Prophet Muhammad, blessings and peace be upon him, called anger a hot coal on the heart of a descendant of Adam. Once he was asked what a strong man was, and he replied, 'The one who is strong is the one who can control himself at the time of anger.'"

It didn't surprise Ike that the Quran mentioned Adam—the one from the Genesis story. Islam claims heritage to the same canon of stories as the other Abrahamic faiths, Judaism and Christianity. However, in Islam these narratives seem to have a different function. For Jews and Christians, religious meaning is inherent in the stories themselves; that is, it's the stories themselves that reveal the character of God and humanity. For Muslims, the stories serve mostly to validate the authority of the Quran's teachings by demonstrating its common origin in humanity's sacred memory. And ultimately, unlike the narrative theology of the Bible, the Quran doesn't show; it tells. Said another way, the moral teachings of Islam share many similarities with those of Jews and Christians, as their ethics are all derived from the same storehouse of stories. However, Judaism and Christianity encourage their followers to use the stories in scripture to cast light in finding the right way along life's path, whereas Islam's teachings are more explicit. This may make right and wrong more black-and-white in Islam, but at the same time more fraught with the dangers and potential evils of any system that tries to legislate morality. It seemed to Ike that the strict dictates in morality and behavior required by Islam and the fact that this demanding way of life occasionally got twisted toward terrorism and evil in the mind of its extremist followers were just two sides of the same coin. In any case, in his estimation mindless, unreflective submission was always potentially dangerous.

"I'd say you did control yourself," Ike consoled. "You didn't act upon your anger. That's what matters, I think."

"I think the Prophet meant more than that," Ismael surmised. "At any rate, just showing anger in this case is what put me in here." Ismael changed the subject. "Ike, what are you going to do with the information you gathered about Street that night? Talk to the police?"

"Doubt if it will do much good, but I'm willing," Ike said. "If you like, I'll talk with your attorney first. Harbuck will know what's best."

"Would you do that? Thanks so much," Ismael acknowledged. "Are you sure you want to get involved in all this?"

"No. Not really." Ike had thought long and hard about bringing up what he knew and about coming to Ismael. "But I do know that I couldn't keep quiet. Not when there's the possibility that what I know could prevent an innocent man from being convicted. Tell Harbuck to give me a call. I'll fill him in."

"Absolutely," was Ismael's response. "And thanks for coming to see me. Right now, I can use all the friends I can get. Maybe that's presumptive of me—thinking of you as a friend. But I am very grateful."

"Sure. We'll see," was Ike's reply. "Glad I came. Can't say as I've ever known many Muslims."

"Well, I know you quite well, Ike," Ismael said, surprising Ike. "That is, I've known about you for years. My mother, Gera, God rest her soul, told me about you. She knew your mother and father quite well. They're the ones who settled her in the United States when she came here as a refugee."

Chapter 9

Ike was startled by Ismael's revelation. Was it true? Seemed unlikely. Baptists, at least as Ike had experienced them, just weren't the type to become involved in humanitarian efforts for people of another religion. No, that wasn't a fair characterization. They might provide aid for refugees—if, concurrently, there was also an opportunity to evangelize. Make converts. Was that what had happened with Ismael's mother? If so, why hadn't his parents ever told him about their involvement in a ministry of settling refugees?

Ike went home directly from the jail and did a little research on the Internet.

He discovered that the Pakistani Civil War, better known today as the Bangladesh Liberation War, started in 1971. That would likely have been the crisis that led Ismael's mother to become a refugee in late 1971 or 1972. This all happened before Ike was born in 1975. He read further.

The UN estimated that ten million people were displaced by that war. Most of them fled into India. The violence took on proportions of genocide. West Pakistan troops were slaughtering unarmed East Pakistanis in the streets, firebombing crowded marketplaces, shooting homeless beggars asleep in the streets, bayonetting small children in acts of blind rage and hatred. The East Pakistanis were provoked to barbarities as well. Tribes turned against tribes, and the Bengalis, the majority tribe, turned against the Biharis, suspecting them of sympathizing with the West Pakistanis. The Biharis, predominately Muslim, were murdered by the thousands.

The displaced of all tribes flooded into India, quickly overwhelming the capacity of the government there to provide for them. The ones who could fled to other countries. Eighty to one hundred thousand of them found their way to the United States and, because of the relaxation of immigration laws here in 1965, were able to come in that large number. Churches from various denominations helped with the settlement of the refugees, including the Baptists.

The historical circumstances fit with the tantalizing tidbit of information that Ismael had shared. What didn't make sense to Ike was why his parents had never shared this particular story. Through the years, Ike's parents had told him about many of their ministries and missionary efforts. He had heard about many to the point that he wearied of hearing them. But never had he heard about this one. This seemed odd to him. Why was he having to discover this part of his parents' history from a complete stranger?

Ike knew enough about himself to know that he would have to learn more. If his family had some connection with Ismael's family, he needed to find out more about it. Though Ismael had come across as an agreeable sort of fellow in their first conversation, Ike still felt a deep reluctance to help Ismael out.

He had felt jaded about Islam since college. It had been fifteen years since he lost a college buddy from Cambridge during 9/11, and time had made him a little more circumspect about that. But deeper and more personal for him was the general hostility of Muslims toward gays. Ike couldn't get past that, and he still harbored some deep resentments toward anyone or anything Muslim.

Perhaps the knowledge that his parents had once helped Ismael's mother out could help him get beyond this emotional barricade. Besides that, Ike was a bit intrigued. Not just about the details of what had happened in 1971 and what his parent's involvement looked like, but more about why it had been kept a secret. Ike had an uneasy feeling that there was some significant history here that, for some inexplicable reason, had been intentionally kept from him.

Chapter 10

Jim Harbuck called Ike the next day. Harbuck was a well-known criminal defense lawyer in town and had gained acquittals in some high-profile cases. As a classmate of Ike's, Harbuck was also one of the few lawyers in town with whom Ike was on a first-name basis. Ike agreed to meet him at his office.

Ike found it interesting that Harbuck had taken the case. Defending a Muslim accused of murdering an eminent citizen of August Valley seemed an unlikely way to enhance an attorney's prestige in town. And Harbuck was all about prestige. Or so Ike had always thought.

The two of them were good friends in high school. They played baseball together and even double-dated a couple of times. All that was before Steve's suicide. After Steve's death, Ike did a dramatic 180-degree turn when it came to locker-room banter about gays. He didn't just quit participating when the group starting teasing someone about being gay. He became a crusader.

At first his circle of friends, including Jim Harbuck, tried to get him to lighten up. He not only refused but got more and more vocal in his opposition when the playful barbs alluded to gays. His closest friends made some effort to avoid joking about the subject, which helped for a while. But not everyone cooperated in toning it down. One day a teammate provoked Ike into a fight. After that happened, many people just started avoiding Ike. Harbuck was one of them. The coolness in their relationship persisted after they both graduated and returned to August Valley to assume their careers. When they encountered each other around town, Harbuck would be civil enough and make conversation, but he always maintained a polite distance. As did many of Ike's childhood friends. It seemed Ike was no longer considered one of them.

"Ismael told me you have some information that might be valuable to his case," Harbuck began.

"Perhaps. Street came to talk to me on the Monday night before he died on Wednesday. He had a lot on his mind."

"What he told you might very well be critical to this case," Harbuck said.

"Only if there's a chance that Street took his own life," Ike countered. "Do you think he committed suicide?"

"I'm not thinking anything yet," Harbuck answered. "I'm trying to get all the facts first.

"No suicide note?" Ike asked.

"No note has turned up yet," Harbuck answered.

Ike told Harbuck about his conversation with Street that evening. Harbuck jotted a few notes as Ike recounted the conversation. When he'd finished, Harbuck leaned back in his chair and sat there thoughtfully for quite a time.

Finally, Harbuck spoke. "You think Street came to see you because he's gay?"

"Yeah, I do. He struck me as someone at the end of his rope—uh, so to speak. Bad taste, I know, considering the way things turned out. I could tell he was upset…and that he took this issue of homosexuality being a sin really seriously. That's something I have some personal experience with, as you know. A gay person feeling tormented by feelings of guilt. I know how it can torture them and what they are capable of doing in their desperation."

"I know you do," Harbuck said. "Steve's death still haunts you, doesn't it?"

"He's always with me, if that's what you mean," Ike said, his reply sounding a little more snappish than he meant it to. Especially since Harbuck's remark came across as an effort at conciliation.

"You know, Jim, I have a hard time understanding why Street would kill himself. If that's indeed what happened. This isn't the eighties. Things are different now than they were for Steve. Times are different, and things are changing. Society is more accepting of gays. Even the church, the last segment of our society to ever get past bigotry and prejudice, is slowly coming around. Some churches, anyway. Why couldn't Street just walk away from a church that wouldn't accept him? A church that condemned him for it? Why be part of a community with such hate-filled practices that are totally inconsistent with the Christ they claim they profess? Why put yourself through the guilt, the hell, by being a part of a community that's so abusive about this issue?"

"I've got no answer for that one," Harbuck said. "I'll have to leave it to you ministers and the psychiatrists to figure out. Right now, my concern is Ismael Hagarson. I appreciate the information, and it does raise some new questions. But the issue of Street's sexual preference doesn't help my client, unless we can prove that it gave someone a motive to kill him or drove him to kill himself."

"Have you gotten any leads on the case?" Ike asked. "I know you're limited in what you can divulge. But maybe if I knew more, I could shed some light on it. Has your investigation turned up anything that suggests my suspicions about Street's mental state might be right?"

"Here's what the police report said," Harbuck said, reaching in his briefcase. "They were dispatched to the store at nine fifteen a.m. on May fifth. Patterson Street had called the police and reported that he came in the store and found his brother Lee dead. The police arrived and found the body lying on the floor. There were bruises around the neck. His hands were secured behind him with a zip-tie. There was a length of rope hanging from one of the rafters. One end had been cut. There was another length of rope lying on the floor beside the body. Patterson Street told the officers that he had cut the body down before he called them and removed the cord from around his brother's neck. Pictures included in the report showed an overturned chair and a broken display case, so these could be signs of a struggle. This could also have been caused by the victim thrashing about as he choked to death."

"That pretty much jibes with the story Ismael told me," Ike said. "Jim, I'm convinced that Street did this to himself. I've got no proof, just a gut feeling based on my conversation with him. Besides, Ismael strikes me as a peaceful chap. Perhaps a little hotheaded, as he proved that night when he talked to Harden. But to do something like this? I can't see it."

"Glad to hear you say this," Harbuck said. "Ismael needs all the support he can get right now. As you might imagine, he's a pretty lonesome fellow in this town right now."

"I can't imagine," Ike replied. "How's he doing? Being stuck in that jail cell—that's got to be torture for him. Also, being away from his family. Tough."

"Yeah, but he'd best stay put. Being at home would only put his family in even greater jeopardy than they already are. I told him to stay where he is. Behave. I could get him out on bond, but he's definitely safer in jail. Once word about this got out, I knew anti-Muslim feelings were going to get stirred up."

Ike knew Harbuck was spot-on. Being suspected of murdering a prominent citizen was one thing. But to be a Muslim accused of that crime...

Chapter 11

Curiosity got the best of Ike the next morning. He decided to visit his mother and bring up the subject of Ismael's mother and the refugee ministry in conversation. *Conversation? What conversation*, he asked himself. His mother had been diagnosed with Alzheimer's two years ago.

Ike's father had died the year prior to that—suddenly, from a heart attack. Looking back now, it seemed clear to Ike that his father's death marked a clear beginning of his mother's slow retreat from life.

At first, she had managed to live by herself in her home. But soon she began to forget things. Ike didn't pay much attention to her forgetfulness until the day that she wandered across the street and couldn't find her way home. A neighbor had called Ike and told him she had found his mother crying in her yard.

Denial is a common way to deal with Alzheimer's disease, the doctor calmly informed Ike, after he did the appropriate workup and made the diagnosis. During the doctor's examination, as Ike heard his mother fail in appropriately answering one screening question after another, he realized just how far into denial he'd slipped.

Soon after that doctor's visit, Ike had to make some tough decisions. As the only child, it fell to him to make the call that his mother needed more care than he could provide. His mother was now in the August Valley Nursing Home.

The nursing home was on the other side of town, but Ike tried to visit two or three times a week. Some days were better than others as far as her memory.

Her dementia was progressing fairly rapidly. Still, on good days, she would re-member people and events that Ike mentioned, and she could recognize and respond enough to make some conversation possible. However, most of Ike's time now with his mother was a monologue. On some occasions, she could string together two-word answers, rarely a sentence. The length of Ike's visits corresponded with his mother's decline in mental faculties, becoming shorter and shorter as she deteriorated. Was that because of his frustration, or sadness, or both? He wasn't sure.

Today, as Ike passed the nursing station, he asked his mother's nurse what kind of day his mother was having. "She griped that her toast was burned," was the reply. "So I guess she's in a good way today, Rev. Benheart. She's still in the cafeteria if you're looking for her."

Hopeful, Ike made his way down the hall. He'd decided not to make a big deal in bringing up the refugee ministry from so many years ago. Just mention it in passing and see if his mother's face registered any recognition of the topic. Often, this was his only clue Ike got that mother was with him mentally when he talked.

The nurse was right. His mother was in a good way today. She had a com-plaint about every subject Ike brought up. The doctor had changed one of her medications without telling her. Becky, Ike's wife, hadn't come by to file her nails. Jake, Ike's son, never came to see her. The usual litany.

Before leaving, Ike promised to come get her this Sunday so she could spend the day with his family. Then, as a parting comment, he said, "Mom, I met Ismael Hagarson yesterday. Not under the best of circumstances, unfortunately. But he told me that you knew his mother, Gera. That you helped her to get settled in the United States. Is that true?"

His mother's face started to redden. Once her temples were in full flush, she began shaking like someone in a rage. Ike had ever seen any reaction like this in his mother.

"That Muslim whore better never get her clutches into your father again!" his mother exclaimed, spitting as she spoke the words. Spoken more distinctly than anything she had said for months.

Chapter 12

It took Ike and the nurse a while to get his mother calmed down. She started screaming, "That bitch," over and over as the nurse wheeled her down the hall, loud enough to upset some of the other residents. Ike walked behind the nurse, apologizing profusely for his mother's outburst, telling the nurse that he had no idea what upset her. This really wasn't a lie. He didn't know what she was upset about. All he knew was he'd struck a nerve.

Ike had only seen his mother behave like the epitome of a good minister's wife. In public, she'd always modeled good "Christian" virtues. Modest dress, good manners, polite conversation. Though in private she could be more forthcoming and honest, he'd never heard her utter profanity. Hearing her do so was shocking in and of itself.

He also knew from the experience of the past few months that Alzheimer's does more than just damage the human brain's capacity to remember and carry out routine mental operations we require for activities of daily living. While the disease is laying waste to our operative functioning, it's also loosening inhibitions. Much like someone under the effects of alcohol, dementia patients are liable to say anything. Like the uninhibited drunk, what his "demented" mother uttered in her moments of indiscriminate frankness might not have been completely logical, but it was likely connected in some way to real life experience.

Ike now knew without a doubt that his mother harbored some mental anguish associated with Ismael's mother, Gera.

But what? What the hell was going on? He needed to clear his head. Get away and think. He wanted a drink.

As Ike entered one of his favorite dining spots in town, an upscale Mexican place, he encountered some of his old high-school buddies around the first table. When they saw him enter, their raucous conversation died a sudden death. A couple of them nodded politely in his direction, but no one invited him to join them. Nor did Ike expect them to. He had gotten used to being a pariah in many circles he used to be part of. Even though it had been fifteen years since he had returned to his hometown and taken up the mantle of a liberal minister, still it pained him at times being shunned by his friends. His punishment for deserting the tribe. Sometimes the pain of being ostracized by his own people was just more than Ike could bear. But not today. Today he really needed to be by himself.

He found a booth near the back of the restaurant where he could sit with his back to other incoming diners and remain undiscovered. He ordered his lunch, pausing for quite some time over the cocktail menu. The thought of dampening some of his tension with alcohol was powerfully tempting. The pressure he felt right now was overwhelming. In the last forty-eight hours, he'd gotten himself involved in a murder case. Then came this outburst from his mother like nothing he'd ever seen. All things considered, he could justify an escape. He would just have to find one other than alcohol.

"My name is Ike, and I'm an alcoholic." The memory of the first time he'd said those words came back to him while he summoned the inner resources to skip over the drink. It was during his second year at Harvard that he began attending AA meetings at the behest of his faculty advisor.

The chip Ike carried on his shoulder in high school remained there through college and into his seminary years. Fortunately, he found more constructive ways to channel his anger other than getting into fights. Rather than blow up every time someone made a joke about gays, he became an activist. He lent his support to the gay-rights group on campus and got involved in the Student Interfaith Movement. Both were wholesome, helpful diversions, but they did nothing to help him deal with the core issue. The only place Ike found relief from the sadness and grief over Steve's death was at the bottom of a bottle.

It was during trips back to August Valley that the alcohol got to be a real problem. There, in his hometown, he felt the sadness more acutely. There reminders of his cousin were everywhere and the horrific way he took his own life. Perhaps Ike could have borne the sadness if there had been someone to share it with. But there was no one.

Being with his mother's family was, for the most part, emotionally toxic. Their focus was almost entirely on their shame. Shame because of the suicide, yes, but more embarrassing for them was of the reason for it. By taking his life, Steve laid bare the family secret for all the community to see. Not one member of the family wanted to take any responsibility for Steve's death. Ike couldn't find one shred of remorse in any one of them. That's what incensed him. Ike was irked both by the family's lack of guilt and by the obsession over their shame of Steve's homosexuality.

Guilt and shame are inextricably intertwined in an emotional field. Guilt is pinned on the source of the shame. The family pinned the guilt on Steve, so he was the source of shame. Ike pinned the guilt on his family, and, since they wouldn't own it, they became his source of shame. And further kindled his anger. Every trip home forced him to escape through either booze or an early departure back to Cambridge. Usually both.

Ike took inventory of his situation. Street, a prominent local citizen who Ike barely knew, had called him and wanted to talk. The guy was confused about how to resolve his religion with homosexuality. The guy never said he was gay, but Ike had suspicions. Street had some property for sale. Ismael, a Muslim, wanted to buy it. Street changed his mind about selling it, or found out that a Muslim wanted to buy it—anyway, the deal was nixed. Street was now dead. Ismael was arrested for the murder. There was circumstantial evidence to implicate Ismael. Ike did the noble thing and let the suspect and his attorney know that Street was distraught right before his death—well, maybe not distraught, but wrestling with some "issues." Ismael, the suspect, had a connection with

Ike's family that he knew nothing about. Ismael's mother, Gera, someone he knew nothing about until yesterday, had a past with his parents. A past that Ismael was not afraid to tell him about. A past that his parents should be proud of—helping out a refugee. However, this past was somehow troublesome—at least from his mother's perspective.

His lunch arrived, breaking his reverie. For a moment, he concentrated on the food.

Returning to his thoughts, he became circumspect. What had him hooked about all this business with Street, the murder indictment, and the connection of Ismael with his parents?

Two things came to mind.

First, he was now committed to proving Ismael's innocence. No, that wasn't quite true. He was committed to proving that Street committed suicide. No, that wasn't quite correct either. He needed to convince himself that an innocent man wasn't being falsely accused of something that he deeply suspected was self-inflicted.

Second, he needed to find out the real story of his parents and Gera. Not just because he was curious. Ike had done enough family-systems work in his ministerial training to know that family secrets hold the key to much of a family's dysfunction. And this situation had secret written all over it.

Third, Ike was also troubled by the idea that he was expending a great deal of effort to aid a Muslim. Troubled by the emotional baggage he was carrying that made him hesitant to render this aid. And troubled that his mother apparently carried some emotional baggage with Muslims too. He might have been slowly losing his mother, but he still loved her, and if something was bothering her, it also bothered him.

As Ike munched on his fish taco, he thought about what potential sources of information were out there for these local events in 1971. Ismael indicated that his mother was dead. Ike's father also. Ike's mother wouldn't be much help. While she had put him on this trail, she obviously couldn't provide much factual information. Just emotional reactions.

There was Ismael, of course. And he had shared his knowledge of their parents' connection innocently and eagerly. He probably wouldn't have done so if he knew of a conflict. Or would he? Nah, Ike dismissed that thought. A guy in jail for a murder rap wasn't going to risk alienating a potential ally by being disingenuous. He would find out more of what Ismael knew in good time, but what Ike needed was someone, a third party, who was around in 1971.

Who else was around then who might have been part of this refugee ministry? Ike knew a few others at this father's church who were active in the life of the church during that time. Ike thought of one in particular, one he knew was still alive, one who brought a wry smile to his lips. Inez White. Unless things had changed recently, she still worked in the church office. Ike finished his last bite and picked up his cell phone. He'd dialed the church's number so many times that he still remembered it even after all these years. He recognized the voice that answered. It was Inez. She agreed to talk to Ike that afternoon.

"What have I done?" Ike asked himself. Inez White. If anyone could give him the inside scoop, it was Inez. She was without a doubt the biggest gossip in town.

Chapter 13

"It's just like old times, seeing you again, Ike," Inez said as Ike entered the church office. "Or should I address you as Rev. Benheart? Have you finally come under conviction for your wayward theology and decided to return to the one true church?"

"It's tempting, Inez," Ike volleyed back, playing his part in their usual repartee. Inez had teased Ike about his liberal leanings ever since he'd returned home after his freshman year of college. "But once you've eaten of the tree of knowledge, there's no going back to the Garden of Eden."

"So, you admit the terrible sin you've committed," she responded. "It's nothing more than the sin of human pride. Thinking you're smarter than God. Repent, and we'll take you back into the fold."

"And pretend that I've never seen the light? Never!" Ike playfully continued. "God wouldn't have given us brains unless he wanted us to use them."

"Well, God tells me to use my brain to study the Bible and listen to my preacher," Inez threw in; then she changed the subject. "You sounded a bit distressed on the phone. How can I help you?"

"Inez, how long have you been a part of this church?" Ike asked.

"Fifty years. Joined in 1966."

"So you were around in 1971 to '72," Ike said. "Did you take part in helping the refugees of the Pakistani Civil War?"

"Oh yes, most everyone helped in some way. Your mother encouraged all of us to get involved. Your parents were very committed to that work. I'm sure they've told you all about it."

"They never mentioned it. At least not that I recall," Ike said, watching Inez's face carefully for any reaction. "I only recently learned about it. Ismael Hagarson told me. His mother was Gera. You don't happen to remember her, do you? I know it's been forty-five years."

A look of both puzzlement and astonishment came over Inez. Though she was rarely one to hesitate in her responses, Ike sensed she was being rather calculating before she spoke.

"What did Ismael tell you about his mother?" Inez answered the question with a question, as if to stall for time.

"Just that my parents helped Gera out when she first arrived in this country," Ike said. "Ismael said she was very grateful for what my parents did for her."

"That's all he said?" Inez responded, caution in her voice.

"Yes, that was all he said," Ike answered. "You know he's locked up right now. Accused of murdering Lee Street."

"Yes, Lee, that poor man. The Streets have always been very faithful to this church. Do you think that Muslim killed him?"

"No idea," Ike said matter-of-factly, not wanting to divulge anything or stray from the subject at hand. "Do you have any recollection of Ismael's mother?"

"Oh yes, I remember her. Quite well. Lots of stories got told about her. Some of the other refugees told us she had been raped during the war. Others just said she had 'loose morals.'

"She was uncommonly pretty," Inez continued. "All the men fell over themselves when they were around her. A Middle Eastern woman was something tantalizing and exotic to men, I suppose. Fancied they could add her to their harem."

Ike could tell Inez was beginning to enjoy this conversation. No matter. He was just glad to see the pieces of the puzzle beginning to fill in. "Everyone knew about this reputation she had?" he inquired, hoping this might explain how his mother had come up with her vivid description.

"Gera made everyone uncomfortable," Inez explained, finally starting to embrace her role as informant. "The men were self-conscious around her, her being so beautiful and a woman of ill repute, and the women were jealous of all the attention she got because of her looks. But really, she was probably lonely. Most of the other refugees had family members with them. She had no one. Until her baby was born, of course."

"She was pregnant?" Ike asked, as another piece of the puzzle fell into place. Pregnant with Ismael, he presumed.

"No one knew she was pregnant during those first few days and weeks," Inez continued. "She couldn't have been far along at all. It only came to light a couple of months later, when she could hide it no longer. After Ismael was born, Gera said the father was a Bangladeshi freedom fighter. That's the story she wanted everyone to believe, anyway."

"But you don't?" Ike asked.

"A woman like that, who knows? Inez replied. "Since she ended up raising the child as a single mother, I guess sticking with that story worked best for her."

"Thanks for telling me all this," Ike said. "Your information has answered a lot of questions for me about a chapter of my parents' life that I knew nothing about. One more thing, though. Do you have any idea why my mother might have been angry with Gera?"

Inez thought for a moment, her mental wheels again spinning. "No, I don't remember anything in particular that happened between them..."

"Okay," Ike replied, preparing to take his leave. "You've been most helpful. Please give my regards..."

Inez, however, wasn't listening to Ike, but rather sat there deliberating. Suddenly interrupting, she continued, "Unless her anger has something to do with how much attention your father gave Gera."

Chapter 14

Two weeks passed since Ismael's arrest, and no evidence came to light that encouraged any hope for dismissal of the case. Harbuck did not ask the judge to release him on bail, because he was right about trouble in town. The anti-Muslim crowd moved their demonstrations from the courthouse to the jailhouse. Protestors carrying signs with messages like "Islam is a religion of violence" and "Mosques house murderers" marched in front of the jail, and their numbers grew. Ismael agreed to stay put, for his safety and that of his wife, Eisha.

Details appearing in the *August Valley Times* were pretty damning for Ismael. He'd been seen entering Street's Department Store the night before the body was found. The victim was hung, known to be a common method of execution used by Islamic extremists. And once it was known that the suspect in custody was Muslim and had a grievance with Street, the pieces came together very well in the public's mind to implicate Ismael. Means, motive, and opportunity had been established, and the court of public opinion needed no more evidence.

To compound Ismael's jeopardy, recent news headlines featured a spate of terrorist attacks, keeping fresh in the public's mind the perception that Islam is a religion of violence. Just the previous week, there was news of a suicide bombing in Pakistan. Women were being tortured and even sentenced to death by

ISIS for not dressing properly. Honor killings. Genital mutilation. Acid thrown in the face. Considering the steady stream of reports the public was subjected to about the brutalities in countries where Muslims comprise a majority, could Americans really be faulted for viewing Islam as a religion of violence?

Ike couldn't help but ponder these facts as well as his own existential dilemma. His life had changed dramatically since coming forth with the information about the conversation with Street, and the consequences of his noble action were causing him a great deal of angst. At moments, this whole episode seemed surreal. He felt tinges of regret for taking action and upsetting his well-ordered life. A self-inflicted wound, he supposed. He tried to remain calm and objective.

Islam might have been getting a lot of bad press now, but as a serious student of history, Ike knew that Islam's record on violence was no worse than Christianity's.

For centuries Christians and Jews lived in freedom and relative harmony with Muslims in Moorish Spain. That stands in stark contrast with the atrocities committed against Jews and Muslims in the name of Christ during the Crusades. The Christians eventually cast the Moors out of Spain, forcing the Muslims to either convert or die. In contrast to that, Muslims conquered the area that is presently Turkey during that same historical period and, after the military campaign, allowed Christians and Jews to stay and peacefully practice their respective religions. That concession continues to this day. Orthodox Christians regarded the region's largest city, Constantinople, as the seat of the Eastern Orthodox Church. Now called Istanbul, the city has remained the center of the Orthodox Church. Based on these and other comparisons, a good case can be made for Islam as the more tolerant and less violent of the two religions. Except when it comes to treatment of homosexuals.

Homosexuals have generally fared poorly under all the world's great religions, but especially under the Abrahamic faiths. Both the Bible and the Quran have passages that can be easily interpreted as condemning homosexual behavior. While the Bible records that God was angered by the activity in Sodom and Gomorrah, there were so many uncivil, wicked, and depraved acts perpetrated in the story that, fortunately, it's unclear which ones incited God's wrath. The story is highly suggestive that God was stirred to anger for other reasons. But when the Quran speaks to the same story, it makes no bones about it. God destroys the people explicitly because of their sexual behavior. Combine the explicit condemnation of homosexuality by the Quran with the fact that Islam is not only a system of beliefs, but also a legal code, and you generate a toxic, dangerous, and often lethal culture for gay people, especially in Muslim-predominant countries.

However, Islam wasn't on trial in August Valley. Ismael was—or was going to be—if some evidence absolving him of this crime didn't come to light soon. Ike got an update on the progress of the investigation from Jim Harbuck the day prior, and there were no new leads. Harbuck pursued every angle he could think of. He had checked with Street's brothers to see if Lee had any enemies from his business dealings who could have been responsible. No threats. Nothing. And Street's family reported no recent change in his mental state. As far as they could tell, Lee was pursuing his usual interests and gave them no reason to think he was feeling threatened. Neither had there been any indication to them that Lee was depressed. The crime lab submitted their report. Nothing at the scene suggested that anyone else had been present. No other new fingerprints. No unexplained artifacts. And the autopsy report confirmed the obvious. Street died from asphyxiation by hanging.

What was really galling Ike about this whole affair was this. Here he was, a champion for the LGBT community, putting himself out there to defend a member of the religion most notorious for its brutal treatment of homosexuals.

Ever since he began working with the Student Interfaith Movement, his principled stance for fair and equal treatment of gay people had put him at odds with Muslims. Now he found himself standing up for a Muslim accused of murdering a gay man. How twisted could fate be? Ike knew he was going to have to visit the issue of homosexuality with Ismael before he would have any peace about sticking his neck out for him.

Harbuck indicated to Ike that he was growing increasingly concerned. At this point all indications were that the murder charge was going to stick. Suicide was the only alternate explanation for Street's death, and, other than the conversation with Ike, nothing else lent credence to that theory. Harbuck had gotten nothing from the family to corroborate Ike's theory that Street was depressed. This case was going to trial unless something else came to light—and soon.

Chapter 15

"How is Harbuck coming with your defense?" Ike asked. After his conversation with Inez, he'd decided it was time to pay Ismael another visit.

"He says he's got new information that might help my case," Ismael said.

Ike wondered if that "new information" had anything to do with what he'd revealed to Harbuck about his suspicion of Lee Street's sexual orientation.

"Ismael, remember when I was first here, and I told you about Street coming to talk to me?"

Ismael nodded.

"Well, I didn't tell you what Street came to talk about," Ike said. "He wanted to talk about homosexuality."

"Okay…" Ismael's voice trailed off, as he appeared to be taking in and processing that tidbit of information. "So, you think I killed him because he might be gay?" Ismael's voice was now oddly devoid of any emotion. Ike thought he sounded tired.

"Well, don't Muslims hate gays?" The question nauseated Ike, but he was determined to follow through with the line of questioning he'd decided to pursue. If he was going to continue to put himself on the line to help Ismael, then he had to know what kind of person he was interceding for.

Ike knew Ismael was a follower of Islam. But that can mean many different things. Ike wanted to know what kind of Muslim Ismael was. What his Muslim beliefs made of him. How this gentle, affable college professor really felt about the violence perpetrated in the name of his religion and how he felt about its treatment of gays.

Unitarian ministers were expected to be well versed in all the world's great religions, and Ike had studied them all. Hinduism, Buddhism, Judaism, Islam, Christianity—all of them have condoned violence during some period of history. But that's history. Just as it is wrong to judge the past by today's standards, is it not also wrong to give one particular religion a pass on today's standards of civility when extremists in its ranks commit atrocities by willfully imposing a fourteen-hundred-year-old code of behavior? While history rightfully grants Muhammad a vaunted place for bringing order to chaotic seventh-century Arabian society, the severe jurisprudence meted out in some Islamic states today that claim to operate by Quranic principles is nothing short of evil.

Christianity had the brutalities and atrocities of its Crusades and its Inquisitions, but contemporary Christians aren't flying airplanes into buildings and lopping off people's heads in the name of their religion. Muslims are. No matter how objective Ike tried to be about Islam, reality bombarded him regularly with a different message. Just look at the headlines on most any given day. Islam seemed to spawn so much of the turmoil in today's world.

A key principle of Unitarianism is the conviction that all the world's great religions have, at their heart, common threads of wisdom and compassion. That conviction was what brought Ike into the Unitarian church and later compelled him to become a minister in that faith. Having escaped the intellectual and emotional straightjacket of a fundamentalist religion himself, Ike knew that a better, more peaceful world could only be created by building community beyond the boundaries of beliefs and ideologies. Was this possible with Islam as well? Ike hoped so, but he had his doubts.

"That's a fair question," Ismael responded, his voice assuming a more objective tone, "considering that in some Islamic countries, homosexuals are put to death. And there is justification for such a punishment in the Hadith, the sayings of Muhammad. But in other Islamic countries, Turkey for instance, homosexuality is legal, and the civil rights of gay people are protected. Muslims in the United States are divided on the issue. Some are tolerant, even supportive of gay people. Personally, I'm ambivalent about it. I think it's a sin, but if someone chooses to live that kind of lifestyle, then that's between them and God. Keep it private, I say. Don't ask, don't tell. Then, whether or not someone should be punished is not an issue."

"Yet you believe that all Muslims in this country should be treated fairly," Ike said, "Be afforded the same rights and privileges as any other group of people?"

"Yes, of course I do," Ismael responded.

"Then that makes you a bit hypocritical, doesn't it?" Ike said. "How can you expect support and empathy for the rights of your minority group, when you're turning your back on another minority?"

"Touché," Ismael responded. "You make a good point. I'll have to consider that. All I can say is religion is one thing. And sexual behavior—behavior that goes against the biological function of sex and God's created order—is another."

"Back to Street and our conversation," Ike said. "He mainly wanted to talk about whether homosexuality is a sin according to his religion. He is—was—Christian. He never said he was gay himself but that a family member was. But I suspect he brought up the subject because of himself and just used a family member as a cover. If we can find evidence that Street was gay and that he was experiencing guilt over it, it would lend support to the suicide theory."

"But finding someone to testify that Street was gay, without any proof that he killed himself, would only add another motive for me to murder him."

"You're probably right," Ike said. "But in the absence of another suspect, suicide is the only other explanation that's going to exonerate you. So we're going to have to pursue this theory."

"We?" Ismael said. "You're going to try to help me?"

"I have to," Ike answered. "My mother and father took on the obligation to help your mother. In my book, that means I'm obliged to try to help you."

"I am grateful, Ike," Ismael said. "As my mother was to your family." Then, almost as an afterthought, Ismael added, "I'm convinced someone got to Street. I mean, before that night. Someone leaned on him to back out of selling his property to us. Maybe even blackmailed him. I wonder if someone found evidence he was queer and threatened to expose him if he didn't back out of the deal."

"A plausible theory," Ike said. "If he felt like someone might be about to out him, and he was already deeply depressed, that could be what tipped him over the edge."

"I'll mention all this to Harbuck tomorrow. Even though I imagine he's already thought of it," Ismael said.

Ike decided now was a good time to change to the other subject he wanted to visit with Ismael.

"Was your mother a Bihari?" he asked.

"Ah, I see you've been doing some research," Ismael replied. "She was part Bihari. That's why she had to flee Bangladesh during the war. The Bengalis were suspicious that all Biharis were supporters of Pakistan during the war and possibly spies. That cloud of suspicion was one reason my mother was forced to leave her beloved Bangladesh. Why she felt she could never return."

After his conversation with Inez, so many more questions were raised for Ike. Who was this mysterious woman named Gera? Why did his mother have such negative feelings toward her? What, if anything, did Ismael know about the nature of the relationship between his mother and Ike's parents? Ike had to find out what Ismael knew.

"So it wasn't the Pakistani soldiers that forced her to leave? It was her own people?" Ike asked, trying to get a better picture of the plight of this woman who had somehow emerged from the past to now haunt his family.

"The civil war between West and East Pakistan turned so many people against each other," Ismael explained. "It wasn't just the West Pakistanis against the Bengalis of East Pakistan. It was also Muslims against Hindus. Even the different tribes of Muslims within East Pakistan turned against each other. Bengali against Bihari—tribe against tribe—Muslim against Muslim. That's why my mother's people were forced to flee. The Bihari were far outnumbered by the Bengalis. They first escaped to India. But being Muslim, they weren't too welcome in India either. That's why many of them ended up coming to America."

"Yet she ended up working for a Hindu family once she was here in August Valley, didn't she?" Ike asked. "The Patels that ran the August Valley Inn?"

"Opportunities were limited for her," Ismael said. "She hadn't finished her degree program. But she was bright and didn't mind working hard. And her English was pretty good. So the Patels offered her a job, and she took it. She did what many immigrants from Bangladesh or Pakistan did when immigrating to America. She passed herself off as Indian, though she resented having to do it. She did it out of necessity. There is a pecking order for refugees to this country, and Indian refugees are better accepted than refugees from Pakistan or Bangladesh. Pakistanis, especially, are stigmatized as troublemakers."

"She became an outcast among outcasts," Ike said.

"That's right," Ismael agreed, his voice starting to crack from his surfacing emotions. "She had to make so many concessions of identity in order to survive. I think that's why, at least in private, she became fiercely proud of her religion and her culture. That was her way of remembering who she was. Preserving her sense of self in a world that tried to make her forget she was Bangladeshi. Forget she was a Muslim."

Ike encouraged Ismael to continue, adding, "You loved your mother very much, didn't you?"

"As she loved me. It was the two of us against the world. Or at least that's how she painted it much of the time. If we didn't have anything else, we had each other. No family came to this country with her, she never married, so in reality it was just the two of us. She was always by my side. Always encouraging me and protecting me. In school, in sports, when the other kids would pick on me, she was always there. She was my supporter. And I became hers."

"She was pregnant with you when she came to America?" Ike ventured, his question duplicitous. He was being ministerial yet also probing for very personal reasons.

Ismael tried to speak, but the words caught in his throat, and he merely nodded in agreement. Then, after collecting himself, he said, "I was born in 1972. May fourth. My mom always told me my father was a soldier and that he was very brave. She showed me pictures of him."

"You might not know the answer to this, but…did my parents know she was pregnant when they were trying to help her?" Ike asked.

"I have no way of knowing," Ismael replied. "She told me about your mother and father and how much she appreciated their help in what was a very difficult time. But I think she lost touch with your parents before I was born. Something happened to change their feelings toward one another. I'm not sure what. I don't think her relationship with your parents ended on the best of terms."

Ismael now had Ike's full attention. "Not on good terms? Any idea why?" he asked.

"Well, I think she got the impression that they wanted her to convert to Christianity. When she showed no interest, they seemed to lose interest in her. I know that's vague, but that's about all I remember her saying about it."

That answered some of Ike's questions but raised others. And it certainly didn't explain his mother's intense reaction to the mention of Gera's name.

Chapter 16

When Ike got home, Becky was holding the phone out to him. She looked exasperated. "It's Patterson Street," she said. "He insists on talking to you—now."

Ike picked up the receiver. "Ike Benheart," he said.

"Ike, this is Patterson."

"Yes, Pat. I was so sorry to hear about Lee. Please accept my condolences."

"Never you mind that," Street declared angrily, loud enough that Becky could hear every word. "Harbuck has been over here talking to me and the rest of the family, asking a bunch of questions about Lee and whether he might be gay. He said you put that idea in his head. My brother's dead, Ike. We're all dealing with a terrible loss. The last thing we want to hear is a bunch of crap about Lee being a fag or something. I'll not have you or Jim Harbuck or anyone else dragging my brother's name through the mud to try and defend that raghead down there at the jail that killed him."

Ike was completely taken aback. "Pat, I've spoken to no one except Mr. Harbuck about this. Lee came to me with some questions about homosexuality. He never said he was gay, and I never assumed he was. But I had to tell Mr. Harbuck about the conversation. I thought it might be relevant in some way to your brother's death. I had to report it."

"Well, Lee wasn't gay. So you and that attorney better just let this go. If not, you're both going to need your own attorney, 'cause you're going to have a defamation suit on your hands. Good night, Reverend."

Ike looked into the receiver a few seconds; then he turned to look at Becky and said, "Sheesh. That guy is intense. What have I gotten myself into?"

"The middle of a murder case," Becky said, with resignation in her voice. "One that is politically charged and likely to get very ugly." After his first visit to Ismael, Ike had told Becky everything about his conversation with Lee Street and why he had to get involved.

"Patterson Street is just upset," Ike reasoned aloud. "He's grieving. He just lost his brother."

"And he's got a lot of power in this town," Becky added. "His whole family does. He's not the kind of person you want to cross."

"The Streets aren't what they used to be. There are plenty of people in August Valley that wouldn't mind seeing them taken down a notch. Besides, I'm not crossing him. I'm just being honest. Telling the truth. Telling what I know."

"I know, I know." Becky knew her husband was doing the right thing, and she agreed with it. But she still had her fears.

Chapter 17

T he next morning over coffee, Ike decided to visit his conversation with Ismael and get Becky's take on it. "Honey, do you remember that speech I gave at the Student Interfaith Movement about the treatment of gays being the litmus test for inclusiveness?"

"You mean the one where you blasted all the liberals for pandering to the Muslims and always giving them a pass over the way they treat gays?"

Ike had given that speech at the height of his fervor about gays being bashed in the name of religion. He was especially incensed with the way Islam always gets a pass in the liberal community, among the multiculturalists, so intent on being accepting and inclusive that they overlook many Muslim cultural practices that marginalize and oppress women, gays, and people of other religions.

"You don't have to remind me how condescending it sounded," Ike replied, pained that this was the way Becky remembered it. "I visited some of the same points I made in that speech with Ismael yesterday when I went to see him."

"You didn't!" Becky exclaimed. "That speech offended everyone—especially the Muslims. You mean you told him your true feelings about Muhammad?"

In that speech, Ike admitted his ambivalent feelings about Muhammad, the founder of and most revered figure in Islam. To this day, he could still recite his remarks about Muhammad nearly word for word:

A fair reading of history tells us that Muhammad brought about a great transformation of the moral life of Arabian society at a time of chaos and lawlessness. In pre-Islamic Arabia, people felt no obligation to anyone outside their family or tribe. Unwanted children, usually girls, were killed, sometimes by burying them alive. Women had no rights and were treated as possessions. Life was cheap; bloody tribal feuds smoldered for years; robbery and warfare were ways of life on the Arabian Peninsula. Muhammad united these warring tribes, brought order and discipline, established certain rights for women and children, and created an empire that would, within a century, not only dominate the world, but preserve much classical scientific knowledge and philosophy through Europe's Dark Age.

But Muhammad was not a Buddha or a Jesus. Jesus and Buddha are admired because they stand above the society of their times and exemplify the best that human beings can become. These two figures are esteemed nearly universally for their wisdom and their teachings. One doesn't have to be a Buddhist to appreciate the value of the way of life the Buddha taught, and one doesn't have to be a Christian to appreciate Jesus's courage and the ultimate sacrifice he made for his convictions.

Muhammad, on the other hand, didn't just speak truth to power. He became the power and assumed the role of a political leader. In doing so, he also became complicit in acts of assassination and even genocide. Establishing order in a chaotic society requires a firm hand, and governing just seems to always end up a messy business.

True, the past can't be judged by today's standards. Muhammad was no more brutal or ruthless than other leaders of his era and probably much less so. But Jesus and Buddha managed to rise above the era in which they lived, and this is what makes them revered in a way that political leaders such as an Alexander the Great, a King David of Judea, or a Muhammad can't.

"No, I didn't exactly go there," Ike said to Becky. "I just confronted him about the general perception that Muslims hate gays and pressed him to tell me his true feelings about them."

"And what did he say?" Becky asked.

"He thinks homosexuality is a sin. But he also said that ultimately its God's place to judge, not his. He advocates 'don't ask, don't tell.'"

"Doesn't sound like he harbors any strong feelings on the issue," Becky said. "That's actually a pretty open and accepting view on the issue, I'd say, coming from a Muslim."

"I accused him of being a hypocrite," Ike countered.

"What?!" Becky exclaimed. "You mean, you're going to get back on that soapbox? Why in the world did you have to go there, with a guy that's got a hell of a lot of other things on his mind?"

"No, that's not why I went there," Ike reassured her. "Believe me; I've learned to stay in my own skin when it comes to that issue. I just had to find out how he really felt, if I'm going to work to prove the innocence of a Muslim accused of murdering a gay man."

"And now, you think you got your answer?" Becky asked.

"Yes, I think so. Ismael didn't get defensive. He even indicated that I'd given him something to think about. That tells me a lot. It lets me know he is capable of rising above what his culture says about homosexuality."

"Your expectations of others are high, as usual," Becky said. "But at least you kept your cool and managed your anger. You're coming along, Ike Benheart."

"I just keep working the steps," Ike said humbly.

"This Doi Maach is delicious," Ismael told Eisha. Doi Maach was Ismael's favorite traditional Bengali dish, chunks of freshwater fish seasoned with many spices and cooked in a yogurt-based gravy, served over rice. Bangladeshi comfort food. Eisha had brought Ismael dinner in his cell, as she had every evening for the past week. It had now been ten days since Ismael was arrested, and they were only now beginning to collect themselves after the shock of that and the total disruption his incarceration had inflicted on their lives.

"Good as your mother made it?" Eisha asked.

"Absolutely. And why not? She gave you the recipe, didn't she?"

"I'm glad to see you have a good appetite," Eisha said. Her husband had lost a noticeable amount of weight since being jailed. "I'm sure it would taste so much better if you were eating it at home." She felt tears welling up in her eyes and turned away from Ismael.

Ismael left his half-eaten dinner on the flimsy TV tray and went to embrace Eisha. "Soon. Mr. Harbuck says this nightmare will be over soon, and I can return home."

With his touch, Eisha completely broke down. Through the tears she managed to say, "But even if you are released, our lives will never be the same again. You will always be that Muslim who was accused of murder. And I will be his wife. There is so much hatred in this place."

"It will blow over," Ismael said, trying to sound strong for her, though he didn't feel it. "Once I am cleared, you'll see."

"The other kids are bullying Bai at school," Eisha reported. "Calling him names like 'sand nigger' and saying his daddy is a 'diaper head.' He almost got into a fight today after a boy knocked his books out of his arms."

"Did you talk to his teacher about it?" Ismael asked.

"She's keeping a close eye out for him," Eisha said. "But she can't be with him every minute."

"Maybe we have to take him out of school for a time," Ismael suggested.

"Has anyone from the Ummah been to see you in here?" Eisha asked, changing the subject. The Ummah is the Muslim community.

"Jahid came. And the imam," Ismael said.

"That's it?" Eisha was incredulous. "The rest are cowards. They call you friend, but they do not come and support you through this, this...disaster."

"I'm only allowed visitors during certain times," Ismael explained. "Besides, it's not safe for them. You've seen the protesters outside."

"Yes, I have to pass them every evening. I have to dress differently now so no one thinks I'm a Muslim. I've completely stopped wearing my hijab." Hijab is the headscarf worn by many Muslim women. "Now it's jeans and blouses everywhere I go. Why American women prefer to stuff themselves into these tight-fitting clothes I'll never understand."

"You are beautiful no matter what you wear," Ismael said. "Women are most elegant in the sari, but right now you are doing the right thing by dressing like you are. It's safer. For now.

"Speaking of visitors, Ike Benheart came to see me again today," Ismael said. "Remember, I told you about him. He is the minister that talked with Mr. Street right before…that night."

"Yes, I remember. What was he here for today?" Eisha asked.

"He really thinks that Street committed suicide. He's cooperating with my lawyer to try to prove it."

"Why does he try to help you? It can only be dangerous for him to do this," Eisha said.

"Because he is a good man, and he wants to do the right thing," Ismael said. "We should trust him, Eisha. Oh, and we have this connection. Or our families do. His parents helped my mother when she first came to America."

"If he can get you out of here, I will shower him with gifts and praise," Eisha said. "I've got to go now. Bai has homework. Go ahead and finish eating. I'll get the plate tomorrow." She kissed her husband and called the jailer to let her out.

After Eisha left, Ismael thought about praying. He wasn't slavishly devoted to the salat, the ritualistic prayer of Muslim tradition done at five prescribed times every day. Though he often attended Friday prayer services with the Ummah, the Islamic community, doing the rote postures and recitations of the traditional salat atop a Mecca-angled prayer rug was not a part of his normal daily routine. Like many Muslims raised in Western society, if asked, he would say he prayed regularly—which he did. But his prayers consisted more of unstructured conversations with God as he understood him. And the God of Ismael's understanding would not want him constantly repeating a mindless ritual.

Since his arrest, prayer offered him some solace. By focusing on God, he could retreat from the unpleasant reality of his current situation for a while. But try as he would, tonight he simply could not discipline his thoughts. Heretical ideas were forcing their way into his inner life.

No matter how much he tried to avoid or deny it, a terrible truth kept hammering on his psyche. He was in jail because of his religion. He was arrested because of the way that Muslims were perceived as a potentially violent people throughout most of the non-Muslim world. It didn't matter that most all the

Muslims he knew were peaceful and good. There were enough rotten eggs in the basket to spoil the entire lot. It didn't matter that he had coexisted peacefully in American society with so many people who knew him as an acquaintance, colleague, and even friend. Even though many of these people knew him as a dedicated academician and family man, this testimony of a lifetime was not enough evidence to overcome the seed of doubt planted in common consciousness by a small handful of extremists.

He could no longer deny his conflicted feelings about the religion of his people. The doubts of the non-Islamic world about the faith he followed had a foundation in reality. The events of 9/11 put those doubts front and center for non-Muslims. And the headlines generated by Al-Qaeda, the Taliban, and ISIS in the intervening years kept it there. And this doubt was now seeping into his own consciousness as well. He could no longer hide under the tent of isolation generated by the Islamic community with its separatist rituals and lifestyle. He could no longer comfort himself simply by saying the problem was not with Islam but with the way a small percentage of Islam's followers chose to interpret it. If this was true, then the entire Muslim community must take responsibility for how Islam is lived and practiced by all its adherents. And in Ismael's experience, this wasn't happening. He'd never heard any serious conversations in his masjid community about the need for reform. Now for the first time he felt an overwhelming sense of hopelessness that his community would ever be capable of doing any sort of critical thinking about itself.

The words Eisha had spoken tonight also gave Ismael permission to continue pressing into some of these dark corners of doubt. She had called the members of the Muslim community cowards for not visiting. She was also curious about Ike's motives for visiting. There was an inconsistency here that Ismael needed to sort out. For the past two weeks, Ike had been here for him, while the response of his Muslim friends had been rather disappointing. If the support he was receiving in this hour of need were to be used as criteria for vindicating a belief system, then Ike's beliefs, whatever they were, certainly trumped those of many in the Muslim community. Given his perilous circumstance, Ismael couldn't help but be hypersensitive to this moral inconsistency. Islam claims theological and moral superiority over all other religions because the Quran is supposedly

God's final revelation. Well, that moral superiority wasn't being manifest in those Ismael was counting on to see him through this crisis.

Ismael tried to dismiss all these thoughts as just an overreaction to the trauma of his arrest and incarceration. Maybe he just needed to spend more time in fervent prayer and in reading the Quran. Maybe then the unshakeable faith that had sustained him throughout his life would return. Time would tell, he guessed. Time. A plentiful commodity for him right now.

Chapter 18

Ike's phone conversation with Patterson wasn't the first time he'd incurred the wrath of the Streets. It happened the first time when Ike decided to leave the fold of the Baptist Church.

The Street family had been members of First Baptist Church of August Valley for four generations. Ike's father, a third-generation Baptist pastor, served as their settled minister throughout the latter third of the twentieth century. Under his leadership, the church experienced phenomenal growth that approached megachurch dimensions, with a membership approaching two thousand and an annual budget nearing five million dollars.

From all indications, Ike was destined to keep the pedigree going. He was born and raised in First Baptist, and the congregation watched with pride as he graduated finished college and headed for seminary at Harvard. Ike's troubles his last year of high school seemingly forgotten, the church expected to get back a well-groomed Ivy League minister capable of expounding on the finer points of theology in terms that would not upset the sensibilities of genteel Southern Christians.

To say Ike was studying at Harvard gave his family and the congregation a sense of pride. However, they would hardly have felt that way had they any idea what transformations his matriculation there was working in the mind and spirit of their favorite son. At Harvard Ike got a taste of the social gospel as well as exposure to the challenging perspectives of critical biblical scholarship. After graduation Ike returned to his home church and assumed duties as an associate pastor. He was determined to teach the Bible from the critical perspective he fully embraced, as well as make the church more inclusive and accepting of minorities and gays. As might be expected, it didn't take long for Ike's progressive agenda to upset the lay leadership of the church and many large donors. Especially Patterson Street.

Ike labored long and hard to introduce the church to his progressive interpretation of the gospel message through Bible studies and occasional sermons, as well as experientially through ministries of social witness. He had one distinct advantage in his efforts to bring about significant change. His father was the senior minister and, in principle, generally supportive. But Ike was no gradualist. He wanted things to move too rapidly for the old guard of the congregation, and so, after only eight months on the job, he was asked to leave. His father, nearing retirement age, did not have the energy or the will to stand in the way of this painful decision. The vote of the church board actually split on the decision to dismiss Ike. And so did the church. Patterson Street was livid when some board members took a differing stance, and he threatened to withhold his substantial financial support.

About two hundred members of the church indicated their willingness to follow Ike on his innovative spiritual journey. These were mostly young families with fewer denominational ties and open to new ideas. At first Ike rejected the idea of starting a new church for fear that in doing so he would be sowing seeds of discord as well as undermining his father's ministry and standing in the community. Although his father could not officially sanction this experiment of reform, informally he encouraged his son to go ahead with what his loyal base of supporters was urging him to do. Under Ike's leadership they started a non-denominational church in an empty storefront building downtown.

At first the members of Ike's new church relished the doctrinal freedom they were afforded with no denominational ties. However, it wasn't long before they realized that there were downsides to this independence. If they were going to achieve their goals and grow as a congregation, they would need to affiliate with a larger denominational body. They were attracted to faith traditions with congregational polity like the Baptists but wanted nothing to do with theology that excluded. They decided to take steps to become a member congregation in the Unitarian Universalist Association. The president of the UUA came to August Valley and, in an event that gained national notoriety, conducted a service where nearly two hundred people were signed into membership.

Next morning Harbuck called Ike.

"Ismael told me you came to see him yesterday," Harbuck said.

"Yeah," Ike replied. "I filled him in on the conversation I had with Street that night. I had to find out how Ismael might feel about Street being gay. That is, if Street really was. I had to find out for personal reasons."

"And how did he feel? What did he say?" Harbuck asked.

"Well, he was mostly concerned that if my theory is correct and we can prove Street was gay, we'd be playing into the hands of the prosecution. They could just use this fact as another motive for Ismael to murder him."

"I'd thought of that possibility also, and that's why I hadn't gone there with my client," Harbuck said. "But I'm glad you did. Go there, that is."

"Well, if my understanding is correct, you've gone there with Street's family," Ike replied, a bit sarcastically.

"What happened?" Harbuck asked. "They call you?"

"Patterson Street did. Said he was going to sue me and you for defamation."

"You worried?" Harbuck asked.

"No. Should I be?"

"No," Harbuck said. "Patterson Street Jr. is doing exactly what I figured he'd do. Blow up. Talk about it. That's what we needed to happen."

"How's that?" Ike asked, though his own thought processes were already whirling and coming up with answers.

"I'd hoped someone in the family might have opened up about Lee's private life," Harbuck continued. "They still might. We need something like that to break."

"I see," Ike said. "I could have used a little heads-up, though, Jim. Patterson Street doesn't mind unloading on people."

"I hope he wasn't too rough on you," Harbuck said with a laugh. "He thinks the whole world revolves around him. A lot of it does, I'm afraid. But I know you, and I know you can handle him."

"I've had practice," Ike said. "He didn't much like it when I split First Baptist."

"I forgot about that!" Harbuck said with astonishment in his voice. "I'd totally forgot. Wow, you've got to be at the top of his hit list now."

"Gee, thanks, Jim. You're really comforting me."

"Sorry, man," Harbuck said, much more soberly. "You okay? I mean, really?"

"Yeah, I can play the game," Ike said. "I'm just not used to playing with the big boys. And with such high stakes."

"You're fine," Harbuck added confidently. "Patterson is all bark, no bite. Man, I'm glad it's you I've got working this with me. You could've made a lawyer yourself."

For the first time, Harbuck was speaking to Ike like the friend he had been twenty-three years ago. Ike felt the guard kept over his feelings all these years release some of its vigilance.

"Never would've happened," Ike said. "I've got this crippling deficiency that would have prevented me. I was born with a soul."

"Ouch." Harbuck feigned hurt. "But at least *I've* got a heart. Apparently, ministers don't have to have one of those. Really, though, you've got the perfect disposition for the legal profession. You're heartless, and you go right for the jugular."

Just like that, Jim and Ike's friendship was restored.

"Okay, that's enough of that," Ike said, trying to move on. "Jim, what motivated you to take this case? A Muslim accused of murdering a Street in August Valley. No way this is a strategic career move for you. Regardless of the outcome."

"A favor to a business associate," Harbuck replied. "At least that's why I was initially called. Then I went and talked to Ismael. After conferring with him, I'm convinced he's innocent. So, I'll do my best to defend him."

"You're going to catch one hell of a lot of flak for it," Ike said. "Like I'm telling you something you don't already know. Religiously, August Valley is deeply conservative. Even by Southern standards. It's like the last bastion of Christian fundamentalism. Judgement has already been pronounced on Ismael, just by association."

"There's no shortage of Bible thumpers around here that spend their time looking through scripture figuring out ways to condemn people," Harbuck said. "I'm going into this with full awareness of the grain I'm going against, Ike. But I'm pretty open-minded. Probably more open than you realize."

"Jim, I can't tell you how glad I am to hear you say that," Ike said, relieved to find that Harbuck was open to a conversation on this subject. "You know though, Jim, it's not going to just be about Islam. This case may end up being about homosexuality as well. If our theory about Street is correct. It's going to be about how the Bible is used to incite hatred against gays. Enough hate to lead Street to take his own life."

"If that's what happened, if Street killed himself because of the pressure he felt from his family and the church over being homosexual, then yep, it's going to be tough. That'll implicate them as accessories in his death. And they won't be willing to accept any responsibility. They'll resist that idea with all they're worth. But if we can prove Street committed suicide, and that's why he did it, they'll experience the guilt. They'll never own it, but they'll feel it."

"I guess now I'm more committed than ever to helping you get Ismael acquitted. If we're able to prove this theory about suicide and the reason for it, maybe that'll open a few people's eyes to the harm they do to gay people when they condemn homosexuality and call it a sin. Not just spiritual harm. In cases like Street's and countless others, physical harm as well. It's a toxic way to be a Christian."

"It's not loving your neighbor as yourself; that's for sure," Harbuck said. "But we're getting ahead of ourselves. Let's work the case. Take it one step at a time. You got any other ideas?"

"Did Ismael mention his own theory," Ike said, "that someone might have blackmailed Street by threatening to out him?"

"That's a distinct possibility," Harbuck said. "But until someone starts talking to us, this case is going nowhere. I want to file a motion for dismissal, and you may have to give a deposition. Before I do though, what we really need is someone else who can substantiate that Street was depressed. I'm going to keep talking to the family. The ones who'll still talk to me, that is. Keep your ears open. Now that word's out to them about what you know, you may hear something before I do. People would rather talk to anyone besides a lawyer."

"Anyone?" Ike asked. "Even a heartless minister?"

Chapter 19

June 2016

Ike was surprised and relieved about the conversation with Harbuck. *That guy has come a long way in his development as a human being*, Ike thought. *Maybe there's some hope for others in this town.*

He remembered another recent conversation, this one with a family member. A cousin, one of the few who were even approachable on the subject of Steve's death and the reason for it. This cousin told Ike, "I don't think gay people should be mistreated. We should love them just like we love anyone else. I just don't approve of their behavior." *At least he is thinking in terms of loving them*, Ike thought. *That's a start. Now, if he would just start exploring further what it might mean to truly love gays like anyone else.*

Ike needed to get back into his ministerial duties. Not just because he was behind on some correspondence and hadn't even started writing this Sunday's sermon. He needed to mostly for his own sanity. The past few days had been incredibly intense. He was helping mount a defense for a murder suspect. He had aroused bitterness in the victim's family. There was this vague family mystery Ismael had made him aware of that he couldn't sort out. He wanted his life to get back to normal. He tried to do that by starting to do normal things. As he started refocusing on what his obligations were for the coming week, he couldn't prevent a wry smile coming over his face. There was no "normal" for the life of a Unitarian minister in the Deep South.

In addition to routine administrative stuff and preparing for the worship service, this week he was scheduled to take part in a roundtable discussion at the college on social justice, perform a same-sex wedding, and march in the gay-pride parade. Being one of the only liberal ministers in town, sometimes Ike felt his time was stretched rather thin. But he had a real passion for what he was doing and found the role he played a constant source of fascination.

This morning, as he planned out the rest of his week in his head on his way to the church office, a thought spilled onto the mental page of this orderly agenda he was working on. *The gay-pride parade! It'll pass directly by the police station with all those anti-Muslim protestors out front. Will there be trouble?* Surely the police had thought about that when the organizers applied for the permit. But what if they applied before Ismael was arrested? He knew he'd better check with someone to be sure law enforcement was prepared. Ike encountered bigotry in the community often, and he knew from experience that many of the same people who were in front of the police station were also opposed to gay rights. Were storm clouds collecting? He put a phone call to the police chief at the top of his things to do this morning.

Ike was running late. The participants in the parade had been told to line up at 2:45 p.m., and it was a couple of minutes to three when he finally found a parking spot. He felt conspicuous, as he always did at these events. He always dressed conservatively, today in a blue dress shirt, slacks, and dress shoes, which made him stand out in the colorful crowd. The lyrics to an old John Hartford ballad, "Natural to Be Gone," came to him. "What's the difference being different, when it's difference now that looks alike." Men in stilettos and fishnet stockings, women with multicolored spiked hair and clad in leather and chains. *The LGBT crowd always tried to outdo each other to see who could adorn themselves the most outrageously,* he thought to himself. Occasionally a participant would go a little over the top with an overemphasis on sex or some outrageous fetish, but most maintained some semblance of decorum and kept it within the bounds of what was family acceptable. Anyway, Ike loved these people! Sometimes he wished a little of this unabashed behavior would rub off, as he considered himself a tad too inhibited and self-conscious. In many ways, these people were like a breath of fresh air after the world of cookie-cutter Christians with whom he had spent much of his life.

He always had to remind himself that all this flamboyance had a purpose. Yes, there were plenty of critics of gay-pride parades and festivals even among the gay community, but few could deny that the LGBT community had made great progress toward acceptance and equal rights by exaggerating and satirizing many of the public's widely held stereotypes. Embracing your enemy's worst criticism and taking pride in it has often enjoyed strategic success. When the word Unitarian was first uttered to describe the founders of his church, it was the worst word its detractors could think of. The founders of his faith tradition took the word and made it a symbol of pride. That dynamic bolstered the religious movement that soon grew into American Unitarianism.

He hurried to get to the starting point on Main Street. Several members of his church were there, and he hurried around to greet them before the parade got started. As he was speaking to one of them, he felt a tap on his shoulder. He turned to find Becky, wearing a rainbow T-shirt. Startled, all he could manage was, "Becky! What are you doing here?" Although his wife's values were liberal as well, participating in marches and protests was not her general mode of operation.

"I'm marching in support of my gay and lesbian friends," she said and then added, "And to keep you from getting into trouble."

"I'm so glad you came," Ike said. "Surprised, but glad."

"If something's going to happen to you," Becky said, "and I'm afraid it might, I don't want it to happen without me being around."

"There's not going to be any trouble," Ike declared. "Chief O'Neal assured me he has put on plenty of additional officers for the parade. He also made the protestors at the jail disperse until we're done."

"Quite reasonable of him," Becky shouted over the sound of the marching band striking up with "I'm Coming Out."

Times were changing, and, even in politically conservative August Valley, organizers of the gay-pride parade found it more expedient to cast the event not so much as a protest march but as a Mardi Gras–type street party. Dozens of religious, social, and charitable groups had floats or banners in the parade, as well as many businesses. Becky and Ike were positioned behind the Unitarian church's banner proclaiming its support by "Standing on the Side of Love." As long as open hostility toward gays still manifested itself in the community on occasion—which it did—organizers found plenty of support for the event as a continuing expression of solidarity.

Anyone who is worried about how their sexual orientation is perceived probably shouldn't participate, Ike thought. He remembered how it was for him the first time he took part. He spent the entire parade wondering if people would think he was gay. As he marched, that was exactly what it felt like when the eyes of onlookers fell on him. That was an eye-opener, to have this felt experience of what everyday life must be like for a gay man in our society. It ended up being one of the most consciousness-raising experiences of his life, and it compelled him to return each year. He could immediately tell that this year, the experience would be different yet again. Having Becky by his side, holding his hand, changed the way that Ike saw the spectators see him.

Ike was gratified to observe an increase in the number of spectators every year. As usual, there were the smattering of gawkers and curiosity seekers. And when the parade passed the main town square, he saw the predictable small contingent of religious protestors from previous years. *Must be the same folks*, he thought, for they carried the same signs. Humorless quotations from Leviticus condemning homosexuality, the constant refrain of their message year after year. In fact, so predictable was their presence that this year some anti-anti-gay protestor added some levity by preparing a sign to hold over the protestors head that read, "These guys need another hobby." Ike held his breath as they neared the city jail. The police chief was true to his word, as the anti-Muslim group was nowhere to be seen.

Ike felt himself relaxing as they marched into the parking lot designated as the end of the parade route. Becky expressed her relief more openly. After relinquishing their banner, they exchanged a few pleasantries with a few other marchers as they filed into the parking area. Just as they were taking their leave to find their cars, a stranger, appearing out of place in a business suit, approached Ike.

"Rev. Benheart?" he asked.

"Yes, I'm Ike Benheart."

"I'm Bruce Massey. I'd like to talk with you in private if I could. I knew Lee Street."

Chapter 20

"Sure," Ike said. After a quick assessment of the situation, he added, "There's a Starbucks a couple of miles away from this chaos. Would you like to meet there?"

Becky was still by Ike's side. She said she had to run some errands before dinner and excused herself. Ike made sure Bruce knew the way to the coffee shop, and they agreed to meet there as soon as traffic would allow.

Maybe Harbuck's strategy is working, Ike thought, as he made his way to his car. Maybe leaking the suspicion about Lee's sexual orientation and Ike's involvement in the case was about to pay off. Maybe this Bruce had some piece of information that would break the case. What did he mean by "I knew Lee Street?" Did he mean he "knew" him in the biblical sense?

After they ordered, Ike allowed Bruce to select seating—to give him whatever degree of privacy he needed.

After exchanging a couple of pleasantries, Ike learned that Bruce lived in Jacksonville, Florida. Then Bruce said, "A couple of days ago, I got a call from Lee's sister, Ashley. She had no idea who I was. Just noticed there were dozens of calls to my number on Lee's cell phone, including one the night he died. She rang the number, introduced herself, and started asking questions."

Ike nodded, leaving the conversation wide open for Bruce.

"She asked me how I knew Lee. I told her we were friends, that we had met at a church convention a few years ago. We both had an interest in music. We sang together at that convention. A sort of impromptu choir. We became friends. Lee had a great voice. Were you aware of that, Rev. Benheart?"

"Call me Ike. I never heard him sing," Ike replied. "I grew up in his church, First Baptist. But I've been away from there for many years. For the past few years, I mostly knew Lee by reputation, as a member of a prominent family of August Valley. As a member of the Street family. But—go on. You were saying Ashley asked you other questions?"

"Yes," Bruce said. "She asked me if I knew he was dead. I said yes and told her I was at his funeral. There was no reason she would know that, however. I didn't speak to any of the family there. They didn't know me, and...well, I didn't see any point."

"Go on," Ike said.

"She apologized for being forward, but she told me his phone showed a call to me the night Lee died, and she hoped I would tell her if he said anything that might have indicated...you know, trouble."

"Did he?" Ike asked.

"I told her Lee didn't sound like himself. That he sounded depressed. I believe you had reason to think the same thing, didn't you, Rev. Benheart? I meant to say, Ike. At least, Ashley indicated you did."

"Then I guess she told you how I got involved in all this, Bruce." Ike said. "About Jim Harbuck, the attorney, asking the family a lot of questions. About Harbuck telling them how I was involved—about my conversation with Lee. About my similar suspicion to yours, that he was depressed. About my suspicion that..." Ike hesitated for a moment. "That he killed himself."

"Yep. And you might be right, Ike. Lee was feeling a lot of pressure," Bruce said, each word coming out slowly, as if he were carefully feeling for the edge of a cliff he feared lay in front of him. "He was afraid."

"Afraid? Afraid of...?" Ike asked quizzically, pretty sure he knew what the nature of the revelation would be.

"Afraid that someone was about to reveal to the world that he was gay," Bruce said, jumping off that precipice into the unknown.

"That was part of my suspicion also," Ike said. "That Street was gay. But I guess Ashley told you that also. I didn't know the part about his fear of being outed. I just sensed that he was feeling a lot of guilt about his sexual identity. Religious guilt."

"Ashley didn't say anything about that part," Bruce said. "Him being gay. It never came up in our conversation. I don't think she had it in her to go into that with a complete stranger. But she told me enough about you and about what Harbuck said that I put it together. What you suspected and what you knew."

"What happened to make Lee suddenly so afraid?" Ike asked.

"Some members of the city council talked to him. About some property sale that they didn't want to go through. You see, the council had this conversation with Lee informally. Off the record. Anyway, in the course of that conversation, one of them said, 'This sale brings up a lot of issues for the council, Lee. We want you to give it a lot of thought before you proceed. We wouldn't want this to result in any damage to your reputation.' That's when Lee's paranoia really kicked in. He got afraid this council member knew he was gay and was insinuating he could reveal that and damage Lee's reputation. That he could bring Lee out of the closet. Shame him in front of his family, his church, the community."

"Thinly veiled blackmail," Ike said.

"Yep," Bruce continued. "Worded in such a way that it could be attributed to any number of things. Said in such a way that he could deny any malice should something happen. Which it did. I wonder how that council member feels about all this now?" There was anger in his voice as he said this, and tears started welling up in his eyes.

"Lee was closeted," Ike said, trying to be sensitive to Bruce while also wanting to get the whole story. "Yet you knew. What was the nature of Lee's relationship with you, Bruce, if I might ask?"

"Lee and I were lovers," Bruce admitted.

Chapter 21

Ike telephoned Harbuck on his way home from Starbucks.

"Jim, you were right," Ike said. "Once word got out, people started talking. And things started happening. I've just had coffee with Lee Street's romantic interest."

"Got time to come by the office and tell me about it?" Harbuck said.

Ike looked at his watch. 6:15 p.m. He knew he'd be late for dinner. "I'll swing by for just a minute. Just need to text Becky and let her know I'll be late."

I've spent this day in two parallel universes, Ike thought to himself. He had marched with people who were openly gay and proud of it here in conservative August Valley. These were self-aware, self-confident individuals taking stock of their courage by utterly defying what were, until very recently, accepted universal norms. From there he had immediately stepped into the secretive world of Bruce and Lee, who had this profound need to conceal their homosexuality and maintain this veneer as aristocratic Christian Southern gentlemen. *Straight* aristocratic Christian Southern gentlemen, that is. Maintain this veneer at all costs. Pay for its loss with their very lives.

"His name is Bruce Massey," Ike reported. "He lives in Jacksonville. He and Street had been together for seven years."

Ike relayed everything he'd learned from the conversation and explicit detail of the sordid meeting with the city council just as Bruce had recounted it to him. Harbuck wrote as Ike talked.

"Whew," he exclaimed when Ike finished. "This thing really blew up in the council's face. Too bad we can't pin Street's death on them. But with Massey's testimony, we just might be able to get Ismael off the hook."

"Massey will have to come out to save Ismael?" Ike asked. "He's closeted too. I don't know much about his life, but obviously he wanted to keep this part of it secret. Doesn't seem right."

"When I file the motion for dismissal, I can request a closed hearing. But as high-profile as this case is, the details will get out. The media will be all over it."

"What'll happen as far as the city council?" Ike asked. "Surely their part in this needs to come out also."

"Let's worry about Ismael first," Harbuck cautioned. "Depending on the judge that hears this, he might ask for a further hearing. But even if he does, I can't see anything happening. Not based on this account. Not in this town. I don't doubt the statement made to Street had malicious intent. However, that would be impossible to prove."

"Another reason I could never be a lawyer," Ike said. "That isn't justice. It's just messing with people's lives."

"I agree," Harbuck said. "It's a fucked-up system. But it's the best we've got. And it sure beats anything the rest of the world has come up with. Don't despair, my friend. It's not over yet. I'll move ahead with the motion to dismiss. Still wish Street had left a note. He would've saved his companion from being exposed and spared a lot of people a lot of trouble."

"Patterson Street will have a shit hemorrhage when he hears about this," Ike said.

"He'll raise all kind of hell. But he'll get over it. At least the part about his brother being gay. The part about the city council, I'm not so sure. If anything can be done to them, Patterson will see to it. He's been at odds with the council ever since his family lost total control of this town. He might try to avenge his brother's death in some way. If you want the council held accountable for what they did to Lee Street, I'd put my money on Patterson, not on some judge.

Patterson's got plenty of lawyers and lots of economic clout. Lots of levers he could pull."

"If Patterson goes after the council, then I'd be right there with him," Ike said. "Hadn't thought of that. We'd be on the same side for a change. Wouldn't Patterson and I make strange bedfellows?"

"You have one sick mind, Ike," Harbuck said. "Go home and have dinner."

Chapter 22

Ike's dinner was cold. Becky warmed his plate while she bombarded him with questions. Ike didn't want to reveal what he had learned about Bruce to anybody except the one person he had to tell. Harbuck. But Becky saved him from having to be evasive. She'd already put it all together.

"I'm not sure I would have figured it out if we hadn't been at a gay parade," she told Ike. "But when that Bruce guy approached you and said he knew Lee Street, my mind immediately went there. This guy looks like a perfect match for Street. Clean-cut. Designer suit. Nice manners. Two peas in a pod."

Since Becky had the key piece to Bruce's identity, Ike gave her the details of his conversation with Bruce. Specifically, how and why Ashley Street had decided to call him and why she had mentioned Ike.

"We need to keep quiet about this until Harbuck gets the charges against Ismael dropped. If the Streets find out there's someone who's going to stand up and say Lee was gay, they'll assemble an army to try and discredit that person."

"I'll not breathe a word," Becky said. "But I don't think the Streets would do that. They knew Lee was gay. At least Ashley Street did."

"What makes you say that?" Ike asked.

"She had to suspect it. Jesus, Ike, she was his sister. Women have an intuition about these things. She made that call on Lee's phone to confirm that intuition. When the person on the other end was male, she knew."

"You're probably right," Ike said. "Lee was apparently one of those middle-aged gentlemen everyone in these parts refers to as a 'confirmed bachelor.' I've learned people often use that as a Southern euphemism for gay. But even if his family had kind of silently accepted Lee as 'different,' they are still going to resist his being exposed. Sure, acceptance of gays has come a long way in our society and has made significant headway even here in the South. But the Streets fancy themselves the cream of Dixie aristocracy, like some poster family for *Southern Living* magazine. They're going to push back. Trust me. I know these people."

Ike spoke plainly with Becky, as he knew he could. Being a native of August Valley, he had the inside track on the pridefulness and prejudices of the towns-people. Also, having lived in the Northeast during his seminary years, he knew it is nearly impossible for anyone not born and raised in the South to understand polite, polished Southern culture. Becky was from the homogeneous Midwest. Living in August Valley was culture shock for her. Even after sixteen years here, she still had little grasp of big-picture items like the unspoken social codes that kept African Americans and European Americans segregated in most of their private associations and certainly every Sunday morning at eleven. This private segregation was entrenched, even though blacks and whites freely integrated in schools, shopping malls, and virtually every other public space. *If Becky couldn't get any handle on that*, Ike thought, *then she's not likely to understand how the high-and-mighty Streets would vociferously defend against the perceived threat to their family honor in this situation.*

"What can they do?" Becky asked. "If this Bruce guy is willing to go public and say he had a relationship with Lee Street, that's it. Why wouldn't people believe him? When something's so secretive and potentially damaging to him, and yet he comes forward and admits it, people will always believe it. People will always believe something scandalous."

"I hear what you're saying," Ike said. "But the Streets can turn Bruce's courageous revelation into their own scandal. Now that gay marriage is legal and grants the couple all the rights of heterosexual marriage, they could say that Bruce is making all this up so that he can be heir to Lee's estate. Or they might say Harbuck solicited some gay guy just to support this cockamamie suicide theory of his just so he could clear his client. There's all sorts of not-so-noble possibilities for this 'out of the blue' appearance of Lee's lover that the Street family can come up with to suit their needs."

"Geez, Ike, you do know these people. Rather, I should say, your thought processes are as devious as you think theirs are. Do all Southerners really think that way? Think the worst of their fellow man? Think everyone is unscrupulous and scheming?"

"Pretty much," Ike replied. "It's all a part of Southern chivalry. Defend our honor at all costs."

"I don't know if I'd have married you if I'd known you were capable of thinking so connivingly," Becky said with as straight a face as she could muster, trying to sound reproachful.

"Can't help it," Ike said, appreciating the tease behind his wife's remark. "It goes with the territory. Down here we're raised to expect the worst of people. And experience teaches us how often people will rise to meet that expectation."

"God, you're cynical, Ike. How did you ever get to be a Unitarian? I thought Unitarians always put their faith in the inherent goodness of humanity."

"I do," Ike said. "But I also recognize that everyone has a dark side, and people will go to great lengths to try to conceal it. I learned that so well growing up in the church. Church. It's the perfect cover for the dark side. Expect the worst from people. Hope for the best, yes. People have a good side too, and they amaze me all the time by their goodness, by failing to meet my expectations. Fortunately, I've lived most of my life in complete astonishment."

"You're right about one thing," Becky said. "I'll never understand the South."

"Hopefully I'm wrong about the Streets," Ike said. "They may accept all this and take it in stride. But I don't expect them to. I just hope Bruce has a squeaky-clean past. If the Streets can dig up anything to silence or discredit him, I expect they'll find it, and they won't mind using it."

Chapter 23

Confident that Bruce Massey's story would serve to exonerate Ismael, Ike turned his attention to his historical research. He thought if he better understood what was going on in 1971, then this business about First Baptist's mission to the Bangladeshi refugees might make more sense. Ismael had confirmed that his mother had to leave Bangladesh because she was on the wrong side of a tribal conflict in a country in the midst of a civil war. But what was life like for these refugees? They were forced to leave everything behind, family, homes, culture, and find a way to survive and begin a new life in a strange land. What other pressures came to bear on them? What other challenges did they face? And how did First Baptist church come to get involved? What compelled them to take a special interest in this particular cause? Ike knew very little about any of this period, neither local history nor what was happening on the global stage. To fully grasp the situation of these refugees, he had to review the history of Southeast Asia back to just after World War II.

The country of Pakistan was created in 1947 when the British colony of India was partitioned as a part of the plan for India to regain its independence. Tensions between Muslims and Hindus in India were such that the Muslims needed their own country. The British carved Pakistan out of two areas of land, one in the northwest corner of India and one in the northeast. These two areas were not contiguous, so Pakistan existed as a divided country, geographically, from 1947 to 1971. It was also divided ethnically and politically, with East Pakistanis generally feeling like they got the short end of the stick. East Pakistan generated by far the greater amount in foreign exchange, yet it received proportionately less in governmental spending and was underrepresented in governmental offices. Dissatisfaction over these and other issues continued to mount between East and West Pakistan throughout the 1950s and '60s. Then came the devastating cyclone of 1970 that hit East Pakistan, killing half a million people. The poor response to this disaster by the central government in West Pakistan led to a strong call for independence by the East, resulting in a civil war between East and West in 1971. East Pakistan prevailed in the war to become the independent nation of Bangladesh, recognized as such by the United Nations in 1972.

During the civil war, the Pakistani military committed atrocities against residents of East Pakistan, murdering hundreds of thousands of civilians as part of a genocide against the Bengali people. People were sought out in their homes and murdered indiscriminately. College-age youth were systematically killed, as the Pakistani military knew this group of intelligent youth comprised a core group fomenting rebellion. They also knew this was the age that would do the actual fighting in any resistance movement. The University of Dhaka became an early target by a surprise bombing. Many students there were slaughtered by marauding troops from the Pakistani military.

Some two to four hundred thousand Bangladeshi women became victims of genocidal rape. The rapes caused thousands of pregnancies. Valiant efforts by the authorities to label these women war heroines were ineffectual. These women knew they would be completely ostracized if they tried to return home when the war ended. Some of them managed to persuade their captors to take them back to Pakistan with them after the war. Some tried to return home and were killed by their husbands. Many saw no other option and killed their own babies or committed suicide. A few who survived the ordeal were able to have abortions. Only a tiny fraction of these "war babies" were carried to term and adopted.

This was the situation in Bangladesh at the time Gera was forced to flee! Ike thought to himself.

Ismael said that she was pregnant with him when she left Bangladesh. Was it possible that her pregnancy had something to do with her reasons for being forced to leave Bangladesh? Had Ismael been told the real story surrounding his conception?

And what about that demented tirade by mother, calling her a whore and a bitch? Though he put little stock in his mother's rantings due to her Alzheimer's, it still left him unsettled. Could Gera have acted promiscuously in some way that incited his mother's anger? It would seem that a newcomer to this country, someone who was looking askance at everyone around her for her very survival, would be on her very best behavior. Being a refugee is such a disadvantaged state from the beginning. Why would she have jeopardized the goodwill of her benefactors by acting inappropriately? Or doing anything that might even seem inappropriate? Didn't make sense.

Or did it? Did she need to curry the favor of someone? A male perhaps? Ike shook his head. He was letting his imagination get away from him. *All this is just conjecture on my part*, he told himself. Surely Ismael's mother would have been truthful with her son about this serious a matter.

But then again, her situation may have been more desperate than anyone could imagine. Anything could have happened to Gera, given the state of the country she left and the uncertain future before her in this country she was forced to adopt, Ike surmised.

What else could he learn—should he learn—about something that had happened forty-five years ago? *Maybe I should just let go of this*, he thought. *I may learn something that brings on more pain than it's worth.*

Two days elapsed, and Ike hadn't heard from anyone about any further developments in Ismael's case. He called Harbuck.

"Jim, what's up? Haven't heard anything. Did you make contact with Massey?"

"Yeah, I talked with him, and we've set up his deposition," Harbuck said. "But something else has come up. We've got a big problem."

"What's that?" Ike said.

"The crime lab that's investigating the case took possession of Ismael's computer," Harbuck replied.

"Okay," Ike said. "They found something they think they can use?"

"I'm afraid so," Harbuck answered. "They found that Ismael has been browsing dozens of websites for ISIS and other links for terrorist organizations."

Chapter 24

"**W**hat?" Ike exclaimed. He was floored.

"I'm afraid this may put a different perspective on the entire case," Harbuck said.

"Wait a second, Jim," Ike said. "I know you asked Ismael about this. What did he say?"

"He said it was all connected with his research," Harbuck said. "Said he's writing a paper about the Islamic State."

"Of course," Ike said with a sigh of relief. "He teaches political science. He's a Muslim. So, if he's going to do research in his field, it seems logical that he might want to make an academic study of the Islamic State."

"And it also makes sense that Ismael might be an angry Muslim that was in the process of being radicalized."

"You *can't* believe that?" Ike protested.

"No, of course not," Harbuck said. "I'm just stating the case the prosecution will make. Can they make a jury believe it? You tell me."

"Un-freaking-believable," Ike responded. "This guy just can't catch a break."

"Nope," Harbuck said. "I'm going to proceed with filing for a summary dismissal. But this is going to hurt our chances for anything happening quickly."

"How's Ismael handling this setback?" Ike asked.

"He's okay, I think," Harbuck said. "Amazingly patient, despite all the turmoil this is causing in his life. It's Eisha that I'm concerned about. She was there last night when I talked to him. She totally freaked out."

"Maybe Becky can talk to her. She doesn't know Eisha except to see her. Our son Jake and their son Bai are in the same class at school."

"Please," Harbuck said. "Eisha needs all the support she can get right now."

Ike didn't visit his mother for several days after the outburst, as he wanted to make sure she had completely calmed down. But today he returned, and if his mother was fairly lucid, he hoped to revisit the topic of his parents' ministry to the Bangladeshi refugees. This time he was going to be more circumspect and not mention Gera at all. When he walked in her room, she appeared more alert than she had been in weeks and actually greeted him with a smile.

After a few minutes catching her up on the family, he decided today may be his best opportunity to broach the subject again.

"Mom, I've been doing some reading about the refugees that you and Dad helped back in 1971," Ike began. "They must have been very frightened by what happened to them back in Bangladesh. Many people were being killed and tortured in the war. Many of the refugees lost family members, I'm sure. Can you tell me anything about it?"

"You don't know," his mother said. It sounded more like a statement than a question.

"No, I don't know, Mom. That's why I'm talking to you about it now. That's why I'm asking you now."

"Mistake," she said. "I made a mistake. We never should have done it."

"But why was it a mistake, Mom?" Ike asked. "You and Dad must have helped many of those refugees find places to stay and settle in and find jobs. I'm sure you did a great service. How could doing good be a mistake?"

"I was nice to those people," his mother said. "I wanted to help. I made your father help. But he didn't want to. I made him."

"Dad didn't want to help refugees?" Ike asked. "That doesn't sound like Dad, Mom. Why did he not want to help?"

"Oh, he didn't want to. At first. He changed his mind. He helped. He helped them a lot. He went there all the time. He helped..." Ike could see his mother beginning to get agitated again.

"Mom, it's okay. Calm down. We don't have to talk about this anymore."

"He helped *himself*." She screamed this last word.

"Mom, let's talk about something else," Ike said hurriedly, hoping to distract her. "We're having a cookout this Saturday at the house. Tim and Diane are coming. Do you want to come?"

"That would be lovely, dear," she said sweetly, and then she just seemed to drift back into her own world.

"Good, Mom. We'll come to get you at eleven. I'll tell the nurses to get you ready. I've got to go now." Ike kissed her on the forehead and departed.

Ike mulled over his mother's limited words as he drove to the church. The information he had gotten from Inez was still fresh in his mind also, and he tried to reconcile that with the tidbits he had picked up from his mother.

It sounds like Mom got caught up in helping the refugees and then tried to impose her enthusiasm on Dad. He wasn't too interested at first, but then "he helped himself." Inez said Mother might have been upset because of all the attention Dad gave Gera. And Inez said Gera was very pretty and acted seductively. If I didn't know my Dad so well, I'd be getting the idea that he might have had a little fling with this Muslim hussy. Ike had to laugh at the thought. But he didn't dismiss it.

Two days later, the day Ike was to go pick up his mother for the cookout, the nurse from the nursing home called Ike and told him his mother was not doing well and that he needed to come right away. He drove directly there. When he arrived at her room, her doctor met him at the door.

"I'm sorry, Ike," Dr. Simmons said solemnly. "Sally has just passed on from this life."

Chapter 25

The funeral took place the following Tuesday. The present minister from First Baptist did the service. Ike gave the eulogy.

Sally Benheart had been involved in the life of the congregation in every church Ike's father had pastored. Many of these churches were within driving distance of August Valley, so several hundred people came to pay last respects. Ike was exhausted when it was over.

Misha, Ike's aunt and Sally's sister, stayed over a few days to help Ike sort through some of Sally's personal belongings.

Misha was the one member of his mother's family whom Ike could actually engage in meaningful conversation.

"Wonderful tribute you gave to your mother this afternoon," Misha said. "You really captured her spirit in those stories you told about her."

"Mom was a woman of great dignity," Ike responded. "She poured her heart into everything she did."

"How much of this stuff do you want to keep?" Misha asked. They were looking at the cardboard boxes that had stored his mother's stuff since she had moved to the nursing home. Ike had kept them in the guest room of his house since he relocated his mother.

"Not much of it," Ike said. "But I want to go through it before I throw anything away. I was right in the middle of a little research project on my parents when Mom died. Now that she's gone, this stuff might be the only place left for me to find any clues."

"Clues to what?" Misha said. "What were you researching?"

"Recently I learned that Mom and Dad were involved in a ministry to the refugees from Bangladesh. Back in 1971," Ike said. "They'd never told me anything about it. But apparently, it was a big part of their life during that time. I've just gotten curious about it; that's all. I tried to talk with Mom about it and get some information, but I didn't get too far with her, as you might imagine."

"I remember Sally talking about that," Misha said. "That was another of those things she really poured her heart into. As you know, Sally needed to feel needed. When she talked to me about it, she would always say how needy those refugees were. Most of them came to this country with nothing but the clothes on their back. That refugee effort apparently gave her a sense of fulfillment, gave her a real sense of purpose. I think it made her feel like she was doing something important on the world stage, like foreign missions. It was like she could be a foreign missionary but still be in her own home every night."

"That sounds like the perfect job for Mom," Ike said. "Yes, she liked feeling needed, and she liked the feeling she was making a real difference in someone's life. She was always talking about missionaries and how much she admired them. Sometimes I got the idea she wanted to be a missionary herself. I could see her doing that. But I don't think Dad would have gone for it."

"No, Abe wasn't the missionary type," Misha said. "He needed his creature comforts. And he had a taste for the finer things of life. I couldn't see him ever consenting to live in the squalor of some third-world country."

"I don't think Mom would have lasted very long in a place like that either," Ike said. "But ministering to these refugees, that would've been ideal. She could go and come from her nice, neat little suburban world as she pleased and still get the feeling she was doing something adventurous, unique, and noble. Like she was little Miss Lottie Moon or something."

"That was her," Misha laughed. "An Americanized version of Mother Teresa."

"I don't want to sound too cynical though, about this mission she was on," Ike said. "Because it was a worthy thing she was doing. Recently I met a child, the son, of one of those refugees she helped. He expressed a deep appreciation to her and acknowledges that his mother's life—and his—might have turned out quite differently if it hadn't been for the efforts and support of that relief endeavor."

"Sometimes we manage to do good in spite of ourselves," Misha observed.

"Aunt Misha, do you have any idea why my mom and dad never talked to me about this?" Ike asked. "You'd think they would be proud of being a part of something like that."

Misha's face suddenly lost all color. "You know something, Ike, don't you?"

"No, I don't," Ike said. "But you do. What is it?"

"I guess it's okay to tell you now, but I feel like I'm violating a confidence," Misha said.

"They're gone," Ike said. "Dead and buried. It's okay. Was my dad having an affair?"

"Maybe," Misha admitted. "I don't know for sure. I just remember your mother writing to me then—that's when I was in college at Vanderbilt—and telling me that she regretted some things she had done. She also wrote me and said she had to forgive your father for something. Next time I got to talk to her, I asked her what was it that she had to forgive. All she would say was, 'Abe got too involved. I pushed him into it, and he got too involved.' Sally never volunteered any specifics, and I could tell it upset her terribly, so I didn't press. I just assumed that Abe got a little too emotionally involved with one of the refugees. That's what it sounded like, judging by what Sally did say to me at that time and the way she reacted. But I don't know. I don't know if Abe actually had an affair, but there was obviously something inappropriate going on."

"Her name was Gera," Ike said. "She was the refugee whose son I mentioned I met the other day."

"You met the son of this woman Abe was involved with. Wow! Did he know—I mean, about his mother's involvement with your father?"

"I don't think so," Ike said. "He knows they lost touch. Obviously, they lost touch. This guy, this son—his name is Ismael—grew up here in August Valley like I did, yet he and I had never met. I've asked him what he knew about his mother's relationship with my parents. He said that something happened to their relationship. He doesn't know what, but his mother gave him the impression it soured because Mom and Dad were trying to make a Christian out of her."

"And she was Muslim, I imagine," Misha said. "Oh boy! I wonder if it would matter to him if he knew? I mean, if he knew that your father tried to share more with his mother than just God's love? Are you going to tell him?"

"Tell him what?" Ike said. "I don't know anything for sure. Besides, what would be the point? No sense in saying anything unless I happen to get some proof."

Chapter 26

"Hello, Becky," Eisha said. "Please come in. This way to the kitchen." Ike had approached Becky with Harbuck's concern about Eisha. Becky called her the next morning. They made a plan to get together for breakfast at Eisha's house after the kids were deposited at school.

"I'll make us an omelet," Eisha said.

"Don't go to any trouble," Becky said. "I don't usually eat much for breakfast anyway."

"No trouble. I have everything out here on the counter. Just made one for Bai. We're going to go broke feeding him. Typical teenager."

"Okay, thanks," Becky replied. "An omelet sounds good."

"Cheese, onion, green peppers okay?" Eisha asked.

"Okay with me."

"While you're waiting, try one of these," Eisha said, offering Becky a platter. "It's a paratha. Bangladesh breakfast food. Sort of a puffed pastry stuffed with potato."

Becky took one and bit into it. "Mmm, delicious. You'll have to show me how you make them."

"It's easy. Next time I'll show you."

"Next time maybe you can come over to my house," Becky said.

"Yes, I'd like that," Eisha said enthusiastically. "I haven't been out of the house much, since…Ismael's arrest."

"Oh, Eisha. This has to be terrible for both of you."

Eisha teared up. "I'm afraid when I leave the house. I feel everyone looking at me now. It's like they know who I am. Who I'm married to."

"So it's easier to just stay home," Becky said.

"Yes. Ismael and I never got out much anyway. Muslims eat only halal food, food that's prepared according to our customs, so there are only certain places we can eat out. And Muslims don't drink alcohol, and that put limits on socializing. But at least I wasn't self-conscious when I went out. Now I have to find some courage just to go to the grocery store."

"Why not take a friend along when you need to go out?" Becky said.

"Sometimes I do," Eisha said, "when it's convenient for them and for me."

"Do you and Ismael have many non-Muslim friends?" Becky asked.

"Some," Eisha said with a sigh, "but not so many as we had when we were at university together. Things change with children. We got busy being parents. It became harder to make connections."

"The Muslim community is a pretty tight-knit group, isn't it?" Becky said.

"They are," Eisha said. "I think that tendency comes from the way some Muslims think the Quran says Muslims shouldn't take non-Muslims as friends. That's not my understanding of what the Quran says, nor is it Ismael's. We welcome relationships with others. While we're talking about this, let me say that I'm so grateful to your husband for what he is trying to do for Ismael. Your husband is a good man. Here, your omelet is ready."

"Thank you," Becky said. "Ike is a good man. Stubborn sometimes, but what man isn't?"

Eisha laughed. "You don't know stubborn unless you know the man I live with."

"It was not an easy thing for Ike to do what he did," Becky said, becoming serious. "Ike took the events of 9/11 very hard. He's always been very open and accepting of other people no matter what their faith is. But the planes used in that attack originated in Boston, where he went to college, and he knew some of the people on board."

"Oh, Becky, I didn't know that," Eisha said. "I'm so glad you told me. That gives me even more respect for what he's doing for my husband.

"I'm so sorry," she continued. "I can understand why Americans might hate Islam. That brand of Islam perpetrated by Osama bin Laden and his Al-Qaeda henchmen, that is. Terrorism in any form doesn't speak for us. I'm glad your husband is able to separate things like that as acts of a few deranged, evil men and in no way represents our way of life, the Islam we embrace."

"Of course," Becky said.

"More coffee?" Eisha asked.

"No thanks. This breakfast was delicious."

"Glad you enjoyed it," Eisha said. Then she teared up again and held up her hand as if she was about to say something. "Becky, I'm so scared right now. For Ismael, for me and Bai. But I'm also angry. Ismael's friends from the mosque haven't been supporting him. Some of the women come to see me, but he's had almost no one."

"Do they think he's guilty?" Becky said, thinking out loud. "Perhaps that's not a fair question."

"No, that is a fair question," Eisha said. "I've even thought to myself that's what they're thinking. The whole thing is just bizarre. This man Street must have killed himself. He was gay, and he felt guilty about that, and maybe that made him do it. But there's no way to prove it. So here's an opportunity to blame a Muslim, and that's what's done. Some Muslims think gay people should die. Some people think if they support my husband, they will be investigated as well. And maybe their computers will be searched also. They have many reasons for staying away. Maybe they're scared, but that makes them cowards."

"It sounds like what happened in Salem, Massachusetts," Becky said. "No one would stand up for the women who were accused, afraid that they would be accused also."

"Exactly," Eisha said. "August Valley is another Salem."

"Not exactly," Becky said. "Ike is standing up for Ismael. And so's Jim Harbuck. The truth is going to come out, Eisha."

"Inshallah, I hope you're right," Eisha said.

"Maybe we should talk about something else?" Becky asked. "Of course, if you need to talk more about this, we can."

"No, I'd rather talk about something else," Eisha said. "This is all I think about, so it would be good to think about something else for a few minutes."

"I was wondering about Ismael's big revelation to Ike," Becky said. "That their parents had this connection from long ago. That's so interesting to me. It's sad that it took these kinds of circumstances for Ike to discover it, but…still, it's a fascinating link for them to make."

"I don't know much about that," Eisha said, "other than what Ismael told me last week when I visited him. Ismael's mother, Gera, was a very proud woman. She had a right to be. She was beautiful. She gave birth to the man who became my husband. But, oh, could she be difficult. If anything got in the way of what she wanted."

"I hadn't pictured her that way," Becky said. "Though I had no reason to form any opinion, really. I only knew she was a refugee and was a survivor from the horrors of a war. You're giving me the impression that your relationship with your mother-in-law might have been a little, uh, 'strained.'"

"That's putting it mildly," Eisha said. "Gera was queen of all she surveyed. She didn't have friends; she had subjects. She didn't carry on conversation; she held court. I know I should be more generous in my opinion of her, considering that she did go through a lot, being forced out of her country and having to leave everything and start all over in a foreign land and all that. But I had to deal with the person she was years later. And she wasn't easy, let me tell you."

Becky was intrigued. She also knew her husband could use this information as he continued to play amateur sleuth with his parents' past.

"How long did you know her?" Becky asked.

"A few years. Let's see; Ismael and I met at Duke University. I met her then. That was around 1993. She died four years ago. 2012. Terrible car accident. She was in the car with a man we thought she might get married to. I certainly hoped they would get married, so she would put her energy and focus into another man besides her son. It was nearly twenty years I knew her."

"You never heard her talk about the war or about being a refugee?"

"No, she never talked about that part of the past. It was like she tried to blot it out. Now, she talked about Bangladesh all the time. But it was always about how great it was, all the good times she had as a child, how much she loved the cuisine, and how much better life was there than it is here. My parents did that too. I think that was a part of how they coped with it. With all they had lost. It was a way for them to hold on to their identity."

While taking all this in, Becky was also engaged in a dialogue with herself. Should she divulge what Ike's mother had said about Gera? On the one hand, she had only just met Eisha, and the idea of saying "My mother-in-law called your mother-in-law a whore" didn't seem like the best way to continue nurturing this relationship. Becky really liked Eisha, and she could see them becoming good friends. In Becky's experience, friendships that arose out of a crisis were often the most meaningful ones, and she could certainly see that happening here. On the other hand, only a couple of hours into the relationship, and Eisha was speaking quite openly and negatively about Gera already, almost inviting Becky to despise her too. *What harm could it do for me to add one more insult?* she thought to herself.

"Ike's mother didn't seem to care much for Gera either," Becky ventured. "It's like she was afraid Gera was trying to take her husband away from her. Does that sound like something Gera would do?"

Without hesitating, Eisha said, "If Gera could get what she wanted by flirting with your mother-in-law's husband, then yes, she would. She was a willful, manipulative person and would stop at nothing to get her way."

"Eisha, if you don't mind me asking, what would Ismael say if he knew you were talking like this about his mother?"

"Since Gera died, Ismael has had his eyes opened a little bit," Eisha said. "Some of the things he's learned about her—well, he's had to take her down off the pedestal. He realizes she had her faults and wasn't exactly a paragon of moral virtue."

Chapter 27

July 2016

"The cartons aren't going to unpack themselves," Becky said to Ike. "I could help you go through your mother's stuff, but I'm not sure what you're looking for. Misha did quite a bit while she was here. Went through her clothes and took most of them to the Salvation Army. Saved you some of the trouble. She said to leave the boxes for you."

"I'll get it done," Ike said. "I know you're ready to get Mom's stuff out of that room and make it a useable space again. Just give me until Saturday. I've got nothing going on then, and I'll sort through it. This project is at the top of my list. But I've had so much to catch up on at the church. With the funeral and all our relatives coming into town last week, I got behind on so many things. Since your conversation with Eisha, I'm more curious than ever about Gera and whatever it was she did to put such a burr under my mother's saddle."

"You really think Sally was jealous of her or might have thought Abe was getting him a little on the side?" Becky asked.

"Everyone who was around then knew something was going on," Ike said. "Mother, Inez, Misha. Even Eisha, Gera's daughter-in-law, said Gera was capable of doing such a thing. From all I've learned over the past few days about Gera and about the situation back then, it's looking quite likely."

"Let's say Abe and Gera did 'hike the Appalachian' together, Ike," Becky said. "What's the big deal? It didn't break your parents up. Why dig it up now? Abe, Gera, Sally—they're all dead. What does it matter? Why try to air the dirty laundry?"

"It matters to me," Ike said. "It changes the way I understand who my parents were, what their relationship was like, the tensions they carried with them, the disappointments they might have endured. Whatever happened was kept a family secret. At least, it was kept a secret from me. That means those who knew the secret possessed a power that was denied to me. I was locked out—in an emotional sense."

"You and that family-systems theory stuff," Becky said dismissively. "I say just let it go."

"And what about Ismael?" Ike said, as a way of coming to his own defense. "Who knows how this information might help him understand things about his mother and some of the things that happened between him and her."

"If you find out there was an affair, surely you're not going to tell Ismael. Don't you think the guy has enough on his mind right now?"

"I may not find out anything unless Ismael helps me," Ike said. "If Sally didn't leave a clue, maybe his mother did. Don't worry; I'm not going to add any angst to the burdens Ismael's already dealing with. You know me; I'll only bring it up if and when it's appropriate. I'm a sensitive guy."

"Yeah, you're a regular Montel Williams," Becky replied sarcastically.

Saturday morning after breakfast, Ike settled himself in at the kitchen table with his coffee and several boxes of his mother's keepsakes. The cartons held pictures, award certificates, newspaper clippings, child artwork—all sorts of reminders from the life of a proud mother, church member, and spouse to a prominent minister. Ike had reason to be hopeful that there would be some scrap of evidence here to either confirm or dissuade him from his hypothesis concerning Gera and his father. Hopeful because his mother was both nostalgic and a packrat. She could never part with anything that had memories attached to it.

Ike focused on the pictures first. His mother was also compulsively organized, and this made it relatively easy to look for any snapshots that might have been taken during the early '70s. All pictures were neatly tucked in albums, all labelled according to date.

There were plenty of pictures circa 1971–72 to chronicle his mother and father's vacations, family reunions, holidays, and church conferences and retreats, but Ike saw no images that might have been taken with any of the refugees. He waxed a bit nostalgic. The pictures helped him fabricate his own emotionally satisfying version of Abe and Sally Benheart's life in the time prior to his birth.

But as the morning progressed, Ike's enthusiasm for the project waned. His primary motive for the chore was bearing no fruit. However, this mental walk through family history and his imagined rendition of his parents' preparental life managed to bring enough satisfaction to keep him going through the boxes. His mother's photos, combined with some oral history of this era he'd accumulated through the years from his parents, allowed him to imaginatively construct a fairly thorough documentary.

It was close to lunchtime when Ike opened the last box. Here, bundled in stacks held together with rubber bands, were letters. He picked up a bundle and flipped through them, noting that the postmarked dates were chronologically arranged. Heart racing, he surveyed bundle after bundle until he found one with 1971 postmarks. There were several from Misha, most of them showing her return address at the Vanderbilt University campus. Ike took a deep breath and began to read.

Sally and Misha corresponded regularly during that time, exchanging three or four letters every month. The first mention of the refugees came in Misha's letter at the end of the letter from July 16, 1971.

Refugees from East Pakistan! How interesting. How many of them is your church group responsible for? What are you doing for them? What are they like? Do they speak English? Can you understand them? It sounds like you're excited about having this unique opportunity to share Christ. Please tell me all about it next week.

The next letter, dated July 24, contained this information:

Thanks for sharing about the refugees. So, they arrived there on July 4th weekend. How appropriate! I hope someone stressed the historical significance of that day to them.

How your heart must have broken to hear their stories about the women whose husbands were killed and those two mothers who lost children in the war. What will women like this Gera you mentioned do to support themselves? At least she's young. What about that older couple, the Choudhurys, who lost all their children and grandchildren and all their worldly possessions? I can't imagine how anyone can find the motivation to go on after such unspeakable loss. All we can do is trust that God will be with them as they try to pick up the pieces and somehow find a way forward.

Are all the refugees Muslim? How has that impacted what you are trying to do for them? Does their religion let them accept the kind of food and clothing you're able to get for them? Do they really roll out their prayer rugs five times a day? Has anyone talked to them about Christ?

What a heavy burden for you to bear, trying to create a whole new life for thirty-two people! I remember where the August Valley Inn is. The church must have blocked off an entire wing to put up that many people. Good thing the church is already set up offering English as a second language classes. If you're having trouble understanding them, sounds like they may need help getting passable English skills so they can get a job.

I'll certainly keep all of you in my prayers. May God bless you all as you feed, clothe, and shelter these unfortunate souls and help them find a way to settle in the United States.

PS, Thought you and your refugees might be interested in this. I read in *Rolling Stone* magazine that the Beatle George Harrison is going to put on a benefit concert for Bangladesh relief next week at Madison Square Garden. Bob Dylan is supposed to be there! You know I'm a huge fan. How I wish I could go.

Misha's letter from August 3 had only one brief reference:

Glad to hear Abe is now helping you with the Bangladeshi refugees. You've always supported him in his ministry, so he should be supportive of things like this that you feel strongly led to do. Maybe after they get to know you and Abe better, they will be more receptive to the Gospel.

Are any of them coming to services at the church? Abe may be just the one to share Christ and the plan of salvation with them.

No mention of the refugees in the letter dated August 12.

Then, here was how the August 24 letter started:

Sally,

I'm so sorry to hear the news about you and Abe. I hope the two of you are able to work things out. Since I don't know the whole story, I certainly won't try to make excuses for him. I will take heart since he told you he's sorry for what he did and you say you think you may be able to forgive him in time.

I know you had a lot of passion for your work with the refugee families and I'm sure that giving it up was a difficult thing to do as well. But all things considered, you're right. You wouldn't want to be around that woman again. Why chance it? You're making the right decision. Move on. There's an ocean of need in this world, and it won't take long for something else to come along that you can pour yourself into.

Abe read several more of the letters, but there was no more mention of either the refugees or Sally and Abe's marital problems.

Ike immediately phoned Aunt Misha and told her of his discovery. She remembered the content of the letters in a general way but had vivid recall only of the part about Abe's emotional and possible physical infidelity and the emotional havoc it wreaked.

"Is there *any* chance you have any of the letters you received from Sally?" Ike asked.

"I'm afraid not," Misha said. "I specifically remember trashing them. I threw them all away because of that one letter. I didn't want anybody in the family to ever discover that Abe had been unfaithful."

Ike had problems sleeping that night. Misha's words in the letters kept tumbling over and over in his mind. The letter confirmed everything he had suspected. But something else was bothering him about the letters. Something that he couldn't quite put his finger on.

Finally, he slept, but only fitfully. Just before dawn he awakened with a start. The dates on the letters! *Something isn't right.*

Chapter 28

It had now been two months since Ismael's incarceration. Still no word from Harbuck about any break in the case. The crime lab had finished their work on the crime scene. They had found Ismael's fingerprints on the door handles, but nowhere else. DNA profiling established Ismael's presence at the scene. Their analysis of his computer revealed that Ismael had made 297 searches to ISIS and other websites sponsoring radical Islam. The background check on Ismael turned up nothing of significance.

Street's blood alcohol was 0.076 percent, indicating that he had been drinking but was not legally drunk. Cause of death was confirmed to be asphyxiation by hanging.

Massey and Ike had given depositions. There was to be a hearing this week on Harbuck's motion for dismissal.

Ike looked through the bars at Ismael as the guard unlocked the door. He was startled at the change in his Muslim friend's appearance since his last visit two weeks prior. Ismael was noticeably thinner, his face pale, his clothes wrinkled, and it looked like he hadn't shaved for a week. He was beginning to look like a terrorist.

"Ismael, how are you, my friend?" Ike inquired.

At first Ike wasn't sure if Ismael recognized him.

"Hello, Ike," Ismael managed to say, as if a light suddenly came on. "Thank you for coming. And thank you for sending Becky to visit Eisha. The visit cheered her immensely."

"Becky told me the pleasure was all hers. You know they are planning to get together again tomorrow?"

"Yes," Ismael said. "Eisha needs friends like Becky. She put Eisha at ease on so many levels. She must look at things positively. Not like the women from the masjid. They see nothing but doom and gloom."

"Well, let's hope that very soon the four of us can sit down together and share a meal," Ike said.

"Deal," Ismael replied.

"You're looking thin," Ike said, to check out Ismael's level of self-awareness. "What's the matter, prison food not agreeing with you?"

"Ramadan started two weeks ago," Ismael said. "I'm fasting from sunrise to sunset."

Fasting during the month of Ramadan is one of the Five Pillars of Islam, the distinct practices that comprise Muslim life—the other four being prayer, alms to the poor, pilgrimage to Mecca, and reciting the declaration of faith, the Shahada. Islam is more of a practice, as opposed to other religions in which belief plays the predominant role in defining an adherent. A Muslim is better identified by what he or she does—that is, by the actions that are a regular part of life. Indeed, one is not considered a Muslim unless these five ritual activities are incorporated into one's existence.

"Of course, Ramadan. I didn't realize," Ike said.

"Eisha brings me dinner to eat after sunset, so I'm pretty much getting by on that. But I really don't have much of an appetite. As far as the beard, it's coming off tomorrow. Eisha keeps forgetting to bring my electric razor. They won't let me have razor blades in here. Can't imagine why. You'd think they didn't trust me."

Ike was glad to see Ismael's sense of humor still intact. "You must eat as much as you can after your fast every day," he urged. "You want to have the strength to walk out of here, don't you?"

"Can't happen soon enough for me," Ismael said. "Or for Eisha. I take that to mean you came to give me good news?"

"I wish I could say yes," Ike said, as he watched the light begin to fade again in Ismael's eyes. "The hearing is this week, isn't it? This thing may be over before you know it."

"No judge who values his career and his life is going to let me go," Ismael said. "This whole thing has become political. Don't forget; if there's one thing I know, it's politics."

"Okay, well, how about if we talk about something else," Ike said. "Maybe it will help to get your mind off your troubles, at least for a bit."

"Sure," Ismael said. "What's on your mind?"

"I have some letters written to my mother, Sally, in 1971 by her sister. I thought you might find them interesting."

Ike had highlighted the relevant passages with a yellow marker. The dates were also highlighted.

He handed the four letters to Ismael.

Ismael read in silence. *It's taking him forever*, Ike thought, but then he recalled that Misha's handwriting was a bit difficult to decipher.

Ismael handed the letters back to Ike. "'That woman,'" he said. "You're convinced she's talking about Gera. My mother."

"Yes," Ike replied.

"Well, that would explain why our parents parted ways," Ismael said. He said this matter-of-factly, as if he was going for dry wit in his response.

"Then you're not surprised?" Ike asked.

"Surprised?" Ismael responded, pausing as if thoughtfully considering how best to explain. "No, not really. I'm not surprised at the possibility my mother would be involved with your father in that way. What I am a bit surprised about is that you don't seem to be bothered about your father's role in this. His unfaithfulness to your mother.

"As far as my mother, those were desperate times. For her. For all those who were escaping the atrocities committed by West Pakistan. Desperate people do desperate things. Was my mother capable of immoral behavior, of seducing a married man? I have no doubt. She would have done most anything if she thought it would help insure her survival. The survival of her unborn child. Me."

"I hear what you're saying, Ismael, but I'm not sure I follow," Ike said. "What possible purpose would her romantic entanglement with my father have served? My father and mother were committed to looking after Gera. Looking after all the refugees. That was their mission. Even if they had known she was pregnant. That wouldn't have mattered. Why would she have seen advantage in getting sexually entangled?"

"I can't say this for sure, but it's something I've suspected all my life," Ismael said. "I was probably a war baby."

"War baby?" Ike really said it more as a statement than a question. "You mean, your mother was raped?"

"She never told me that. I put it together after I grew up and started learning about the war and the hundreds of thousands of women who were systematically raped by the Pakistani army. The women who got pregnant by these rapes were total outcasts. They had few options. They couldn't go home. Their families would have rejected them. Some of the women committed suicide or had the baby and then killed it.

"My mother didn't do either of those, thanks be to God. She could have had an abortion or put me up for adoption, I suppose, but she didn't. The maternal instinct is strong, I guess, even for a woman who has suffered the horror of rape. Instead, like other women trapped in this way, she tried desperately to find some other solution that gave her unborn baby, me, a 'legitimate' father."

Ike paused, trying to take all this in. "So, if what you're saying is the way things happened, then your mother was trying to trap a man here in the United States into thinking he was the father. Still doesn't quite add up. Why go after a married man? Why not someone single? Surely that would have made things a lot simpler."

"Maybe there weren't any single, eligible men around, and she took what opportunity she saw," Ismael said. "Maybe she thought she could convince your father to leave your mother. Maybe she fell in love with your father. Who knows what happened? These things I'm saying are only possibilities. I don't know any of this. I don't even know for certain she was raped. It's just something that was likely in those circumstances. Very likely possibilities, given the desperation of the time and the resourcefulness of my mother."

"I'm with you now," Ike said. "You've lived a good portion of your life with the suspicion that you might be a war baby?"

"That's right," Ismael said. "My mother showed me pictures of my father and told me he was a hero of the resistance and that he was killed, and that's why she ended up coming to the United States. But the story just doesn't add up. There was never any contact from any family of this man who was supposedly my father. Whenever I was around my mother's aunt, the only one of her family that survived the war, she never talked about my father. All Mother had was a picture of this man. I think she made him up. Another way that she tried to give me a father and give my life legitimacy—as anything but the product of a rape."

"And you never tried to approach your mother about these suspicions?" Ike asked.

"Never had the heart," Ismael said. "Knowing my mother the way I did, I just couldn't bring myself to do it. She had this dignity that she protected all the time. But it was a fragile dignity, and I wasn't about to be the one to shatter this facade she worked so hard to build and maintain."

"Wow, Ismael," Ike exclaimed. "What has it been like for you, to live with the probable knowledge that you were a war baby?"

"It is what it is," Ismael replied. "I have a good life. That is, I *had* a good life—until a month ago. I always felt loved. My mother provided for me, made it possible for me to do what I wanted to do. She sent me to college. What would it matter, in the great scheme of things, if my father was a rapist? I hate it for what my mother suffered and the scars she bore. But me? It's been all right. I wouldn't be here if it hadn't happened. That's a strange thought, isn't it? But definitely something to think about."

"Ismael, there may be yet another wrinkle in the picture," Ike said. "Did you notice the dates on the letters?"

"Nah," Ismael said sarcastically, adding, "You'd think I would've, considering that someone has obviously marked through them several times with a highlighter."

"You terrorist," Ike said playfully.

"You infidel," Ismael responded, dishing it back to Ike.

"Seriously, now, when did you say you were born?"

"May 4, 1972."

"Not possible," Ike said. "Not possible if your mother was pregnant when she arrived on July 4, 1971. That's ten months.

"Well, I've got the birth certificate," Ismael said. "Something must not be right about the dates in the letters."

Ike couldn't help but smile as he said, "Either that, or you're not a war baby after all."

Chapter 29

Ike wished there was something else he could do. Harbuck's motion for dismissal was denied. The judge set a date for trial. August 20.

At the hearing Harbuck also requested that Ismael be released on bond. This was granted. The protests had died down, and Harbuck thought Ismael would probably be okay at home. The attorney was also concerned about the physical condition of his client, and he wanted Ismael to look healthier if he was indeed going to appear in court.

Though Ismael was released from jail, Harbuck advised him not to appear in public under any circumstances and to remain confined to his house. At least at home he would get regular meals and not be subjected to the constant intimidation of the penal system.

Now that Ismael was released, visiting him would be much easier to arrange. Ike planned to make himself more available to his friend once he got settled in at home. Visits might be just the distraction he needed. Or he may just want to be left alone. Ike would do whatever Ismael thought was in his best interests.

The past month had been a pivotal one in Ike's spiritual formation. He actually enjoyed Ismael's company. Ismael was proving to be a good guy and fun to be around. Ike was developing a personal relationship with a Muslim. This made Ismael not only a friend, but also a sympathetic figure. The connection Ike felt to his friend and the respect he was developing for him were becoming a part of his conception of Islam.

The first thing Ike noticed as a result of this budding friendship was the way he heard news reports. The bombings, beheadings, and mass shootings continued to be reported nearly every time he was around a TV or computer screen. But when the word *Islam* appeared as a part of the identity of the perpetrator, his mind did something quite different with the information. With that word *terrorist*. His mind still registered as much disgust at the horrific act as ever. But rather than lump it all together in a mental basket labelled "Islam," he began to split the actions of these deranged sociopaths from those of the Islamic community. Entirely. Ismael, Eisha, and by extension Muslims in general, rather than being lumped in with all Muslims, became victims of these atrocities as well.

As is the case with anyone we think of as friend, Ike began to assign increasing importance to Ismael's safety and well-being. Every negative headline tying the word *radical* together with Islam increased the jeopardy of Ismael's situation. Anything that further threatened his friend further distressed Ike. This simple split that occurred in Ike's mind severing terrorism from Islam cleared the way for him to form a more realistic and (hopefully) healthier perspective. What at first glance might appear to be a subtle shift in perception was actually seismic. The forging of a friendship had, at least within the confines of Ike's mind, taken 99 percent of the world's 1.4 billion Muslims and moved them from being potential perpetrators of terrorist acts to being their victims. Amazing what putting a human face on a stigmatized group can do.

Ike was becoming increasingly comfortable with Ismael because of his delightful sense of humor. Despite being in jail, despite living in the shadow of a potential murder conviction, despite this most recent revelation that he may have been fathered in a rather mysterious way, Ismael could still crack jokes with Ike. *What a remarkable person Ismael must be,* Ike thought, *to have such an inner fortitude and self-awareness that enables him to separate himself from his situation and not allow it to swallow him entirely. This guy's fear and anxiety have to be off the charts, and yet he manages to exhibit a healthy wit. What informs that? Where does Ismael's courage come from through all this? How is he maintaining his sense of agency and not allowing the circumstances to swallow him up?* If it had anything to do with his faith, Ike wanted to learn more.

Ike knew that Muslims were expected to remain sober. Not just in the sense of not drinking alcohol and getting intoxicated, but also not giving themselves to excesses of laughter. Ismael shattered Ike's stereotype of the dour Muslim and prompted him to do a bit of reading on the subject of Muslim humor.

The Quran said almost nothing about it, other than to say that God is the giver of both tears and laughter. The sayings of Muhammad, the hadith, are a bit more explicit, with the Prophet reported saying "laughing too much deadens the heart." Excessive laughter indicates that the sincere Muslim is being manipulated or charmed by someone's wit or has given himself or herself over to frivolity; that's the supposed sentiment behind this teaching. Whether that truly elucidates what the Prophet thought about the jocular has been hotly debated over the past fourteen hundred years. There is general agreement that humor in Islam should not insult or offend anyone, or promote indecency or immorality. Beyond that there is no clear consensus as to whether fostering a sense of humor should be considered advantageous or detrimental in the development and expression of character. Just what constitutes "excessive" is rather vague. Often the funniest people in the world are dry witted, never even cracking so much as a smile. Given the ambiguities on the subject, Muslims in general tend to maintain a certain decorum when it comes to joking, and expressions of amusement tend to be somewhat restrained.

Since in Ike's view most of the problems in the world were caused by people who took themselves and the causes they promoted too seriously, he had no problem with a Muslim who had a sense of humor. Ismael could laugh at himself and the absurdity of what the provincial world of August Valley was throwing his way right now. Ike admired this and considered it a clear indication of character. Ismael didn't deserve what he was being handed.

These weren't the only attributes persuading Ike to want to help Ismael. There was also Ike's own sense of integrity. He had ample reason to believe in his heart of hearts that Street had killed himself, making Ismael an innocent bystander. Ismael was simply the wrong person caught in the wrong place at the wrong time.

Ike was putting the final touches on a sermon for the next morning. The subject for tomorrow: forgiveness. No shortage of inspiration for this subject; he'd collected plenty through his years in ministry, both having to forgive and having to be forgiven. Ministry functions well to keep one humble.

Ike wasn't a procrastinator. He liked to write his sermons several days in advance. He detested working under the demand of a deadline and never felt satisfied with his work under pressure. Given normal circumstances he would have had all his sermon preparations done long before now. But the past few weeks had been anything but normal.

He didn't often stay late at the church, especially on a Saturday night, but Becky had gone out to a farewell dinner with a group of women from her office, so he biked over to the church to get some exercise and to finish his sermon. He looked at his watch. It was 8:53 p.m. *Becky's probably home by now*, he thought. *Better wrap this up and get home.* He never dwelled much on his safety, but he tried to be sensitive to his wife's increasing concern due to events in recent days. She would be worried if he didn't get home soon.

Ike hit the print button on the computer. While the printer was spitting out the pages of his manuscript for tomorrow, he reshelved the reference books he'd been using and stuck his notes in his backpack and shouldered it. When his sermon finished printing, he gym clipped the pages together and headed for the sanctuary, intending to leave it on the lectern on the way out. Ike liked to have everything in place for the service in the morning when he arrived. As he locked his office, he was startled by the sound of breaking glass. It was coming from somewhere close by. The sanctuary!

Chapter 30

*S*omeone's breaking in, he thought. *I'd better call 911.* Before he could react further, he heard the sound of furniture being overturned, followed by much giggling and loud whispering, then more crashing sounds. Vandals, he realized. Of course. If it were burglars, they'd be trying to work quietly. The church had been vandalized previously, only a year ago. That time the culprit appeared to be children; it had mostly consisted of broken windows and egging of the outside walls and doors. This sounded like more thorough work. The work of someone larger and stronger.

The way the building was situated, Ike knew he could look out his office window and see the parking lot and one window of the sanctuary. He still had the key in his hand, so he unlocked the door he had just locked and went back in. More crashes, like the sound of glass and pottery breaking. *The vases in the vestibule,* he thought. Then a hissing sound like an air compressor. Peering out through the blinds, he saw flashlight beams crisscrossing the one wall of the sanctuary he could see from this vantage point and the shadows of at least two people moving around. *They're spray-painting the walls.* From there he turned to look out in the parking lot. *If they're driving a car, maybe I can get the license plate.* There was no car, but he did see two bicycles, hastily leaned against trees.

Kids, he thought. *Probably teenagers. They parked there and went around to the back of the sanctuary to break a window where it wouldn't be visible from the street.*

Which meant they would probably go back out that way when they had sated their lust for destruction.

Ike thought quickly. He dismissed the thought of calling 911. He knew from the experience last year that law enforcement would take their sweet time in coming. Even if they dispatched a squad car immediately, the perpetrators would likely be gone by the time the police arrived. What he really wanted was to catch them in the act and see who it was so they could be identified. But he wasn't at ease with the idea of walking directly into the sanctuary. Though doubtful they would be armed, there was no way to be sure, and he wasn't about to do something that foolish. *If confronted directly they may panic*, he thought, *and in a panic people are capable of anything.*

He hatched a better plan.

First, he slipped out through the door at the opposite end of the building where his office was so he could come up to the bicycles from the woods and complete darkness. He grabbed the bikes one by one and pushed them off into the woods where they would be difficult if not impossible to find in the dark. Then he went back in the building and pushed the button on the nearest ceiling smoke detector. This immediately set off the shrill sound of its alarm. Simultaneously, the sanctuary went dead silent. Just for a couple of seconds. Then there was the pandemonium of loud whispers and shuffling feet. Ike quickly stepped back out to the parking lot and rushed to assume a position near the trees where the bikes had been. There, just in the edge of the woods, Ike found a strategic position behind an oak tree with a trunk large enough to conceal him.

To get out of the sanctuary the way they had gotten in, through a broken window on the back of the building, they would have to come around far side of the building from Ike's office. This was their shortest route and would take them right past Ike's present position. He expected they would be passing his way in mere seconds as they scrambled out the back of the sanctuary and circled around to find their transportation. Sure enough, just as he slid into the shadow of the oak, two boys came tearing around the building running at breakneck speed.

As they approached the tree where they expected to be able to retrieve their transport, one of them shouted in absolute panic, "Where's the bikes? Oh my God! What do we do, what do we do?"

The other one said, "Ricky, shut up! Something's not right. We better run. The cops will be here any second."

Then the one named Ricky said, "If we leave our bikes, we're dead. They can use them to identify us."

Ricky Wood. Of course. Once Ike heard the first name, he immediately recognized who it was.

They ran around for a few seconds, looking for their bikes with hysterical frenzy, shining their flashlights this way and that.

"You look over that way. I'll look over here," Ricky said, as he headed toward Ike.

Ike waited until Ricky started to circle the tree he was hiding behind to show himself. Ike went the opposite way around the tree and stepped in behind his vandal.

When Ricky realized someone was behind him, he froze. Then he screamed and tried to run. Ike was ready for this and grabbed his arm. After Ricky's scream, Ike could hear the rapid footfalls of the other boy running wildly down the street.

"Hold on, son," Ike said as calmly and authoritatively as he could manage under the effects of his own adrenaline rush. "I'm not going to hurt you."

"Mr. Benheart. I mean, Rev. Benheart, you scared me to death. I-I didn't mean...I'm so sorry that..."

"So sorry that what? That you were destroying my church?" Ike said, releasing his grip on the teen.

"I didn't mean to destroy it. We were just having a little fun. I'll pay for it. Please don't tell anybody. I'll do anything; just don't tell anybody."

"I'm afraid I'm going to have to tell your parents. Now tell me who that other boy was."

"Wes. Wes Hill. Jake knows him, too. We're both in his class."

"Yes, I know Wes. And I know his parents, too. Okay, I'm going to need to talk to both your parents. But it might go better on both of you if your parents hear about this from you first. Confession is good for the soul. You have your father call me. I know you'll do that for me, won't you?"

"Yes, sir," Ricky said, completely dejected.

"For right now, I'm keeping your bikes. I'll see that they're returned to you in good time."

"Yes, sir," was all Ricky could manage, now that he had been cornered into polite mode.

"Okay, you can go now. Can you get home on foot okay? I would give you a lift, but I don't have my car with me."

"Yes, sir, I can get home." Ricky turned and sullenly walked away.

After Ike could see Ricky well down the street, he made his way toward the sanctuary. He needed to assess the damage. As he walked and began to collect his thoughts scattered in the excitement, he remembered what day tomorrow was. Sunday. Would the sanctuary be in any condition for the church to hold a service?

Ike fumbled in the dark with his keys until he found the one for the sanctuary door. When he swung it open, the smell of oil paint greeted his nostrils. Once inside, he felt around for the light switch and flipped it on. The first sight grabbing his attention was red and purple graffiti spray painted all over the flat beige walls. Antigay hate messages with most every four-letter word in the redneck lectionary.

There was also glass from the broken window strewn across the floor and several of the chairs. Shards from several broken vases and some pottery also littered the floor. Chairs and tables were overturned, but on initial survey these appeared mostly undamaged.

Kids don't learn to spread messages of hate like this on their own, Ike thought. *They pick it up from the community. From the culture. Catching a couple of kids in the act and punishing them isn't going to do anything to address the systemic bigotry in evidence here.*

Before touching anything, Ike turned on all the lights and took several pictures with his cell phone. He debated with himself about what to do next. Calling Becky and telling her he was running a little late took first priority. He assured his wife he would be home in a few minutes. His next thought was to call the chair of the building-and-grounds committee and report this. But after giving the whole affair some more thought, he changed his mind. Ike turned out all the lights, secured the doors, picked up his backpack, found his bicycle, and started for home.

He'd made an executive decision. He wasn't going to tell anyone. Yet.

Chapter 30

Ike weighed the course of action he was embarking upon as he rode home. Could he live with himself if he followed through with what he was contemplating? Was it the right thing to do, given the circumstances? While he wouldn't be lying, he would be withholding a significant truth. But he wouldn't be doing it for selfish reasons, but for someone else's good. *Actually, I've already begun*, he considered, *because I said nothing about the vandalism to Becky. I can't confide this to her. There's no sense in involving her. I can't confide it to anybody.*

Ike continued giving the whole matter a great deal of consideration. In the whole scheme of things, if he followed through on this plan, would he be acting unethically or immorally? He knew that if he was discovered, it would appear that way. *The hell with it*, he said to himself. *If my plan works, it will serve a much greater good.*

When Ike got home, he went upstairs and checked in with his wife. She was ready for bed, so he kissed her good night and told her he had to run to the convenience store for something. Another white lie. Because when he got in his van, he headed back to the church with a flashlight in hand. Once there, he located the bikes, loaded them in the back of his van, and drove home. He did stop by the store and pick up some milk, just to ease his conscience a bit. Then he quickly drove home and hid the bikes in the garage. Exhausted by this point, he went upstairs, showered, and went to bed, comfortable in his decision after all his mulling over it for the past hour. He just hoped he would be able to sleep a little. Tomorrow was going to be an interesting day.

The first call came through at nine the next morning. It was Dell Wood, Ricky's father.

"Rev. Benheart?"

"Yes."

"This is Dell Wood. I understand my son Ricky got in some trouble last night."

"What did Ricky tell you?" Ike asked.

"He said Wes had some painting to do at your church, and he wanted Ricky to help him," Wood said.

He's trying to make light of this, Ike thought. "We certainly appreciate Wes and Ricky wanting to help out. But I wish they'd consulted us about what colors to use. Purple and red just don't go well with our decor."

"Listen, Rev. Benheart," Wood said. "I'm so sorry this happened, and Ricky is very sorry. I'd be more than willing to pay for the damages. And Ricky will be punished; I can assure you of that. When I'm finished with him, he'll learn a lesson he'll never forget about damaging someone else's property."

"Did Ricky tell you any of the things they wrote on the walls?" Ike asked.

"No, we didn't go into that," Wood replied. "Can't we just chalk this up to the rambunctiousness of teenage boys and let it go at that? Both of the boys have said they're sorry, and I believe their confession is sincere. We're willing to make amends to your church."

Yeah, Ike thought, *they confessed once they were caught and had no choice*. "The messages they wrote were addressed to the gay and lesbian members of our church," he said. "Some very colorful and degrading stuff. Very hateful. If this were reported, I'm pretty sure it would qualify as a hate crime."

"We certainly don't want that to happen, Reverend. Ricky is basically a good boy. He's just impulsive, and sometimes he lets his friends be a bad influence. But we'll do whatever it takes to make this thing right."

"Well, Mr. Wood, I can appreciate your situation. I really can. My son, Jake, is the same age as Ricky. Wes, Ricky, and Jake are actually in the same class. I'm not insensitive to what's going on here. I know what it's like to be the father of a spirited teenage boy."

"Then you're willing to keep this just between us and not report it?" Wood asked.

"I have no control over what my parishioners do," Ike said. "I didn't report it, but someone will be arriving at the church most any moment now, today being Sunday, and I imagine the first thing they'll do is call the police."

"Of course," Wood said. "But you're the only witness, right? You're the only one who has to know the real story."

"You want me to lie?" Ike asked.

"No, I wouldn't ask you to do that," Wood said. "Just play a little dumb. Don't say anything. The police won't be able to figure out who did it. They never do in cases like this. I'm just asking you to think about the future of these two boys who got in a little too deep. Let's give them a second chance."

"That's right," Ike said. "You probably hear about things like this all the time. You're still on the city council, aren't you?"

"Yes, I'm just finishing my second term," Wood answered.

"Okay, Mr. Wood, I'll give the boys a second chance if you can answer me one question."

"Certainly. I will if I can," Wood said.

"Which member of the council told Lee Street that they wouldn't want his reputation to be damaged if he sold his store to the Muslims?"

Silence. Ike waited a long time for Wood to respond. He knew Wood's mind was racing.

"I'm not sure I know what you're talking about, Rev. Benheart."

"I think you do," Ike said. "But I want you to think this through carefully. I'm not asking you for any information about what transpired between Street and the city council. I already know what happened. I just need a name."

"Jones. Jerry Jones. He's the one that made the statement to Street."

"Thank you, Mr. Wood. That's helpful. And thank you for arranging an anonymous contribution so that our church can take care of this vandalism damage. Your generosity will certainly be appreciated."

The next call Ike was expecting came within minutes. The lay leader for today's service had arrived at the church and discovered the damage. She had already called the police, and they were on their way. *Good*, Ike thought. *Hopefully, they will come and investigate and be gone before I get to the church. That way I won't be questioned.*

He suggested an alternate plan for the service that morning to the lay leader. Since the sanctuary was unsafe and unfit, they could hold an outside service in the garden area behind the building. The weather was beautiful, without a cloud in the sky. Given the circumstances, his lay leader was fully supportive of this idea. She and Ike talked briefly about moving the altar, getting enough chairs set up, and other logistics this switch in locale involved. After they hung up, Ike started thinking about how he would deal with this violation of their sanctuary space in the context of a worship service. What kind of remarks could he incorporate that might be helpful to his congregants, especially the members of the gay and lesbian community? Everyone would be curious about the damage and could look through the windows and read the graffiti on the walls. There was no way to get it covered over in so short a time.

A minister is at no time more needed than this, he thought. His role was to usher them through the psychic trauma of this violation of their sanctuary, their safe and sacred space. What kinds of things could he say that might help them make sense of it and bring some comfort, some healing? The sermon he'd already prepared for this morning, on forgiveness, actually seemed rather appropriate given the current circumstances. The dynamic of forgiveness, as he planned to present it this morning, requires the victims to honor their own feelings. Allow themselves to feel anger. That shouldn't be too difficult for Ike to do given his own feelings about this whole incident.

Forgiveness given too easily or too quickly, without proper reflection on the damage that's been done, may not be forgiveness at all but merely denial. The more Ike thought through the process of forgiveness as he had it outlined in his notes, the more he looked forward to leading the service. He anticipated worship being a therapeutic experience for him as well.

Chapter 31

Becky stood in front of her dresser mirror fussing with the collar on her blouse. Now that Ismael was home and Ramadan was over, her family had been invited to dine at the Hagarsons' tonight. She looked forward to the evening but was a little nervous. She had never met Ismael. Neither had Ike made the acquaintance of Eisha. She had no concerns about Jake and Bai. They were classmates and had several common interests.

Her dress was purchased specifically for the occasion. She had done some research on the Internet about the dos and don'ts of visiting in a Muslim home. One of the first things on the list of dos was to dress modestly. No dresses or blouses that showed cleavage. Since she was rather full-figured and well-endowed up top, she knew she wasn't going to be comfortable wearing anything from her closet.

"Honey, did you pick up the flowers?" she shouted to Ike. He was in the bathroom shaving with an electric razor.

"Got 'em," Ike shouted back. He turned off his razor and looked out the door. "Everything's going to be fine. Ismael is going to like you, and you're going to like him. You know, you're going to a lot of trouble just to have dinner with a murder suspect."

"I hope you plan to tone the snarkiness down just a bit this evening," Becky said. "Eisha doesn't know you either. Give her a chance to get to know you before she has to figure out how to take your impertinent sense of humor."

"I'll be my usual charming self," Ike said as he straightened himself up and assumed a dignified air in front of the mirror. He was completely naked.

"I just hope Eisha doesn't have to live in regret for the rest of her life for inviting us," Becky said. "Were you planning to wear something a little more formal than that?" she asked, eyeing her husband's completely exposed anatomy.

"Maybe I should," Ike said playfully. "But then what would you and Ismael possibly find to talk about?"

As Ike began to dress himself, Becky's tone became more serious.

"Do you think Ismael is going to want to talk about his case? The trial?" she asked.

"I don't think he'll avoid the subject," Ike said. "After all, it's sort of the elephant in the room. Then again, he may not. I suspect the reason they invited us over, at least partly, was to be a distraction. I'm not going to bring it up. My plan is to let the conversation go where it needs to go. Just be present to them."

"Thank you for saying that," Becky said. "Eisha and I are becoming good friends. I feel for her terribly right now. I've only seen her once since Ismael got home. Having him there has helped, but she's still a wreck. Someone left a note on her car windshield last week. It said, 'Leave America. Go back to your own country. Kill your own people.' She hesitated about telling Ismael but decided she must. She's trying to protect him too."

"You know, Becky, I think, in a hundred years or so, when people look back on the times we're living in, they're going to talk about the war on terror and how the Muslims were treated in this country, and it's going to be clear to them that so much of the violence resulted from our lack of acceptance and our fear of their differences. Our country has always prided itself in being a nation of immigrants. But you wouldn't know it by looking at the way they've been treated. The Irish, Catholics, the Jews, they've all been the feared group during some period. We rounded up the Japanese and put them in internment camps. But each of these minorities prevailed and came to be more or less accepted. It'll be the same with the Muslims. What we're doing by becoming friends, in some infinitesimal way, will help speed that process up."

"I'm totally with you on that. But my concern is right here, right now, and seeing this whole dark, ugly thing come to an end for Ismael and Eisha.

"It will," Ike said. "In the meantime, all we can do is be supportive. Let's go have dinner."

Ismael greeted them at the door. Ike was amazed at the change in his physical appearance since his visit to the jail some ten days prior. Now clean-shaven, a couple of pounds heavier, with color returning to his cheeks, he gave an impression of renewed confidence.

"Ike, so good to see you, my friend. You must be Becky. Very glad to meet you. Hello, Jake. Please come in. Shoes go over there."

"Ismael, being a stay-at-home dad seems to be agreeing with you," Ike said. "Eisha is really fattening you up."

"She really is a marvelous cook," Ismael said, patting his stomach. "Wait till you try her biryani. That's what we're having for dinner. We can't wait for you to try it."

"Here, we thought these might help brighten your day a bit," Becky said, handing the flowers to Ismael.

"Thank you so much," Ismael remarked.

"Your house is beautiful," Ike commented, surveying the Persian carpet in the living area, a samovar in one corner, and various other Indo-Asian accent pieces tastefully displayed.

"You are too kind," Ismael said. "Jake, Bai is upstairs. You're welcome to go see what he's up to. And Eisha's in the kitchen, Becky, if you want a chance to see how she prepares the biryani. Come, step this way, and I'll take you. I'll ask Eisha to put these in water. Ike, please have a seat. I'll be right back."

Becky identified saffron, cloves, cinnamon, and ginger as just some of the spices in the aroma wafting from the kitchen.

As Becky entered the kitchen, Eisha was slicing cucumbers. She immediately dropped her cutlery and hurried over to embrace her. Eisha was dressed in a light-blue sari. This was the first time Becky had seen her in something other than Western cultural attire.

"It's wonderful for us to finally have our families together," Eisha said, her eyes beginning to well with tears. Quickly she composed herself. "Come, I will show you how we prepare our favorite meal."

"It smells delicious," Becky commented, following Eisha to the counter.

"It's biryani," Eisha said, pointing to the large steaming copper pot she'd just removed from the stove. The lid was still in place, and there was a bread-like crust around the lid as if the ingredients were trying to burst from the pot. "This is called Hyderabadi biryani. It's made by what's called *dum* style. We do this by putting this bread dough around the rim of the pot before we put it over the fire. This seals in all the wonderful tastes from the spices." As Eisha described this process, she removed the lid of the pot. A large cloud of steam escaped, magnifying the mouthwatering aromas.

"How long has the pot been cooking?" Becky asked.

"Only twenty-five minutes," Eisha answered, "but the meat we marinate overnight. With some biryanis, you cook the meat and the rice separately. But this one everything cooks together. It's quite simple, really. A one-dish meal. When the spices all cook together like this in dum style, it makes plain rice taste like a delicacy." Eisha took a large wooden spoon and stirred the layered ingredients, mixing the meat into the rice.

"Here's a list of all the ingredients," Eisha said, handing Becky an index card with the recipe.

Becky read the ingredients. Mutton, salt, garlic paste, chili paste, cloves, sautéed onions, cumin seeds, cinnamon bark, mace, nutmeg, saffron, yogurt, lemon juice, rice.

"So, you just marinate the meat overnight..." Becky said.

"Then, thirty minutes before you plan to eat, put all the ingredients in the pot—rice on top, seal it with flour dough, and cook."

"Wow, it is easy," Becky said. Eisha had set aside a spoon of the biryani, now cool enough to taste. She handed it to Becky.

"I can do easy," Becky said; then she tasted it. "Mmm. Good. Ike may be getting more home-cooked meals in the future."

Ike looked around the sitting area while Ismael took the flowers to the kitchen. Some pictures on the credenza attracted his immediate attention. They showed a remarkably attractive middle-aged olive-skinned woman, usually in a *kameez* and a headscarf, sometimes a sari, always with a young boy at various stages of development. Ike studied the woman intensely. He was totally captivated by the pictures and failed to notice that Ismael had made his way back into the room.

"She was very beautiful, yes?" Ismael asked.

"Indeed," Ike replied. "There is almost a hypnotic quality to her appearance. Her eyes. I've been hearing so much about this woman for the past few weeks. Now I have an actual picture for my mind's eye. A lot of things make more sense now that I have a visual on her."

"How she could turn a man's head, you mean?" Ismael said. "She could do that. I began to notice, even before I went through puberty. She had no trouble being the center of attention. Even when she didn't want to be. Which wasn't often."

"I think you said she worked as a hotel manager," Ike said. "Was that always her career?"

"She started at the bottom in the lodging industry," Ismael said. "Housekeeping. She worked for the Patels at that motel where the church put her up as a refugee. She gained their trust, and they started letting her work the desk. Worked her way up. It wasn't long before other opportunities came along. She was master of giving the good first impression. That will take you a long way in a business where the contact with clients usually only amounts to about ten minutes."

"Any idea why she never, uh, remarried?" Ike asked, hesitating over his words.

"I have some ideas about that. I want to show you something that might help you understand."

Just then Eisha entered the room and informed the men that dinner was ready.

"It can wait," Ismael said. "I'll show you and Becky right after we eat. First the biryani."

Chapter 32

"There are dozens of different recipes for biryani," Eisha explained, delighted that her guests were eating heartily. "In Bangladesh and India, there are restaurants that specialize in biryani. It can be made with fish, shrimp, chicken, or beef. In India, many people are vegetarian, so there they will sometimes use lentils in place of the meat."

"There are so many theories about where the dish originated," Ismael said. "Probably it came from the Mughals. There are credible sources that show it being served from the Mughal royal kitchens."

"The Mughals?" Ike asked. "Forgive my cultural ignorance. I missed that class in world history."

"The Mughals ruled India for nearly 300 years, up until, really, the British East India Company took over India in the nineteenth century. Much of the art and architecture associated with India, Pakistan, and Bangladesh came from the Mughals. Think Taj Mahal. That was built during the golden age of the Mughal empire."

"All Mughals were Muslim?" Becky asked.

"The leadership was," Ismael explained. "Most of the empire they ruled remained Hindu, however. The Mughals usually didn't interfere in religion and local culture. The most prosperous region of their empire was the Bengali delta, the area that today is Bangladesh. It was our golden age as well. Bangladesh is the breadbasket of South Asia, and for much of history our delta country prospered. Unfortunately, because of the civil war and natural disasters, you know - cyclones and floods, most of the world today thinks of Bangladesh not as a breadbasket but as a basket case. Things are improving, however. A country that can produce a Nobel Prize winner like Rabindranath Tagore has the genius to rise and prosper again. But, Eisha, I'm afraid I'm boring our guests with this history lesson. Ike, I understand your church was vandalized last weekend."

"Yep," Ike said. "Probably some young punks. They broke out a window and sprayed messages all over the walls. Gay-bashing messages. Some really colorful words and phrases in lovely pink and purple pastel."

"It's been a week for hateful messages," Eisha said.

"Oh, Eisha, that's right," Ike said. "Becky told me about the note on your windshield. I'm so sorry you've had to endure that kind of abuse."

"Ike, I've been thinking about something you asked me at the jail. You asked me how Muslims can expect support and empathy for their minority rights when we turn our backs on another minority. Gay people. That was food for thought, my friend. And I'm coming around on that issue. I believe that Muslims are not only going to have to start being more accepting of gay people, but we're going to have to start being active in our advocacy of them. I've been reading about so many instances where gays have spoken out for the Muslim community. More of us need to stand up for them. I'm beginning to see that my attitude of staying at home and keeping my virtue has really been rather cowardly."

"Well, right now you don't have much choice in the matter other than to stay at home," Ike said.

"That's true," Ismael replied. "But I hope you hear what I'm saying."

"I do," Ike said, "And I really appreciate your change of heart."

"Well, I've had a lot of time to think these past few days," Ismael said. "And being on the receiving end of oppression makes you more sensitive to the plight of others."

"Doesn't the Quran say Allah makes excellent everything he creates?" Ike asked.

"Oh, goodness," Ismael said. "Now this guy is going to quote my own holy book to me. You infidel."

"You terrorist."

"Okay, guys, I'm going to exert my influence here as a liberated Muslim woman and break this up," Eisha said. "Ismael, didn't you have something you wanted to show Ike?"

"Yes, dear," Ismael said. "I've been rather anxious to show him."

"Well, has everyone had enough to eat?" Eisha asked, looking around.

Becky had learned through her research of proper etiquette that they should leave a little food on their plate as a sign that they had had enough. Otherwise a good Muslim hostess will keep refilling the plate. She had clued Ike in on this custom as well so he wouldn't feel any pressure to gorge himself if Eisha kept piling the food on. This went against the grain of the way they were raised, as both their parents had insisted they clean their plates; however, they managed to waive their previous training for this occasion. They both nodded yes and expressed again how much they had enjoyed the meal.

"Okay, then," Eisha said. "Ismael, why don't you take Ike into the den while I clear the table?"

"Let me help you, Eisha," Becky chimed in.

"Thanks. If you could grab some of the plates."

Ismael ushered Ike into the den and then went upstairs to retrieve something. The women busied themselves in the kitchen. A few minutes later, they all joined Ike and sat around the coffee table.

"This is something I just discovered since I was released from jail," Ismael said, as he put a Bible on the table in front of him. "The last time Ike visited me there, he showed me the letters he found in his mother's things. The ones from his mother's sister. Well, that inspired me. When I got home, I went back through this trunk of my mother's where she kept her treasures. The trunk is about the only thing of hers I held on to. Anyway, I found this."

Ismael tenderly picked up the Bible, opened the front cover, and located the title page. The yellowed page opposite, in large letters, read, "This Bible is presented to," and written in on the line below was "Gera Hagarson." Just below that it said "by the First Baptist Church of August Valley, Georgia. July 5, 1971."

"The Bible given to her when she first arrived," Ike said. "This must have meant a lot to her. It looks worn."

"She had it tucked away in the trunk right underneath a copy of the Quran," Ismael said. "A Quran a relative sent her from Bangladesh. The one her father gave her as a child."

Then Ismael opened the Bible up to where something was tucked between the pages. A piece of white cloth and a neatly folded sheet of paper. He removed the cloth first and opened it up. It was a man's handkerchief. Monogrammed in stylistic blue lettering at one corner were the initials A. B.

Ike took a deep breath. Ismael handed the handkerchief to him. "Do you recognize this?" Ismael asked.

"Oh, yes," Ike replied. "It's one of my father's. He always had one of these tucked in the pocket of his suit." Ike stared at the memento and sat in silence for several seconds before passing it to Becky. "Ismael, may I ask what this means to you?"

"Before I answer that, let me show you what else is here." He unfolded a plain piece of notepaper, creased only once. Tucked inside was a lock of jet-black hair. In the neat, flowing handwriting of a woman, the note said, "Ismael— God has heard my affliction." A date was written in the upper right corner. May 11, 1972.

"May eleventh," Ismael said. "The seventh day after I was born. That would have been the day of my *aqiqah*. My naming ceremony. It's our custom for babies to be named on the seventh day after birth. A celebration is held, and the baby's head is shaved. The parents thank Allah for the birth of a healthy child."

Ike noticed that the Bible was opened to the book of Genesis. He picked it up and found the passage he was looking for. The notepaper and the handkerchief had the right page bookmarked.

He read from Genesis 16:11: "And the angel of the Lord said unto her, 'Behold, thou art with child and shalt bear a son, and shalt call his name Ishmael; because the Lord hath heard thy affliction.'"

"My mother named me after the traditional ancestor of the Arab people. The name given to a child is carefully thought out in our tradition. We believe that the name that's chosen helps shape the character of the child."

"Ismael—God has heard my affliction," Becky said. "Your mother wrote that. That meaning of the name must have been important to her as well."

"Yes," Ismael said. "And the name of the father of the biblical Ishmael was a part of her decision too, I think."

"All the evidence we have seems to suggest that," Ike said.

"Yes, that our husbands are half-brothers," Eisha said to Becky in a hushed voice.

Chapter 33

On the way home, Ike wanted to be alone with his thoughts. Becky wanted to talk. Jake, sitting in the backseat playing a video game, was totally oblivious to both of them.

"I just can't believe this happened," Becky said. "It's like some story you read about on the Internet. Somebody finds their long-lost sibling. And here it's happened to you. Ike, aren't you excited?"

"You know I like Ismael," Ike said. "He and I are becoming good friends. But brothers? I've been preparing myself for this news ever since I started asking questions and poking around in Mom's things. But now that we're pretty sure it's true, I don't know. Maybe I've just got to give myself a chance to get used to the idea."

"I know it's a shock," Becky said. "But I just think it's soooo interesting."

"Maybe Ismael and I should have our DNA tested," Ike said. "That way we'd have proof."

"That's a great idea!" Becky said. "Can they do that? Prove you two have a common parent?"

"Yes, it's called linear consanguinity testing," Ike said. "I've been reading up on it."

"So you've been thinking about having it done," Becky said. "Ever since you suspected…"

"No, I'm only joking," Ike said. "I'm not thinking about it. I just wanted to see if it was possible."

"You thought about it enough to do all that research, but you aren't thinking about actually doing it?" Becky asked. "Or should I say, thinking of suggesting it to Ismael. I guess he would have to want it done as well." After a long pause, she said, "I just don't understand."

"It's one thing to know it's possible to test for this," Ike said. "It's another to want it done."

The precariousness of Ismael's situation clouded Ike's thoughts and cast a dark shadow over any excitement he tried to muster about Ismael's latest revelation. He was tempted to ask Becky why should he get excited about finding out he had a brother when that brother could very well spend the rest of his life in prison or maybe even face the death penalty. But since Becky had seemed to thoroughly enjoy the evening, Ike thought better of visiting that dark scenario.

It also surprised Ike how upbeat Ismael and Eisha had been. *If they invited us over to be a distraction, then we succeeded admirably*, he thought. *The anticipation of showing us the handkerchief and the note may have also diverted their attention from the indictment.* Despite what loomed on the horizon, the Hagarsons had managed to pull off a wonderful immersion in Bangladeshi culture. Amazing they were able to focus their thoughts and energy enough to put on a dinner party, he marveled. Quite a demonstration of character and emotional discipline.

Ike was also preoccupied with this fresh evidence of his father's affair with Gera. To Ike, the fact that Gera had held on to the handkerchief, this souvenir of a relationship all those years ago, meant it was more than just a one-night stand. She had feelings for him. They shared some depth of affection.

Dad must have been a very passionate person. Ike smiled to himself as he tried to picture his father being seduced by Gera. Maybe that wasn't how it happened. Maybe he seduced her. That was even harder for him to imagine. Gera was vulnerable, Ike reminded himself. All alone in a strange country. His father may have seen an opportunity and taken advantage of an innocent and defenseless woman. But from what he had learned about Gera from others, and from her countenance in the pictures, she didn't strike Ike as the innocent and defenseless type at all. She was most likely the aggressor, Ike decided. He was basing this mostly on his knowledge of his father, a man who never appeared too comfortable around women.

Still, if Dad had an affair and got a woman pregnant, wouldn't he have done the noble thing? Seen that she was cared for? But did he know? Maybe their paths never crossed again. Ike hadn't thought about that until just now. But he supposed it could be possible. Mom would have done everything in her power to make sure Dad stayed away. No doubt she kept him on the short leash after this happened. Again, he smiled to himself as memories of his parents flooded back.

But there was still an unanswered question. A big one. Inez had the impression that Gera was pregnant when she arrived in this country. Ismael had had that impression too when Ike first talked to Ismael about Gera. Ismael had spoken about her pregnant state as if it was a commonly accepted fact. But now Ismael conceded that he must have been conceived well after his mother's arrival. Most likely late August or early September 1971. Yet for some reason, there existed this notion that Gera was pregnant on arrival. But why?

Part II

"And God heard the voice of the boy; and the angel of God called to Hagar from heaven, and said to her, 'What troubles you Hagar? Do not be afraid; for God has heard the voice of the boy where he is. Come, lift up the boy and hold him fast with your hand, for I will make a great nation of him.'" (Genesis 21:17–18 [NRSV])

Chapter 34

June 1971

They called it Operation Searchlight. The central government of West Pakistan ordered its army to invade East Pakistan to put down the Bengali nationalist movement. Pakistan's president, Yahya Khan, said, "Kill three million Bengalis, and the rest will eat out of our hands." In the stealth of night on March 25, 1971, the Paki army marauded the streets of Dhaka, killing indiscriminately. Shanties in the poorer parts of the city, the walls of which put up no opposition to Paki bullets, were riddled by machine-gun fire. Pedestrians, caught off guard, were shot down en masse. Students and academics were specifically targeted, as the army moved quickly on Dhaka University, bombing dormitories and murdering the youth in large numbers.

Once the army gained control of the city, they began the door-to-door searches. Any male young enough to join the army was likely shot. Women were rounded up and taken to camps and repeatedly gang-raped. Children were killed or left to fend for themselves. The soldiers mastered the art of cruelty and became more and more effective in their genocidal campaign as the days passed. By mid-May the Paki army had secured the major cities.

These actions infuriated the Bengalis, and they formed a provisional government across the border in Calcutta, India, and started a resistance movement called the Mukti Bahini, or freedom fighters. The Mukti Bahini gained control of large portions of the Bengali countryside and from there began a prolonged program of guerrilla operations on the fortifications of the Paki army in the cities.

This was the situation in the newly formed country of Bangladesh the first week of June 1971, as Gera and her father sat in front of their transistor radio every evening listening to radio free Bangladesh for any word of encouragement. Gera's father, Nazir, was the head chef at the Intercontinental Hotel Dhaka, a prominent luxury hotel in the political district and host to many political events leading up to Bangladesh's independence. With the start of the war, the International Red Cross declared the hotel a neutral zone. This had done little to dissuade the fears of father or daughter. Nazir Hagarson was ethnically a Bihari, which made him suspect by both the Bengalis and the Pakistani troops. Reports filtered in to the upscale Dhanmondi neighborhood where they lived that the Paki army was doing random searches of homes looking for residences that might be harboring Mukti Bahini operatives or be outposts of guerrilla operations.

Like most citizens of the new country, Nazir hoped the Mukti Bahini would prevail and succeed in establishing a new republic. He had witnessed the atrocities committed by the Pakistanis firsthand. And by virtue of his profession, he was within earshot when governmental officials of the Pakistani occupation held high-level meetings in his dining halls, talking their strategies and speaking so casually about inflicting casualties on the civilian population of the city. These things made him a nationalist. He felt such contempt for the government and military officials he was often obliged to feed at the hotel. Yet he stayed at his post, deeming that course of action not only the safer of his limited options, but also affording him further chances to eavesdrop on Paki politicians and military commanders. Whenever he thought he heard information of strategic importance, he passed it on through his nephew who was active in the resistance movement.

The news over the wireless in late May gave Nazir and Gera occasional reason to cheer. A successful ambush of an army convoy. Word that the city's power grid had been sabotaged, followed by a confirmatory loss of electricity. Father and daughter celebrated these small victories with the radio broadcasters.

Nazir was born and raised in one of the poorer areas of Calcutta. Life presented him with few ingredients for success. Though opportunities for success were almost nil, somehow he created a way. With a little luck, a hefty portion of spunk, and a dollop of street smarts, he had put together a career in the culinary arts. Imminently resourceful, he parlayed this trait of character to carve out an enviable life for himself.

He worked diligently to ingrain these same traits into his daughter. Since his wife, Gera's mother, died thirteen years ago, he'd done everything in his power to give his daughter the best education, both academically and in the ways of the world. Though he loved her more than life itself, he tempered his affection with a generous helping of tough love. If he had anything to do with it, she was going to be tough-minded and practical. He wanted her as prepared as he was for whatever life threw her way.

Being raised in a masculine world, Gera grew up learning to think the same way as her father. While growing up, they spent a great deal of time together in the kitchen. Gera picked up most of her father's knowledge of the culinary arts simply by immersion in his world. For the past couple of years, she had also been working on a degree in business at the university with the hope of one day going into business with her father.

Though Nazir loved his daughter deeply and hoped to keep her close, she was now approaching twenty-one years old. He knew that soon he would be losing her to a young man. Gera had two suitors vying for her affection when the war started. One had been missing since the attack on the university and was presumed dead. The other, named Abir, worked for a multinational corporation and had not been heard from since the end of April. A mutual friend of his and Gera's told her he had joined the resistance forces gathering across the Indian border in the town of Agartala.

Nazir listened to the broadcasts with the future of his city and his livelihood in mind; Gera filtered the same news for any potential hints of harm that might befall Abir. When the invasion started at the end of March and she heard of the bombings on campus, she could not rest until she got word about her student beau. When that word came, it left little hope. He had been seen on campus just before the massacre.

The first of June, the broadcaster announced news of particular interest to Nazir. A blast had been heard at the Intercontinental Hotel earlier that evening. Significant damage was done to the structure, and there were several casualties.

"Babu, the resistance has attacked your hotel," Gera announced to her father, who stepped back in the room from the kitchen. "There was an explosion. And there are casualties."

"I hope they got the bastards they were after," Nazir said grimly, "and none of the staff were hurt."

"Please don't go back to work," Gera pleaded. "It's too dangerous."

"Don't worry; there's no way I can return to work now. Everyone on the hotel staff will be under suspicion as an informant to the resistance. There is no doubt about it now. We have to leave."

"When?" Gera asked.

"Tonight. We'll go under the cover of darkness. Go pack. Just one bag. And get your passport."

"But, Babu, what about Kazmir?"

"I'll ask Ms. Choudry next door to feed her. There's no way we could take a cat with us. We knew the day might come when we would have to leave. Now go, hurry!"

Gera went upstairs and started pulling clothes from her closet and throwing them on the bed. She asked herself what she should take. She couldn't think. Too many other thoughts were crowding her mind. Tears were streaming down her face. She was about to say good-bye to the only world she had ever known. Her well-ordered mind, never failing her before, was completely shutting down. Unable to focus, she walked around the room in a daze, opening and closing drawers at random.

The doorbell rang and jolted her out of her emotional stupor. From upstairs she heard her father answer it.

"Good evening, officer, may I help you?" she heard her father say.

"Are you Mr. Hagarson, employed at the Intercontinental Hotel?" asked the officer.

"Yes, I'm Nazir Hagarson."

"You have been accused of spying based on the testimony of Abir Mallik."

Abir! Gera's heart leapt. And then it sank.

"I have no idea what you're talking about," Nazir said. His voice sounded calm but barely audible.

"Turn and face the wall, Mr. Hagarson. You have been accused as a traitor and a spy and found guilty."

Gera heard two shots fired and then the sound of a body collapsing onto the floor.

She ran down the stairs in complete shock and utter abandonment of any thought for her own safety.

"Father! No!"

When she got to the bottom of the stairs, she fell over his crumpled body. A Paki military officer and another man in uniform stood over her as she kept screaming "No" between violent sobs.

"This is what happens to mukti bastards," the officer calmly announced.

After a few moments, the other soldier, apparently bored with Gera's intense grief, asked, "What should we do with her?"

The officer reached over, grabbed a handful of Gera's hair near her scalp, and forcibly turned her head so he could see her face. He gave her whole body the once-over.

"Take her to the major," he ordered the soldier. "He'll know just what to do with booty like this."

Chapter 35

The look on the officer's face stunned Gera out of the pit of her grief far enough that her instincts of self-preservation kicked in. Never had she encountered such a countenance of evil. The two men handled her roughly as they forced her into a sedan. The pain in her arms from their grasp and the ache in her head from striking the frame of the car convinced her emotions to take a backseat for the moment and let her focus on survival.

She managed to take note of the direction they were moving before the soldier gagged her and put a black hood over her head. Her head was really throbbing now, but she forced herself to use the senses remaining to her. The car had just turned onto Mirpur Road when the hood went on. *We're headed to the university*, she thought. She knew she must concentrate on how far they traveled. The sounds of the city might also offer her some clues as to where she was being taken.

The car never turned until a few seconds before they reached their destination, about twenty minutes from her home. Once the car was parked, she was taken forcibly into a building. From the sound of the wooden door opening and closing, Gera guessed they were at a house. Once inside, she deduced they were traversing both wood flooring and carpet from the sounds their feet made. They half dragged her up a flight of stairs. Then she was made to sit, and the hood was removed; however, the gag was left in place. Her throat was parched, and the throb in her head had reached the intensity of a jackhammer.

She looked around. They were in some sort of lavishly furnished makeshift officer's quarters. The large desk in front of her had a fireplace behind it with a mirror above the mantel. In the mirror, she could see shadows on the ceiling cast by the two men who had killed her father and apprehended her. There was a sofa to either side of her with soft fabric upholstery. Scattered about the room were valuables of all sorts. Jewelry, paintings, small sculptures, randomly placed as if they had been brought into the room and unloaded at different times. A table in the far corner of the room was overflowing with stacks of money, several wallets, and a few purses. Gera remembered the officer's words, "He'll know just what to do with booty like this." This room must contain the "booty," the spoils of war. Her fellow citizens' hard-earned money. Their life savings. So much for the Pakistani president's ardent claim that the country must not be divided as his justification for the crackdown. These soldiers were mercenaries. In it for the money. And from what Gera saw in the room, they had made off with quite a haul.

Gera heard the officer bark some sort of orders to the soldier. Obediently he moved to take his post by the door, Gera noticed, as she followed his shadow in the mirror. Gera then heard the officer leave the room, descend the stairs, and slam the front door as he exited the building.

The soldier remained still for a time, but in a few minutes Gera could hear him moving. He came within her peripheral vision. The table with all the money was drawing him like a magnet. He moved quickly but carefully, pausing every few steps as if to listen for approaching footsteps.

When he got to the table, he scanned it quickly and grabbed one of the wallets. He turned and headed back to his post behind Gera, passing by her close enough to whisper, "Tell anyone, and I'll chain you up at the rape camp myself."

Gera had heard rumors about the rape camps. Women chained down and repeatedly raped and beaten until they died from either their wounds, starvation, or exposure. The specter of this horror threw her mind back to another atrocity. Her father in the pool of blood. *Father is dead.* Her heart was only beginning to absorb the reality of this abominable act.

Suddenly there were approaching footsteps on the staircase in the hall behind the soldier. The door opened. The sounds of the soldier coming to attention. A salute, possibly. "Relax, comrade," the newcomer said. *Is this the major?* Gera wondered. The soldier's reply, "Yes, sir," led her to the conclusion that it was.

"I hear you have brought me something more precious than diamonds," the major said, walking around the chair to face Gera. He was tall, well-built, with rough, chiseled features. And the worst acne scars Gera had ever seen. He was also drunk.

He put his hand on Gera's chin and held her face up so that she could meet his gaze. Then he put his hand in her hair and lifted it to his nose and inhaled.

"Yes, comrade, you and the lieutenant have done outstanding work tonight. It will be my pleasure to have her as my company tonight. Now go and take your post outside, and let no one enter the building. Except the commander, of course, should he show up."

The soldier left. The major removed her gag.

"Your men killed my father," Gera said hoarsely. "Shot him in the back like cowards." She was determined not to cry.

"Shot him like a spy. Like the mukti bastard he was. Telling the traitors about our secret meetings at the hotel. A bullet in the back was too good for him."

"What have you done with Abir Mallik?" Gera asked.

"We captured him last week. Sneaking into the city to do mischief. Naughty boy. He paid for his crimes against the country as well."

"You killed him too?" Gera asked, amazing herself at how evenly the words came out.

"No, but we had to get the information out of him. We have ways we do that. You can have him back now if you want. But I don't think you would recognize him."

So that's it, she thought. *They tortured him until he's totally disfigured. Or he's lost his mind. Or probably both.*

"What are you going to do to me?" Gera asked. One part of her mind was preparing herself for his answer, another coming to grips with yet another loss. Abir. Her one remaining reason to look toward the future.

"That depends on you, my pretty thing," the major said with lust in his eyes and a wicked smile on his lips. "If I enjoy my night with you, I just might keep you around. If you resist, then I'll turn you over to my men. They're not so gentle as I can be." With these words, the major came over and put his lips on hers. Gera had to resist the urge to slap him with every fiber of her being.

She was repulsed by the smell of whiskey on his breath. In her fear of this man, the best she could manage was a cold impassivity. Apparently, at least for the moment, that was good enough for him. After the kiss, he backed away slightly.

"There, that's a good girl. We're going to get along just fine, you and me."

He came back toward her, this time more aggressively, shoving his tongue in her mouth. Though the alcohol stench threatened to overwhelm her, she yielded to him. After what seemed an eternity, he backed off for air.

"You've got the makings of a good recruit," the major murmured, his face flushed from both lust and booze. "Let's adjourn to the bed and see how well you perform under fire."

Gera had a glimmer of hope. She had enough experience with men to know that they had difficulty performing sexually once they had a certain amount of alcohol in their system. And this man appeared to have a blood alcohol level well over the impotence threshold. *Maybe he'll even pass out once we get in bed*, she thought. Gera continued to play along as the docile sex partner.

Unfortunately, the major held his alcohol well. He had no trouble performing. Gera's only consolation lay in how expeditious he was. A few thrusts and it was over. It was at that point the major proved himself less than Superman. His thirst for both alcohol and sex now slaked, he completely passed out.

Good, she thought. *But what do I do now?* The major was still on top of her, and he was a large man. She decided to wait a few minutes and let him really get comatose, and she would try to roll him off of her. Gera was fairly athletic and, with her adrenaline really flowing, managed to push him over. She waited a few more minutes. He remained asleep.

Next, she went to the bathroom and washed out the major's semen the best she could with only her hands to work with. If by some miracle she got away alive, she sure as hell didn't want to have a pregnancy to deal with.

Could she possibly escape? Against all hope, she dared to think it possible. First, she surveyed the rest of the upstairs of the house as quickly and quietly as she could. She dared not go down the stairs, both because of the noise her feet would make on the stairs and the fact that she had no idea whether there might be other soldiers quartered there.

She found another bedroom with a window that opened to the back of the house. She tried it. It opened! Looking out, it was a long way to the ground. The terrain around the building sloped away from the house at a good angle. She estimated it to be a drop of at least twenty-five feet. Too far to jump, she surmised. Still, she thought about it. The prospect of a broken leg was infinitely better than being the major's whore. But she had to be able to get away once she hit the ground. She opened the window more fully and stuck her head out. By the streetlights and that of a three-quarter moon, she was able to see a trellis covered with a thick growth of ivy on the outside wall of the house adjacent to the window. She reached an arm out the window to test if she could reach it. She could. It felt sturdy enough to support her. She could climb down. At least part of the way. Escape appeared possible!

But what could she do next should she make it to the ground in one piece? She thought of seeking out one of her friends and asking them to hide her. But because she didn't want to endanger anyone else's life, she quickly dismissed this possibility. She was a fugitive of the war now, the soldiers would come looking for her, and this meant she needed to get out of the country.

She would have the advantage of a head start, but not for long. The Paki army was everywhere in the city, and once the major woke up, he would send out alerts to block all escape routes. *Think,* she commanded herself. *Outthink this bastard.*

When the British partitioned India along religious lines to create the separate countries of India and Pakistan, they barely kept the landmass of India contiguous. Northeastern India is connected to the rest of the country by a very narrow strip of land along Bangladesh's north border that, at its narrowest point, is only eighteen miles wide. This choke point is called the Chicken's Neck. Geographically, this means India borders Bangladesh on three sides— east, north, and west. The Bay of Bengal, part of the Indian Ocean, is the fourth.

Since the country of Bangladesh is really a delta, formed by three rivers flowing toward each other, traveling overland from Dhaka, where Gera was, to the closest major city in India, Calcutta, requires crossing many rivers by ferry. To avoid the time-consuming and toilsome process of ferry travel, many travelers opt to go east and catch the train that goes up, over, and around Bangladesh through the Chicken's Neck. This railway, built during the British Raj, is also referred to by the name of this narrow passage.

Gera decided this was her best option also, to work her way east and hope to catch the Chicken's Neck in Agartala. If she could get to the train station there, she would be as good as in Calcutta. Her father had friends in Calcutta. Calcutta was the only place she could think of that offered her any support, given the events of the past few hours.

Gera would need food and other things for the journey. But going back to her house was not an option. When her absence came to light, that was the first place the soldiers would search. And there was no way she could face her father's bloody corpse again.

She crossed the hall into an upstairs room on the front side of the house and checked on the soldier standing guard at the front door. He was still awake but was smoking a cigarette and did not appear tuned in to his surroundings. Still, she had to be extremely careful and keep her decibel level below that of the night creatures.

Then she reentered the room where she was first escorted. Without hesitation, she went to the table with the money and selected a stack of the larger-denominated notes. She estimated how many bundles she could conceal under her kameez, grabbed them, and went back into the bedroom to dress.

Before slipping her outfit back on, she secured the money in her undergarments. That accomplished, she grabbed her shoes but did not put them on. Then she padded barefoot as quickly and quietly as she could back to her escape route. Opening the window as widely as it would allow, she took a deep breath of the night air and then looked down and found a grassy spot on the lawn to toss her shoes. That done, she reached over with her left hand and grabbed the trellis. Then she put her left leg out the window and searched through the ivy with her toe and found a good hold. Taking another deep breath, she swung the full weight of her body out the window. The trellis held. Now she had a hold on the trellis with all four extremities.

The climb down went slowly. She had to let go and replant her feet through the ivy into the holes in the trellis by feel alone, and the ivy was so thick that there weren't many spaces wide enough to admit her foot. After fifteen minutes, she had only moved about five feet. And the process was more tiring than she realized.

Another fifteen minutes and she was almost halfway. This heartened her. She took another deep breath and lowered her foot once more. Suddenly the wood lattice where her other foot was planted gave way, and she was unable to hold herself up with her arms alone. With the snap of rotting wood, Gera fell backward into the night.

Chapter 36

The shrubbery broke her fall but scratched her back and legs severely. She also had the wind knocked out of her. It took her a few minutes to recover. But her arms and legs survived intact. She lay still, listening to see if the sound of her fall might have carried around the building to the soldier standing guard. After several minutes, as no guard came to investigate and she could fill her lungs with air again, she stood up. She could walk without pain.

Her captors had brought her down Mirpur Road, and the house where she was held was very near that busy thoroughfare if her deductions while blindfolded were correct. If she could make her way to Mirpur Road, there was a good possibility she could hail a rickshaw even at this late hour. But which direction to go to get there? She didn't dare venture back into the street this close to where she was held captive.

She looked at the night sky. Mirpur Road was illuminated well. The horizon glowed more brightly in one direction, so she headed that way, slipping through the yards behind the large houses that lined this side of the street. Some had fences, but none she couldn't negotiate quickly. With each barrier she crossed, she felt her chances for escape improving.

Soon a familiar landmark on Mirpur Road appeared. She would still need to be careful. A woman appearing alone at night either attracted suspicion or made her a target. She tried to stay in the shadows.

It had to be well after midnight by now. Fortunately, there was still some pedestrian traffic in this sector. She got into the flow of the foot traffic and tried to walk close enough to a group in front of her headed in the same direction so as to appear a part of them. She looked for a rickshaw stand.

Not much farther down Mirpur, she found a driver looking for a fare. He appeared young and extremely thin. As Gera approached, he asked, "Lady need to go somewhere?"

"To the ferry at Bhairab Bazar," Gera said, sizing up this fellow as trustworthy.

"Lady, that's at least eighty kilometers. No can do in a rickshaw," he said.

"Then take me as far as you can. I'll get another ride from there or walk," Gera said with determination.

The rickshaw driver paused as if in thought. "I have an uncle with a car. He can take you there. But he doesn't like to be bothered at night. It will cost you."

"I'll make sure he is paid well," Gera answered. With what she had in her clothes, money was the least of her concerns.

"He'll want a hundred rupees for his trouble," the driver said.

"If he can get me there before dawn, I'll give him two hundred," Gera said. "And a hundred for you."

"Get in, lady," he said. "That's no problem. You will be there in three hours."

The driver pedaled furiously down Mirpur Road a short distance and then turned west. Not the direction Gera wanted to go, but she figured this must be the way to the uncle's house. Another mile or so and they entered a run-down sector of the city. The driver pulled up to a dilapidated house.

Panting, the driver said, "Wait here."

He went and banged on the door. No response. He banged again. Nothing. Then a shouting voice from inside, moving toward the door.

The door flew open. "What?" came from the man inside. He saw the rickshaw driver, and his face registered recognition. If this was the uncle, he was built nothing like his nephew. Very short and heavyset.

Gera saw them exchanging words excitedly. She figured the driver was trying to convince his uncle that she was good for the money. Two hundred rupees was more than a day laborer could earn in a month. Given her present situation, she would have given him a thousand to take her there. But she didn't want to suggest how much money she was carrying for fear of appearing an easy mark for a high-stakes robbery. While she was alone, she reached underneath her clothes, took out a few notes, and put them in a more accessible place.

The uncle closed the door and returned in a few moments fully clothed.

The two men approached her. "Uncle says he will take you there. But he wants one hundred rupees in advance."

Gera was glad she had moved the money. She reached in her kameez and, deliberately revealing she had more than one of the hundred-rupee notes, peeled off one and held it out to him. "Are you sure you can have me there before dawn?"

"Yes, no problem," he said, taking the note. "Very good. I'll get the car."

He disappeared into a nearby alley. In a few moments, a pickup truck emerged.

"That's your uncle's car?" Gera asked.

"Car not running. Truck is better anyway. It will get you there. Don't worry; I'll ride in back."

The uncle pulled up and went around and opened the door for Gera. She stepped in, and they were on their way.

As promised, they arrived at the ferry landing just before dawn. The sky was brushed with hues of magenta. Other colors of the spectrum melded into orange near that bright anticipatory spot on the horizon awaiting the sun's first rays. The smells of her delta country were most pronounced here, at the river. Each year the rivers overflowed their banks, depositing their fertile silt, mingling it with the ancient accumulations of decomposing plants, completing nature's perennial cycle of fecundity.

Cars were already lining up in the queue for the ferry. Gera thanked the driver and his uncle and paid them. Then she hurried toward the dock, hoping to be in time for the first crossing of the day.

She purchased her ticket and was one of the first allowed to board. She took a seat near a family with two small children.

The mother was opening a tiffin carrier and doling out breakfast to her family. During the harrowing events of the last twelve hours, Gera had had no chance to focus on anything but her grief and her escape. Only now could she realize how hungry she was. She instinctively reached in her pockets. All she found there were the remaining notes and a couple of tamarind sweets. Not much to assuage the gnawing in her stomach. She got an okay from the mother and offered the sweets to the children.

Within a few minutes, the ferry was loaded and ready to cross. Just as the lashings were about to be loosened for casting off, a squad of uniformed men started to file aboard. Paki soldiers!

Gera panicked. There was nowhere to hide. If they were looking for her, she was trapped.

The men walked slowly around the ferry as if searching for something in particular. They were questioning people as they went.

One of the soldiers approached Gera. "Are you traveling alone?" he asked.

Gera hesitated. If she said yes, there would be more questions.

The mother of the two small children said, "She's my sister. Came along to help with the children."

The soldier looked intently at the woman and then eyed Gera again. She hoped he could not see her heart thumping wildly in her chest.

After a few seconds, the soldier scowled and moved on to the next group. Gera could finally release the air in her lungs. She mouthed a thank-you to the woman who had just saved her life.

Chapter 37

After her experience on the ferry, she decided to travel the thirty-mile distance from Bhairab Bazar to Agartala on the back roads, using rickshaws and walking. She didn't know if she could handle any more encounters with enemy soldiers. Her endurance was nearing its limit. Fortunately, the kind mother on the ferry had shared some dal and flatbread with her. Otherwise she would not have had the energy to make it. She searched in vain for other food throughout the day.

It was late afternoon by the time Gera arrived at the train station. She had made it to India! Still, there was no way she would feel safe until she was aboard the train.

She checked the train schedule. The next train headed north through Chicken's Neck was at five o'clock. Only forty-five minutes from now. She purchased a ticket.

There was nowhere to sit, so she leaned against the wall to save whatever energy she had left. In the minutes of her wait, she assessed the multitudes in and around the station. Those few who had a purpose in their step were likely her traveling companions. Others were standing about as if expectant someone would be coming to pick them up. Many looked like they had been here for days, either disappointed in their plan of escaping, or here because they had nowhere else to go.

Typical of Indian trains, the locomotive lunged into the station late. At 5:48 p.m., Gera boarded and found a seat in the back of her compartment. All the tension she had accumulated over the past eighteen hours dissipated in an instant. Having nothing to rest her head on except her arm, she slumped against the window, covered her face with her head scarf, and sobbed herself into a fitful sleep.

The ride to Calcutta took fifteen hours. Gera was so tired that she managed to sleep intermittently during the first half of the trip. The last half she was completely miserable from hunger pangs.

She tried to focus on formulating a plan for when she arrived in Calcutta.

She would have to make finding food her top priority. Then she would try to contact Sayeed, a friend of her father's and her closest contact in Calcutta. Sayeed was well connected in the city and her best hope for help in picking up the pieces of her shattered life.

Gera had no trouble locating food once she arrived at the Calcutta train station. There were vendors everywhere. In a city with a recent influx of three million refugees, entrepreneurs abounded. Dozens of improvised stands were selling food to anyone with hard currency.

She found a stand preparing mutton *kabiraji*. Her mouth watered as she watched the cook combine the minced mutton with the spices and then pop the cutlet in a deep fryer. As the meat cooked, he drizzled the egg batter over the cutlet to make a crispy coating of the egg net. Once done, he placed the mutton kabiraji on a cardboard platter and served it with green chutney, *kasundi* mustard, and onion.

She ate enough to fill her stomach for the first time in two days. Next, she ventured about, trying to locate a telephone. She had some difficulty getting Sayeed's number, as he no longer resided at the place she remembered. Once she made the connection, he volunteered to come immediately and pick her up at the train station.

A short while later, she heard the welcome sound of her name being spoken in the form of a question.

"Gera?" The voice came from behind her. She turned to see a young man she barely recognized. She had not seen Sayeed for almost a year.

"Sayeed! Thank you so much for coming."

"Gera, you look terrible," Sayeed said before thinking. "I mean, you look tired. Let me take you home so you can get some rest. Where's your luggage?"

"Oh, Sayeed, there isn't any." She looked down and began to cry. He came and put his arm around her. For a few moments, he didn't say anything. When she recovered a bit and turned her face toward him, he asked, "What happened?"

"The Paki soldiers murdered Father. They came to our door and called him a spy and shot him right there in our house."

"Inna lillaahi wa innaa ilayhi raaji'oon. We surely belong to Allah, and to him we shall return," Sayeed said. "Oh, Gera, I'm so sorry. I had no idea. You ran away?"

"The soldiers took me prisoner. But I escaped. I knew they would come looking for me, so I fled across the border to Agartala and immediately took the train here."

"Nauzobillah. May Allah protect us," Sayeed exclaimed. "Come, let's get you home. We can talk more in the car if you want to."

Sayeed escorted Gera to his family's car. Sayeed now lived with his parents in an extended-family arrangement. She had stayed with them before and felt comfortable there. All she wanted right now was a bath and a long night's rest.

Once they arrived at his house, Sayeed ushered Gera straight to the guest room. He told her he would make excuses for her to his family. She showered, collapsed across the bed, and slept uninterrupted for twelve hours.

The next morning Sayeed and his family were just finishing breakfast when she appeared in the kitchen. Gera made light of her captivity. If anyone in the Muslim community ever suspected she had been raped, she would be labeled as woman of low repute and made an outcast. Though Sayeed was part of a more modern and enlightened generation, he was also part of a family and a community, and she knew it was best not to confide in anyone. She decided to focus instead on reassessing her situation, exploring her options, and soliciting advice. Sayeed was not the great source of comfort and optimism she had hoped.

"Calcutta has always had enough poor to keep the streets full," Sayeed said. "Now they are stacked on top of each other. The city is bursting at its seams."

"More people means there's more need," Gera said, trying to better understand the situation. "Surely there is something I can do."

"If you want to work for nothing, then yes, there is plenty to do in the refugee camps," Sayeed said. "But if you want to support yourself, go somewhere besides Calcutta. There are other cities in India where you can find work." Then, as a joke, he said, "Of course, people with means are getting on ships and going all over the world. There's a boat of them leaving tomorrow for the United States."

Gera didn't take it as a joke. "Do they have any more room?" she asked.

"Well, I don't know. They were taking three hundred, I heard. It's too late for that one, I would say. But there will be another sailing in a month or two."

"I want to go," Gera said, with a determination that came from deep within her. "Now."

"We can check," Sayeed said, "but there's just not enough time to get you all the documents you'll need, get you clothes and luggage."

"I have money," Gera said. "And I have my passport."

Gera got the last berth on the sailing from the port of Calcutta to Savannah, Georgia. After securing her ticket, Sayeed took her shopping. She purchased a suitcase, a couple of saris, and a few toiletries and, with a total sense of abandonment, set sail in search of some better dimension to life. Anything, even the total unknown of a foreign country, was better than the hell she had experienced over the past seventy-two hours.

Conditions aboard the boat were much better than Gera thought they would be. The food was good and plentiful, and she helped herself to it. Her cabin was very cramped, but she didn't mind since little of her time was spent there. She wandered the decks of the ship, using the twenty-six long days on board to rest up from her ordeal, to grieve, and to reassess. For the most part, she stayed to herself. She sifted through the former goals she had set for her life and found a couple for which she could still muster some enthusiasm and energy.

Gera suffered the same psychological effects any rape victim has to endure. Shame and self-blame tried to gain a foothold in her psyche. She experienced flashbacks and occasional nightmares. Having endured such a trauma, she now understood why so many women never manage to regain their self-esteem and go on with their lives.

Fortunately, Gera had a defiance of spirit that enabled her to get some perspective on the assault. In spite of her inner anguish, she was not going to let the experience define her. Instead of internalizing the trauma and taking responsibility for it, she managed to focus her anger where it needed to go. Toward her assailant. She blamed; she cursed. She also nursed her anger toward the Paki officer who had murdered her father. She would get back at them the only way she could. By not letting them break her spirit. That resolve, more than anything else, allowed her to survive with her sense of self-worth intact. She had persevered, had freed herself from her captors, and was determined to start a new life for herself in a completely new world and culture. Her resilience came from more than good coping skills. The same remarkable strength of character her father had possessed was hers also. The whole experience of the war, her father's murder, the rape, somehow made her stronger, more assured that she had the inner fortitude to take on whatever the world was going to throw her way.

Though Gera maintained a solitary existence for much of her voyage, she did make friends with another woman, Tahira, much older than herself, who was also traveling alone. Tahira had lost her husband, a professor at Dhaka University, in the initial bombings during Operation Searchlight. An educated woman herself, she had traveled extensively with her husband.

"I wonder what life is like in the United States," Gera said. "Have you ever been there?"

"No, we never had the opportunity to visit, my husband and me," Tahira answered. "But we spent some time in England. The cultures are similar, I've been told. Male dominated. But in these cultures, women have many more rights than in our country. And more opportunities for jobs, for education. Even though I had a university degree, there were few chances for me to use my education at home. I don't know if things will be any different in America. But at least there I won't be bound by what the men in my family want."

"You have a son?" Gera asked.

"No, no children." Tahira smiled to show she felt no inadequacy because of this. "There was only my brother and my husband's brother. It was expected that I would move in with one of them after he died. The idea of having another man rule over my life was just more than I could stand. My husband was a good man and very kind and supportive. But my brother and brother-in-law not so much. They are very traditional. Their wives aren't as happy as I was. If they don't have respect for their wives, how much less would they have for me? I would just be another burden for them to bear, and I would be expected to be grateful, to be submissive to them, to know my place. I would rather be dead than be dependent on them. Whatever awaits me in America, no matter what the hardships, has to be better than that."

"Family is a safety net in our culture," Gera said. "It's good to have them there when you need them. But it also means there is no respect for individuality."

"No honor for the individual," Tahira added. "Everyone is expected to up-hold the honor of the family. Our culture of honor. That, more than anything else in our society, prevents change. Prevents reform. When you must always make sure you fit in, always maintain belonging no matter what, you are con-trolled, and nothing will ever change."

"You are hoping you can be an individual in America?" Gera asked, encour-aged to find another woman who felt some optimism for what lay ahead of them.

"Maybe," Tahira said. "We're going to another culture where everything revolves around upholding the dignity and reputation of men. White men. Our part of the world endured that for nearly a hundred years when Bangladesh was a part of British India. There are ways to be true to who you are and still make your way in that kind of world. Respect the limits the culture will place upon you, but don't be afraid to take risks. Be bold. Be who you are. Define your own honor. You're young, and you'll have far more opportunities than me."

"Where in the United States are you going when we land?" Gera asked.

"Chapel Hill, North Carolina," Tahira said. "And you?"

"August Valley, Georgia."

"We'll both be in the South," Tahira said. "Plenty of people there are ances-tors of slaves. They survived a system of oppression. So will we."

The ship Gera was traveling on was an old ocean liner from the British India Line. It was scheduled to be decommissioned after this, its final voyage. When India was a part of the British Empire, there was heavy demand for sturdy vessels like this to transport passengers and cargo between these countries. Following India's independence in 1947, the need for massive transfer of goods and people began a gradual decline, and, one by one, these grand vessels were converted to cargo ships for other routes or taken out of service and scrapped. That was the situation of the small liner Gera sailed on. Once capable of carrying over one thousand passengers, most of its deck and hold space was now dedicated to cargo. Only three hundred passenger berths remained.

One of the few features remaining to passengers aboard the ship was a small library. There Gera located a book describing her port of destination, Savannah. She learned that the area around the city where she would disembark was known as the "low country," the phrase magnifying her nostalgia for her delta home. Savannah's founder, the English general James Oglethorpe, formed his plan for the city while still at sea on his first voyage to Georgia. He envisioned a colony to give debtors from English prisons a second chance to make a life for themselves. Georgia was to be the place where Gera was planning to stake out her second chance at life. Thinking of her new home in light of Oglethorpe's founding vision gave her some comfort. She tucked this little tidbit of information about Georgia away in the recesses of her psyche.

For most of an afternoon, she dwelled over the many pictures of Savannah's landscapes and architecture. It looked like a beautiful place, with its planned layout of city squares and wide streets lined with overhanging oak trees. However, she doubted there would be much opportunity to take in much of it. The plan, as she understood it, was for the churches to meet the refugees at the port and transport them directly to their respective cities. In her case that city was to be August Valley.

The ship sailed up the Suez Canal and crossed the Mediterranean, and by the time it was midway across the Atlantic, Gera had come to some sense of peace with all that had happened and was in a pretty good place within herself. And then she got ill. Violent nausea and vomiting. The ship's doctor gave her medicine for seasickness that helped very little. When she arrived in Savannah, she kissed the ground, so glad she was to finally be off that boat. But the nausea didn't abate. Not only that, but she was several days late for her period.

Chapter 38

July 1971

Gera held her breath as the customs agent inspected her luggage. Inside the hems of the few garments she had purchased in Calcutta were forty-four of the one-hundred-rupee notes she had appropriated in the major's quarters. During the crossing she had passed some of the time carefully sewing the notes in by hand. She risked deportation if the money was discovered, but it was a risk she thought worth taking. Without it, she would have few options should she fare poorly in America. It wasn't that she was short on optimism. She was just being tough-minded and realistic, just like her father. As a single woman traveling alone, she felt she needed an escape hatch.

It came as no surprise when an epidemic broke out among the refugees. The illness started soon after the church bus picked them up in Savannah and deposited them at the motel in August Valley. None of the refugees seemed immune to this one. Homesickness.

All the refugees had losses to count. All had lost their homes. Many others besides Gera had lost loved ones. But most could count themselves fortunate to have one or more family members with them. Gera, however, was alone.

It had now been a month since her father's murder. The twenty-six-day ocean crossing had given her a lot of time for reality to sink in. She had lost everything. Her vision of the future was gone, wiped away by the vicissitudes of war. During the long days at sea, she had made some progress toward reenvisioning a future for herself, only to have these fresh hopes now dashed by the prospect of a child to birth and raise.

She had no regrets about her decision to come to America. Here she was far away from the war and the tribalism that she and her father continually had to deal with. If she had stayed in Calcutta or some other area of India, she would have had opportunities, but nothing like what the United States offered. If she was fated to be an unwed mother, she would rather deal with the cultural stigma associated with that in any place except her home country.

Honor is so important in the Muslim world and in a Muslim country. And it's women who bear the burden of that honor. In a culture of honor, a woman who becomes pregnant out of wedlock is a source of shame no matter what the circumstances that led to the pregnancy. She will be rejected by her family, by her clan, and by society in general. In many places, she will be marked for death by the family, the cultural practice known as honor killing. Family honor trumps any notion of human dignity or human rights. These practices did not originate from the teaching of Islam and have no basis in the Quran. Culture alone dictates these subhuman barbarisms. They originated in the ruthless medieval world of patriarchal domination and are only maintained today because the male leadership is paralyzed with fear, fear of losing what little hold on power and control remains within its grasp.

Gera still wasn't sure how she felt about the pregnancy, but at least here in the United States she could sort out her feelings without fearing for her life or that of her unborn child. For that, she would be eternally grateful to the patronage of First Baptist Church of August Valley and the individuals in that church who made it possible for her to be in this country.

The church proved itself to be a model of organization and efficiency. Each refugee was given an instruction packet with lots of information about services available in the city, several forms to be filled out, and an itinerary for a series of orientation meetings to be held at the church. Each of the sheets in the packet had some verse from the Bible at the top of the page, verses such as "Go ye therefore and make disciples of all nations, baptizing them in the name of the Father, and of the Son, and of the Holy Spirit."

A woman named Sally Benheart coordinated the volunteer activities for the refugees, making sure everyone got to where they were supposed to be. Gera soon learned that this take-charge woman was the minister's wife. Sally quickly earned Gera's respect for her dedication to the refugee cause. She was a woman on a mission, and she worked tirelessly to see that everyone under her patronage got the attention they needed.

What Gera didn't appreciate was the way Sally ignored anything having to do with the cultural and religious life of the refugees. Sally gave no consideration to the dietary restrictions of orthodox Muslims. She was dismissive when one of the refugees requested time in the schedule for *maghrib*, the prescribed prayer after sunset, stating that she had plans for the group to pray together.

After just a couple of days, Gera concluded that Sally was trying to make converts of the refugees. The more time passed, the more convinced Gera became of Sally's ultimate intention to make Christians of them. With each passing day, Gera trusted her less. After a while, Gera began to think of Sally's actions as dishonest. It was like all the care and concern she was lavishing on the refugees amounted to no more than a bribe.

However, Gera also recognized that the refugees were benefitting tremendously from many of the things the church was doing. The refugees were given food, clothing, and shelter, classes to help them with their English, vocational counseling and placement services, and child care while they took training classes or interviewed for jobs, all provided at no cost and always with a smile. Gera tempered her smoldering disgruntlement and gradually accepted that enduring the proselytizing was just the price the refugees had to pay for the services provided.

One evening, toward the end of the two-week orientation, Gera was milling about in the fellowship hall while refreshments were being served when she overheard part of a conversation Sally was having in the next room.

"You really ought to come out and visit with the refugees, Abe," Sally said. "They are, after all, children of God, too."

So, she's talking to her husband, Gera thought. *The minister.*

"They are," Abe said. "And they deserve to be treated like children of God. With dignity and respect. Trying to convince other people their religion is wrong and ours is right isn't what Jesus wanted us to do."

"What about the Great Commission to preach the gospel to all nations?" Sally asked.

"This group of refugees isn't a mission field," Abe said. "This is a captive audience. These are people escaping a war. You've offered them a foxhole. Any conversions, if you get any, would be foxhole conversions. And those kinds of conversions aren't too reliable."

"Well, what about John chapter fourteen verse six? 'I am the way, the truth, and the life. No one comes unto the Father except through me.' These people are condemned unless we teach them the truth. I've heard you say the same thing yourself in some of your sermons."

She talks to her husband like this? Gera thought. *Muslim women don't question their husbands like this. Certainly not if their husbands are respected authorities.* Understandably, Gera was having trouble getting a handle on some of the cultural differences in gender relationships, especially within a marriage.

"Not exactly the same thing," Abe said. "I'm not sure Jesus meant that everyone was going to hell who doesn't believe the same things we do. I think Jesus was talking more about actions than beliefs. That we 'come to the Father' by how we treat others, not by making sure a person has some correct set of beliefs. You and I have had this conversation before, Sally. You know how I feel about this."

"And you know how I feel, too," Sally said. "I know you weren't too keen on the church taking on these refugees. But what's done is done. They're here now. We're going to take care of them. And we're going to make sure they hear the good news about Jesus."

This sounds to me like a marriage in trouble, Gera thought. *This woman is not being respectful of her husband. He's not going to put up with this.*

"Certainly take care of them," Abe said. "That's not why I opposed the project. I opposed it because I know how different their beliefs are and how foreign their ways are to ours. And I knew that many of you wouldn't understand and respect that and would end up trying to Christianize them."

This is a wise man, Gera thought. *At least he makes an effort to understand that we come from a different world than he does and is respectful of our differences.*

"Abe, I haven't asked you for much in our marriage," Sally said. "I've always been the respectful wife, haven't I? Respectful of your authority as the head of our house and as the pastor."

"You have," Abe said. "You've been right there for me in our marriage and in my career."

"Well, I'm asking you for something now," Sally said. "Taking care of these people is very important to me. It gives me a sense of purpose. It makes me feel like I'm really doing something meaningful. Not like the silly things people usually ask the minister's wife to do. I'm asking you to help me in doing this work. Just show that you're supportive of what I'm doing."

"Okay, okay," Abe said. "What do you want me to do?"

"Come out and mingle with them," Sally said. "Come out to the motel tomorrow for a little while. Some of them have found jobs, and we're going to help them move into an apartment."

"Lead the way," Abe said, and he followed his wife out into the fellowship hall.

"Abe, this is Gera," Sally said. "Gera, this is my husband, Abe."

"Nice to meet you," Abe said.

"For me as well," Gera said. "You're the minister here, aren't you?"

"Yes, I'm the shepherd of this flock," Abe said. "Sorry I haven't been around more. It's a busy time for our church, and our volunteer ministry team is well trained. I understand they are taking good care of you."

"I've been well taken care of," Gera said. "And I'm so grateful to all of you."

"Gera is our earliest success story," Sally said. "She's already found a job and a place to live. This weekend we're going to help her get settled into an apartment."

"Wonderful," Abe said. "Your English is very good. I imagine that helped you in finding a job."

Sally, sensing that her husband was relaxing into the conversation, left Gera and Abe and moved on to check on others.

"I learned English from an early age," Gera said. "And yes, my employer was impressed that I understood English so well. Though I don't know how much use I can make of it working in housekeeping at a motel. But it's an income until I can find something else."

"What did you do in Bangladesh?" Abe asked. "Before the war?"

"I was a student at the Dhaka University. And I helped my father in his business."

"What business was that?" Abe asked.

"Cooking," Gera replied. "My father was a well-known chef in my country. He traveled a lot, and I often accompanied him on his trips. He spoke several languages and encouraged me to learn them as well. He's the reason my English is as good as it is."

"What is your native tongue?" Abe asked.

"Bengali. That's the real reason my country is at war. Because of language. Right after the British divided India and created Pakistan for the Muslims in 1947, the government of West Pakistan declared that Urdu would be the only official language. In East Pakistan, what is now Bangladesh, most everyone spoke Bengali. This meant the Pakistanis were trying to suppress our language and our culture. The Bengali Language Movement started right after the partition as a protest against these government actions on language. The protests got to be violent, and in 1952 several people were killed. Our resentment of the Pakistani government grew and grew, and led to the war my people are now fighting for the independence of the Bengalis."

"What other languages do you speak?" Abe asked. "Parlez-vous français?"

"Oui, monsieur," Gera said, her face lighting up with excitement at finding a fellow linguaphile.

Gera learned that Abe's mother was French and had taught him her native tongue from an early age.

Gera and Abe, both thrilled to find someone with which to speak a language they both cherished, conversed in French for the remainder of the evening. This was how their relationship started, in the safe, innocent intimacy of shared thoughts through a language that no one else in the room understood.

Chapter 39

Gera still had not experienced menstruation. It had now been more than six weeks since the major violated her. Her nausea passed once she had been on land a few days, but she was developing other symptoms suggesting pregnancy, especially heaviness in her breasts. A home pregnancy test indicated positive. She decided it was time to get an appointment with an obstetrician.

She gave a lot of thought to the possibility of abortion. Given the circumstances, she expected a competent physician could easily be located who would be willing to perform one. And this solution made sense given all the other challenges she faced in starting a new life for herself in a new country.

But something in her resisted. It wasn't so much that the idea of having a child appealed to her, even though she was willing to admit to herself that she was painfully lonely. Her reluctance came more from the basic respect she had for life. The idea of willfully terminating a human life, one that had done nothing to deserve a death sentence, was a decision she did not have the constitution to make.

She also considered having the baby and putting it up for adoption. There were agencies that would help her should she choose this option. But the idea of carrying the pregnancy and going through the pain of childbirth only to give up the baby at the end was not a decision she thought she could make either.

After careful deliberation, she resolved to keep the baby and raise it as her own. She would tell the child his or her father was Abir Mallik, a man who had suffered nobly and was most likely dead now, all in the war for the independence of Bangladesh. Explained in this way, not only would her child have a father he or she could be proud of, but this story might salvage Gera some shred of respect within the refugee Muslim community. None of the other refugees had known her before they boarded the ship together in Calcutta. Some might still have their suspicions, but Gera hoped that in the shared suffering brought on by this war, her people might give her the benefit of the doubt and cut her some slack. Even though human beings tend to think the worst of each other, Gera had enough faith in human decency to think them also capable of granting mercy.

When Abe and Sally showed up at the motel the next morning, several other church members had already arrived. One of the primary needs of the refugees was transportation. Job interviews, doctor visits, access to social-service offices, locating more permanent housing—all these things and more required a car. Sally and her coterie of volunteers coordinated a sign-up list and made sure everyone got to where they needed to be.

Gera emerged from one of the motel rooms just as they were parking. She appeared anxious.

"Abe, could you please come and speak to Mr. Syed?" Gera asked. "He's very upset. Neither he nor his wife speaks much English, but I can interpret for you."

"Certainly," Abe said.

"Go ahead and talk with him," Sally said. "I must get Eva Mustafi to her job interview. I should be back in half an hour."

Abe accompanied Gera to the Syeds' room. As he entered Abe saw an older Muslim woman, probably in her sixties, standing beside her husband, who was sitting in a chair with his head between his knees, sobbing uncontrollably. The woman was trying, unsuccessfully, to console her husband.

"Mr. and Mrs. Syed," Gera said in Bengali, "this is Reverend Benheart, the minister of the church that is taking care of us. He is here to help. Can you tell him what happened?"

With the appearance of a stranger, Mr. Syed tried to compose himself. He told Gera the story again he had already shared with her before Abe arrived, holding up a small, ornate book as he talked. As he talked he looked alternately from Gera's face to Abe's.

Gera translated. "This is my Quran," Mr. Syed said. "It was given to me by my father. I have read it every day and protected it all my life. Now look at it. It's ruined. I spilled a carton of juice on it this morning. Living in this motel room, we have very little room to put things. When I opened my suitcase, it tipped over the juice, and it ran all over the table."

When Gera had finished, he began crying again.

"I'm so sorry this happened," Abe said, looking directly at Mr. Syed. Then, to Gera, he said, "There may be more to this than just a soggy Quran. Ask Mrs. Syed if something else has happened."

Gera spoke Abe's words to Mr. Syed and then turned and questioned his wife as instructed. Mrs. Syed told Gera that their daughter had been kidnapped and later killed in the war. Details of her fate were sketchy, but likely she was raped and tortured before she died. The rest of their family lived in one of the villages that were razed by the Paki army. Facts were sketchy, but, best they could determine, all of these family members were now in a mass grave.

As Gera heard the story of the Syeds' daughter, she couldn't suppress her tears. Abe, while focused on Mrs. Syed as Gera recounted the atrocity, also picked up on Gera's wounded state and reached over and gave her hand a little squeeze as she continued to interpret.

"I have no words to offer for such terrible pain and loss," Abe said, deeply affected himself by what he was hearing. Gera relayed this message to the Syeds. Abe sat there for some time in silence, allowing everyone in the room to have their feelings without any compulsion to try and fill the void with some platitude.

In a few moments, Abe asked Gera, "These horrors occurred some time ago, though the pain has not lessened, I'm sure. But I have to wonder if there might be something else, something that's occurred since the Syeds arrived here."

Gera turned again to Mrs. Syed and inquired about a more recent upset. Mrs. Syed related something to Gera, and soon Mr. Syed added a few sentences of his own.

After Gera heard what the couple had to say in its entirety, she turned to Abe. "Mr. Syed is also worried that he will not be able to find a job. He can't understand English, and he is old. He's been to several interviews, but no one wants him. He feels useless."

Abe considered this new information. "Tell him that if he is willing and able to work, I will see to it that he finds meaningful employment." Gera shared this message with Mr. Syed. Registering understanding, he then nodded a grateful thanks in Abe's direction.

Once outside, Gera expressed her thanks to Abe for his intervention.

"I hurt so for those folks," Abe said. "Such unspeakable tragedy. Now, at their age, they must try to carve out a new life in this strange place. I can't begin to imagine what they are going through."

"You restored some hope for him," Gera said. Her respect for this man was growing by the minute.

"Whatever we can do for them will not be much to replace what they have lost," Abe said. "But we'll do what we can."

This dialogue of empathy for the Syeds gave them permission to look directly into one another's eyes. Both saw the genuine compassion each held for this unfortunate couple. But in that gaze, something much deeper and more powerful was also being exchanged.

Before either of them could say more, Sally made her return known from the other side of the parking lot.

Gera had never been in the presence of a man like Abe. Emotionally present. Emotionally perceptive. A person with strong convictions and at the same time sensitive to the feelings of others and the needs behind those feelings.

He was handsome but not remarkably so. Whatever deficiencies he had in physical appeal he more than made up for with an animal magnetism. The self-assured way he conducted himself stirred Gera's memories of her father. But

Abe was not old enough to be her father. She estimated him to be just a few years older than herself. He also aroused another longing within her, one that Abir Mallik had gratified somewhat. Though Gera clearly saw the futility of dwelling on what could never be, she couldn't help herself. Given all the pressure and uncertainty in her life right now, she could not help but give herself the little luxury of fantasizing about being with Abe Benheart.

On Saturday morning Sally came to the motel to help Gera move into her new apartment. Gera had found one that was both convenient to the motel where she would be working and near a bus stop. She planned to take the bus to work until she could afford a car. The apartment was furnished, and Gera's possessions were few. Most of her clothes fit into the one suitcase she had brought with her from Calcutta. Still, she needed a ride to get to her new lodging, so Sally volunteered to drive her.

Gera took this opportunity alone with Sally to ask her for a recommendation about an obstetrician in the area. When Gera brought up this need, Sally pressed her for all the facts. Knowing Sally the way she did, Gera prepared herself for Sally's nosiness. She had already decided that, since she needed to confide in someone, she would tell Sally about her condition. Sally was more than happy to suggest someone and made the call herself to her gynecologist for the appointment. They could not see her until the latter part of next month, but Gera was to call if she had any problems in the meantime.

Abe showed up at the motel just as Gera was checking out. He followed the two of them in his own car to Gera's new home.

"This place is going to work out fine for you," Sally assured Gera as they walked in her modest apartment. "But you're going to need several things to set up housekeeping. I can take you to the store after we get you settled in."

"Thank you, but I think I'll be able to manage," Gera said. "There's a store just up the street."

"But you haven't gotten a paycheck yet," Sally said. "And we have funds set aside for this purpose."

"All right," Gera conceded, knowing how useless it was to argue with Sally. "Just give me a few minutes to get my things unpacked and think about what I might need."

"Abe, take the suitcase upstairs," Sally commanded. "Gera, show Abe which bedroom you want it in. I'll go check your kitchen and start making you a list."

Once upstairs Abe and Gera made small talk as Gera took a few clothing items out of her luggage and hung them up or put them in drawers. When she finished, she zipped up the suitcase and attempted to put it on the top self in her closet.

"Here, let me help you with that," he said as he rushed to her aid. As he reached over her to grab the suitcase, their bodies brushed against each other. Then their eyes made contact. They held their gaze for quite a few seconds, only to be interrupted by Sally calling from downstairs.

"Gera, are you about ready?"

At the sound of his wife's voice, Abe backed off and gave himself a moment to let his head clear. "I'm coming," Gera shouted back to Sally, looking once again at Abe. He turned his head away, as if he could not bear another bewitching look from her.

Abe chanced one more glimpse in her direction as he made his way to the door, a glance that seemed to convey his helplessness in her presence. Then, without any good-bye, he hurried down the stairs. Gera heard him announce to Sally that he had to get back to the church.

Gera went to the grocery store with Sally, but she must have appeared to be a total scatterbrain. She couldn't escape her memory of the hungry look she had seen in Abe's eyes. What was she to do? She knew he'd be back. There was just no way what had passed between them this morning was going to be the end of it. What was she going to do when he returned? Here, Abe's wife was devoting all this time and energy to helping her, and yet she could not escape this flood of carnal thoughts she was having about her benefactor's husband. She hated the major for getting her into this, she hated Sally for being so nice, but most of all, in this moment, she hated herself.

She wandered the grocery store like a zombie, checking items off the list Sally had prepared. Dishwashing liquid, paper towels, broom and dustpan. *Maybe*, she thought, *it's time to implement my backup plan.* She still had the money she had taken from the major's stash. She had more than enough money to get a plane ticket back home. That was the only noble and courageous way she could think of to get herself out of her circumstances now. Better to face war and keep one's self-respect. But she couldn't. There was still the pregnancy, which now weighed on her like a ball and chain.

That evening about dusk, Gera heard a knock at her door. She hesitated, because she knew it was him, and she knew it was still within her power to put a stop to this. But that possibility existed in theory only, because there was nothing in her now that could summon the will.

She opened the door. They gazed at one another only long enough to find the passion still burning within the other, and instantly they were in each other's arms.

Chapter 40

A be stayed with Gera as late as he dared.

After he left she started bleeding. Rather heavily. Was she about to lose the baby? She shrugged her shoulders when she felt the cramps and noticed the blood clots. Nothing would surprise her anymore. She told herself she didn't care one way or another. She did, but her feelings were so mixed up. One minute she had reconciled herself to having the baby and being happy about it; the next she thought of all the possibilities in her new life if she wasn't burdened with a baby. And now, further complicating her emotions, Abe was in her life. That muddled matters infinitely more. Her feelings were in total turmoil.

One minute she felt elated. The next guilty. Abe was the most kind, gentle, understanding man she had ever met. But he was married. The hunger she felt when she was in his presence rendered that inescapable fact irrelevant. Abe was alive and available, a comforting presence to occupy the huge void left by both her father and Abir. The guilt tugged on her, but it was losing the battle within her conscience. The respect Gera once had for Sally had already faded, even before she ever laid eyes on Abe. In the drama created by her and Abe's torrential love, Sally was now occupying the position of poor victim. Gera's disdain for Sally was instantly transformed to scorn the very instant Abe had surrendered to his desire.

The bleeding stopped the next morning, just as quickly as it had started.

Their torrid affair lasted barely two weeks. During that time, they met as often as Abe dared under the cover of darkness. Unable to wait, they careened immediately to bed, seeking refuge from their separate, individual loneliness, finding solace in this sanctuary of the flesh. But soon passion succumbed to guilt. Pain overtook pleasure. On their last evening together, they talked openly about their feelings. Abe admitted that his marriage to Sally was currently unsatisfying. His decision to marry her had been a sensible one at the time he made it, when he was totally consumed with career and advancement. Sally was, in his estimation, a good woman and had all the credentials to make a good minister's wife. And she had played the role to perfection. Her support had been instrumental in advancing his career. But vital parts were missing when it came to them sharing any sort of inner life together. Sally was for the most part unreflective about life and about her motivations. She always did what she thought was expected of her, and this was, for the most part, satisfying to her. As their marriage progressed and they moved to larger and larger churches, she increasingly busied herself with project after project, and he compensated for their lack of intimacy by retreating more to his study to think, read, and reflect. They had grown apart.

Gera told Abe about witnessing her father's murder, the news about Abir, and the rape. She openly acknowledged her intense loneliness because of these losses and the fact that she was now an unaccompanied Muslim woman, looked upon with intense scrutiny and suspicion. She stopped short of telling him about the pregnancy. Sally would tell him all about it, Gera figured, but if she had already revealed that news to her husband, Abe made no mention of it.

Each of them had been at a fragile crossroad when they met. A description does not excuse, only explains. They would part with guilt but not regret, disappointment at the ending of their affair but gratitude for its memory. For these few days, they had experienced mad, passionate love and complete fulfillment—a completeness that few people are fortunate to ever discover in a lifetime.

Abe returned to Sally, confessed his sin, and asked for forgiveness.

Gera went to the obstetrician in September. She was getting worried because she was at least twelve weeks along and felt no movement from the baby. After some tests, the doctor reassured her that it was too early for that to happen. She was only four weeks along, and the pregnancy was doing fine.

Counting back, she realized that she had conceived (again?) the last night she was with Abe. Once she got over her shock and came to grips with this news, she made the most of it. She was tough-minded and practical. Just like her father.

Abe Benheart is a good and honorable man, Gera thought. *I am proud to be bearing his child. But I'll do or say nothing to come between him and his wife. He can never know that he is the father of my child.*

Chapter 41

July 2016

Through the synchronized labor of two contractors and the work of some volunteers from the congregation, the damage from the vandalism at Ike's church was repaired, and the sanctuary was made safe and ready for services the next Sunday. Ike chose "love is stronger than hate" as the theme for his sermon. He incorporated a building rededication into the litany. The service was so well attended that extra chairs had to be brought in to accommodate everyone.

Ike had seen a lot in his twenty years in the ministry, and few things surprised him anymore. But one thing that never ceased to amaze him was how crises of one sort or another always seemed to bring people together and bring out the best in them. All week congregants came by offering to help with the cleanup and painting, some of whom had not been to a service in months. Once word of the incident got out in the community, pastors from other churches came by with offers to help as well. Donations for the repair work flooded in, and by the middle of the week the church had more than enough money to cover the estimates for the work. This was before even taking into account Del Wood's generous contribution.

The incident had brought on an interesting twist of fate. The board of the church now had to deal with a very gratifying problem. It would have to decide what to do with all the extra money.

With all the extra activity at the church this week, the tension over Ismael's situation, and the excitement over Ismael's revelation, topped off by the revival atmosphere at the church service that morning, Ike was exhausted by the time he got home after church. All he wanted to do was eat lunch and take a nap. After he changed clothes and inhaled a plate of leftovers Becky had heated up, he was headed toward the bedroom when his cell phone rang. He noticed the number was from another area code and just let it ring. In a few seconds, the phone gave its indication that the caller had left a message. Before lying down, he played it back.

"Ike, this is Bruce Massey. I may have some important information. Please call me as soon as you get this message."

The message acted like a shot of adrenaline. Ike immediately dialed Bruce's number.

"Hello."

"Bruce, this is Ike. I got your message. What's up?"

"Ike, this is going to sound crazy, but since the thought came to me, I just can't get it out of my head. I thought I'd better tell somebody. Lee may have left me a note at his family's cabin."

"What makes you think he left you a note?" Ike asked.

"We used to leave notes there for each other all the time," Bruce said, "until our cell-phone service got better. We used to meet at the cabin on weekends. It's at Park Lake, which is part ways to Jacksonville. Lee would always check to make sure none of the family was using it. But we still had ways of signaling each other just in case someone showed up unexpectedly. We left each other these notes, so we could communicate without his family knowing anything."

"It's been seven weeks since Lee died," Ike said. "Don't you imagine his family's been there during this time?"

"Most likely they've been there," Bruce replied. "They always used it a lot during the summer."

"Then wouldn't they have seen a note?" Ike asked.

"Nope," Bruce said. "We had a special hiding place. Used to put notes there all the time. Not so much in the past couple of years, though. That's why I didn't think of this possibility sooner."

"When will you be able to go to the cabin to check and see?" Ike asked.

"I've just returned from there," Bruce said. "Figured Sunday morning was a good time to go, since Lee's family would be at church."

"And did you find anything?" Ike asked.

"Couldn't get in," Bruce answered. "Couldn't even get in the gate. All the locks have been changed. Makes me wonder if they suspected I might have a key."

"Maybe they found a note, and that's what clued them in," Ike suggested.

"I doubt it," Bruce said. "They'd never have any reason to look in this place."

"Where is it?" Ike asked. "I mean, where you hid the notes?"

"There is a ship in a bottle sitting on the mantel in the great room. There's a cork in the bottle, and the neck of the bottle has a label on it so anything stuck in there is not visible. We put our notes in there."

"Bruce, are you thinking, by some chance, that Lee might have left you a note there telling you he was going to kill himself?"

"All I'm saying is it's possible," Bruce said. "I think somebody needs to go and check. Maybe you could contact Ashley, Lee's sister. You know, the one who contacted me, and get her to look."

"I don't know if we can trust Lee's family to tell the truth if they were to find something there," Ike said. "They're convinced the Muslim killed him. They don't want to admit Lee was gay, and they sure as hell don't want to admit he committed suicide."

"What do you suggest we do?" Bruce asked.

"Call Harbuck, the attorney," Ike said. "When he hears this, he may want to get a search warrant."

Ike promised Bruce he would let him know if they found anything and then hung up. *No nap for me this afternoon,* Ike said to himself.

Chapter 42

Ike immediately phoned Harbuck and told him the story. Since the note wasn't going anywhere, if there was a note, and Harbuck didn't want to rile the judge by calling him on a Sunday afternoon, he told Ike he would get a search warrant first thing in the morning. He also asked Ike keep his morning free so as to accompany them when Harbuck and the sheriff's department went to the cabin. Harbuck said he could get this okayed by telling the sheriff only Ike knew the exact location for them to look. Besides, he had some suspicion Ike would want to be there. He was right about that.

The following morning a convoy started out from the August Valley courthouse headed for Park Lake. A squad car, followed by the separate cars of Patterson Street, Harbuck, and Ike. Harbuck said Street wasn't too pleased when the officers served the warrant, and at first he blustered about, calling his attorney. "But he came around," was the way Harbuck put it.

The cabin was located deep in the woods down a couple of miles of winding dirt roads. From the entrance gate, Ike could see the cabin situated on one of the larger recreational lakes for which Park Lake was known for. The Street property was quite large, and its waterfront had its own cove. No neighbors anywhere in sight along the waterfront. *A perfect place for two lovers to meet clandestinely*, was Ike's first thought.

The convoy stopped. The officer and Street got out of their cars, unlocked the gate, and swung it open so everyone could drive in.

The cabin was made with wood siding, painted sea blue, and trimmed in white with a porch spanning the entire front. The porch had wooden rails, and several rocking chairs were in residence. It appeared to have been originally built to resemble the seaside quarters of a ship's captain, as there was a large ship's wheel hanging on the front of the building. The entire party parked, got out of their cars, and approached the front door. The lock appeared new and shiny, in contrast to all the other metal fixtures. Street fumbled through a large key ring with dozens of keys till he found the right one. He opened it unceremoniously and stepped in. Everyone followed. The entire cabin was decorated like the inside of a ship. A large stone fireplace was immediately visible when they stepped into the great room. There, on the mantel above, was the ship in a bottle. Ike could barely contain his excitement. He waited for Harbuck to give him a nod before he moved toward the mantel. Harbuck told the officer that Ike might know the whereabouts of some evidence in question, and then motioned for him to proceed. Ike went to the mantel and uncorked the bottle. He slipped his finger in. There was something there!

A rolled-up piece of paper. His fingertip found the distal end of the paper, and he pressed it against the side of the bottleneck and slowly pulled out the paper. Everyone gathered around as he unrolled it and then unfolded it. It was a handwritten letter signed "Lee." There was no letterhead or date.

Bruce,

Strange thing, you being the only person I wanted to write and tell about this. You—the only person who ever understood me. The only one who ever loved me for who I am. For a long time, you have been my only reason to go on living. I'm writing this to you because I want you to know that you had nothing to do with causing me to take my life. I had to write to you because I know that if anyone can understand the why, it would be you.

I should be telling everyone else. I should be telling the ones that hurt me. Maybe if I wrote to them, I could make them feel sorry for making me feel so bad. I thought about leaving them a note. But I don't want anyone to feel guilty. I don't want anyone to feel the way I feel. No one deserves that. Not even them.

I know how hard it has been for you to live our secret. I've shared that misery. Hiding ourselves away so no one in our families could ever feel humiliated or shamed. We always talked about moving away, finding a place where we could live together openly. We dreamed that dream, but it was not meant to be.

You know I've had reservations about our relationship because of my faith. Our love has made me feel so guilty, but not guilty enough to stay away. No one should have to feel guilty about love. That's not right. That tells me that I'm not right. Something's wrong with me and that guilt is now closing in, squeezing me from all directions. Like a thick fog I can't escape.

I have good reason to believe they know about us now. I've heard you say, "So what if they find out?" You might can bear that trial. I can't. We live in a world that doesn't respect our bond. And I no longer desire to live in such a world.

We've lived in exile these past seven years, on the remote island of this hideaway. But even here we've been afraid someone might come by and discover us. So, we put messages in this bottle, like castaways. That's a good word, for me anyway. Castaway. That's what it's felt like. I've been cast away.

Every time I came here these past seven years, the first thing I did when I arrived here was to put my finger in this bottle. When there was a note here, my heart would sing. It sang even if it was just a grocery list. Because I knew it came from you. And because we had this secret place, even though it was just the neck of a bottle, it was something we could share and a way we could meet and nobody else in the world would ever know about it. One place that was all ours.

This will be the last message we'll ever share in this way. I'm about to be rescued from the torture of my existence. And if God can forgive

me, I'll be waiting for you. Across my ocean of despair, on some tran-
scendent shore.

Forever yours,

Lee

After Ike finished reading the letter, he handed it to Street. Street read in silence, taking his time over every word. When he finished, his hand with the
letter fell to his side, and he looked off into space. Harbuck brought him around
by asking if he could see the letter. Street surrendered it without any protest.
Harbuck read enough to satisfy himself that it contained convincing language
for a suicide. Then he handed it to the sheriff and asked him to take it into custody as evidence.

Everyone stood around in silence, giving Street as much time as he needed.
After a few minutes, Patterson Street turned around and smiled, saying, "Well,
that about wraps it up, doesn't it, boys. Let's go home."

After Street locked up and everyone headed back to their cars, Ike waited
until Street got in his car and went over and tapped on the windshield.

"Pat, I'm sorry," Ike said. "I truly am. Whenever you're ready to hear who
pushed your brother over the edge, give me a call."

Chapter 43

On the way back to August Valley, Ike called Harbuck. Harbuck saw Ike's number on caller ID.

"Okay, Ike, who gets to tell Ismael first, you or me?" was the first thing out of Harbuck's mouth.

"Why don't we both tell him?" Ike suggested. "We know where he is. Are you headed to his house now?"

"Absolutely," Harbuck said. "I'm headed there as soon as we get back to town."

"Good," Ike said. "I'll be right behind you. It's great having the chance to finally be a bearer of good news."

"Amen to that," Harbuck said.

"How soon can you get the case dropped?" Ike asked.

"I'll file another motion for summary dismissal this afternoon. This one should stick. Since I've already done it once, the paperwork should be easy. Should be on Judge Preston's desk in the morning."

"Jim, the note was written to Bruce Massey," Ike said. "I know it's now critical evidence and all, but shouldn't we let Bruce see the note before it's shared with the world?"

"I can get a copy," Harbuck said. "Will that suffice for now?"

"Sure," Ike said. "I think I should deliver it personally. I'm not looking forward to that visit nearly as much as the one we're about to make."

All Harbuck could say was, "Understand that."

Ismael and Eisha were ecstatic when Harbuck told them.

They had many questions, mainly concerned with how soon they could get their lives back. The attorney informed them that, if there were no hitches in the legal system, the case would be dismissed in a day or so. No, he didn't think there would be any hitches. Then the media could be informed, and, hopefully, the dark cloud that had been hovering over the Hagarson home would dissipate. Harbuck suggested that Ismael give the news a chance to filter out for a few days before he appeared again in public. Ismael gave the attorney no argument on this.

After Harbuck had given Ismael and Eisha the opportunity to ask all their questions, he told them he needed to depart so he could get the legal proceedings underway. Ismael embraced the attorney and thanked him profusely for all he had done. Eisha expressed bountiful gratitude as well, but she confined hers to verbal expressions, keeping to her culture's norms regarding physical contact between the sexes.

After Harbuck left, Ike had a private moment of congratulations with the couple. Then he issued Ismael and Eisha an invitation to a celebration dinner at his house.

"Becky and I want your first trip out into the community to be to our home," Ike said. "As soon as Harbuck gives you the green light, we're going to have you over. We have so much to talk about. Right now, though, I know the two of you need to hold your own celebration and let your friends and family know the good news. I'm outta here."

The next afternoon Harbuck called Ike to let him know that all charges against Ismael had been dropped. He also informed Ike that he had obtained a copy of the suicide note. Ike could come by and pick it up anytime. Ike called Bruce and arranged a visit to Jacksonville the following day.

Ike located Bruce's residence from the address. Bruce lived on the twelfth floor of a waterfront high rise on the St. John's River. *He's done well for himself as a real-estate agent,* Ike thought as he surveyed the well-appointed lobby of the building. Ike took the elevator up and knocked.

"Ike, come in."

"Hello, Bruce."

"Just have a seat," Bruce said, motioning to the living area of his flat. "What can I get you to drink?"

"Just a soft drink for me," Ike said. "But please, feel free to pour yourself something stronger."

"Ginger ale okay?" Bruce asked.

"That would be great."

The large room had all-glass walls on two sides with a stunning view of both the river and the cityscape. Ike looked around. Furnished tastefully in a modernist style with plenty of chrome and glass, it was just what Ike would have expected in the digs of a middle-aged bachelor. *Bruce has a flair for decorating, or he hired someone who does,* he thought as he took in his surroundings. Ike took a seat on the white leather sofa and absorbed himself with the view while Bruce busied himself in the kitchen preparing drinks.

"I love your place here," Ike said in a voice loud enough to be heard into the kitchen. "What a view."

"We've been very happy here," Bruce said, "Muffy and I. Muffy may make an appearance in a few minutes. She's pretty shy around strangers."

About this time a long-haired white cat peered around the corner from a hallway.

"She's just appeared," Ike said. "Is she friendly?"

"Just let her come to you," Bruce said as he came in the room with a drink in each hand. "If you try to approach her, she'll run away. She won't scratch or anything. Just timid."

Bruce sat down, and the cat came and curled up in his lap.

"On the phone yesterday, you said you and the attorney found something at the cabin," Bruce said, opening the conversation to the topic foremost in both their minds.

Ike said nothing but merely reached in his pocket and pulled out a copy of the note from Lee Street. He handed it to Bruce.

Bruce unfolded the note, took a deep breath, and read.

When he'd finished, he calmly folded the note up and attempted to hand it back to Ike. Ike could not read the emotion on Bruce's face.

"No, it's yours to keep," Ike said, refusing to take the paper. "That's only a copy. We'll give you the original once all the legal proceedings are over."

"He said if anyone could understand the why, it would be me," Bruce said. "I wish I could say I did. Understand why he did this. But I can't say that I do. Not really. I can give you a whole list of the reasons Lee might have been depressed. He had some setbacks in his investments and in his business affairs. His family wouldn't listen to him and tried to make him be something he wasn't. He felt persecuted by the church every time the subject of homosexuality was raised. Then the city council started pressuring him to stop the sale of the store, when he had hopes that the money from that sale might help him right the ship. But to make him do this? To make anybody do this? It's hard for me to get my head around the idea of anyone destroying the precious gift of life."

"So, you really didn't see this coming?" Ike said. "The suicide, I mean. You said at our first meeting that you thought the city council might be blackmailing Lee by threatening to out him."

"Lee and I talked about that," Bruce said. "I'd been trying to persuade Lee to go away with me for some time. To get the hell away from that toxic situation he found himself in with his family, the community, his financial affairs, and his church. But he just wouldn't do it. The hole just kept getting deeper and deeper, and even when I offered him a rope, he couldn't—or wouldn't—climb out."

"You were offering him a lifeline—including financial support—and he couldn't bring himself to take it?" Ike asked.

"I've done pretty well for myself," Bruce said. "I'm not rich, but I've got enough saved that I could've supported us. But Lee was too proud. His brothers were enormously successful in business, and Lee was determined to prove that he could be as well. Things didn't work out as well for him. He still had his part of the family business that he could fall back on, but Lee would never go to his family and ask for help. He was just too prideful."

"Going away with you would have been like admitting defeat," Ike said. "From a financial standpoint, I mean."

"That's exactly it," Bruce said. "Lee said he dreamed about us going away together one day as well. But he wanted to do it on his terms. To leave victoriously. Not in disgrace."

"The machinations of the city council were a double whammy to Lee's dream," Ike said as he took up the thread of Massey's thought process. "He took their words to mean they might expose his sexual orientation. But by going along and not selling the property, he then saw no way out of his financial predicament."

"You've got it," Bruce said. "I knew Lee was depressed about all this. I just didn't know how depressed. I should have known. Lee was right about one thing. I did understand him better than anyone. But I didn't understand him well enough to see this coming."

With those words, Bruce's composure broke and he started sobbing uncontrollably.

Ike arrived back in August Valley late that afternoon. He didn't normally read the newspaper, preferring to get his news online. But today he wanted a hard copy. He stopped at the first convenience store he saw that had a vending machine outside.

There, printed in large letters, was the headline he hoped to see.

"ALL CHARGES DROPPED IN STREET CASE."

And under that, it read:

"August Valley University professor cleared after suicide note found."

Ike immediately phoned Becky.

"Seen the paper?" he asked her.

"Yep," Becky said. "I've got a half-dozen copies sitting on my desk here at the office. Everyone brought one in, wanting to talk about it. We aren't getting much work done today."

"You don't mind, do you?" Ike asked.

"Not a bit. How did things go with Bruce today?"

"The guy was all broken up, as you might imagine. He gave me a little more clarity on why Street decided to off himself. I'll tell you all about it when we get home. When do you want to have Ismael and Eisha over?"

"Friday night works for me," Becky said. "I know we said we wanted them to make our house their first outing, but I'd rather wait till it's not a school night. They would probably prefer that as well."

"I'll call now and invite them," Ike said.

The next evening the call Ike was hoping for but not expecting came. *He would pick now to call me*, Ike thought as he glanced down at the caller ID on his cell. Ike was in the middle of a contentious board meeting at the church. The repairs to the church building had been completed over a week ago, and everything had been paid for, but now the board was split on what to do with the surplus of monies that the church had received to take care of the damage from the vandalism. When Ike realized who the caller was, he excused himself from the meeting and stepped outside.

"Hello."

"Ike, this is Patterson Street. Hope I'm not catching you at a bad time."

"No, Pat, now is fine. What can I do for you?"

"You said something about knowing who pushed my brother over the edge. I'd like to hear more about that if you're willing to share what you know with me."

"Sure, we can talk, Pat," Ike said. "How about tomorrow morning?"

"Okay," Street said. "Where?"

"How about here? At my church? Say around nine a.m.?"

"I'll see you there," Street said and hung up.

Ike went back into the meeting, but he wasn't much good to the board in working out the money issue. His thoughts were on steeling himself for what he was going to attempt in the morning.

Chapter 44

The next morning Street walked into Ike's office like he owned the place. *No wonder this guy is so successful at business,* Ike thought. *He can intimidate the hell out of anyone, just by the way he walks into a room.* But today Ike knew he had the upper hand. He had information that Street didn't and couldn't acquire by any of the formidable means at his disposal. Street might be daunting, Ike admitted, but he was at a disadvantage in this conversation. And Ike wanted to make sure Street stayed that way. Rehearsing what he was going to say and anticipating every response he might hear had kept Ike from sleep most of last night.

"Come in, Pat," Ike said cheerfully. "Welcome to the Unitarian Universalist Church. I didn't think I'd ever live long enough to see you come through our doors."

"You won't," Street shot back. "Not for a church service. Or whatever it is you call what you do here. If you'll just tell me whatever it is you think you know, then I'll be on my way."

"Now, Pat," Ike said, "I'm afraid you might have been misled. I don't know anything. All I've got is hearsay. Certainly nothing that might hold up in a court of law. But it comes from a fairly reliable source, though it's a source that I'm not at liberty to reveal."

"So that's how you're going to play this," Street said. "I might have known you wouldn't shoot straight with me. Anyone who would split up a church by manipulating people the way you did and insisting on having things your way. I shouldn't be surprised you'd call me here to spread more gossip. I haven't got time for this," Street said as he rose from his chair.

"Relax, Pat," Ike said, starting to relax himself but still guarding his words. "Let me just tell you what happened. Then you can do with it whatever you like."

"Well, what is it?" Street said impatiently.

"The city council had an unofficial meeting with Lee a few days before his death," Ike said. "They had some concerns about Lee selling the department store down on Main Street to the Muslims. I imagine you already knew this and knew some people were concerned about a mosque springing up in downtown August Valley."

"Yeah, that's not news," Street said. "Lots of people in this town are against having a mosque here. It doesn't surprise me the city council would try to discourage it."

"Do you think it was right for the city council to use its influence to coerce a citizen into discriminating against someone?" Ike asked.

"No," Street said. "I don't think that's right. But the city council doing something like that doesn't surprise me. There are some real sleazebags on that council. Believe me; I've had my share of run-ins with them. Now, truth be known, I don't have any particular affection for the Muslims either. But they're here, they're citizens, and as long as they behave themselves, they deserve to be treated just like everyone else."

"I'm glad to hear you say that," Ike said. That was the sentiment he had hoped to hear Street express. "So, if the Muslims still wanted to purchase the property, you would have no problem selling it to them?"

"Not really," Street said. "As long as they were willing to pay the asking price and their credit was good, fine with me."

"Muslims don't use credit, Pat. They pay in cash."

"All the better," Street said. "I like doing business that way."

"I'd really like to see the Muslims get the site for their mosque," Ike said. "And what I hear you saying is that you don't have a problem with it."

"Yes, yes," Street said. "What are you driving at, Ike?"

"Well, in that meeting with the council, one of the members of the council said to Lee, 'This sale brings up a lot of issues for us. We want you to give it a lot of thought before you proceed. We wouldn't want this to result in any damage to your reputation.'"

"They blackmailed him," Street said.

"That was my take on it as well," Ike said.

"Who said that to Lee?" Street asked.

"I don't know," Ike said. "All I can tell you is the gossip I heard from my fairly reliable source that I won't divulge."

"Understood," Street said.

"Jones. Jerry Jones."

"Sounds just like something that son of a bitch would say," Street said angrily. "I'll take the whole lot of them to court for doing this to my brother."

"You're free to do whatever you want with this information," Ike said. "But my legal sources tell me such action won't go anywhere."

"Don't worry," Street said. "I've got lots of other ways I can deal with them."

"I sort of get the feeling you're not too fond of the present city council," Ike said.

"You have a gift for understatement," Street replied.

"I know how you can get back at them." Ike suggested.

"How?" Street asked.

"See that the mosque gets built," Ike said.

Chapter 45

Friday night, as Ike and Becky welcomed Ismael and Eisha into their home, Ismael handed Ike a gift wrapped in bright-blue foil paper. "This is a little token of our appreciation for all that you and Becky have done for us these past several weeks."

"Thank you, brother," Ike said, accepting the gift.

"It'll take me a while to get used to you calling me that," Ismael said.

"Let's all go in the living room," Becky said, gesturing to the room that opened up beyond the foyer. "Everything will be okay in the kitchen for a few minutes while we talk."

After everyone sat down, Ike handed the present to Becky. "Honey, why don't you do the honors?"

Becky unwrapped the package. It was a cookbook entitled *A Taste of Bangladesh*.

"Oh, thank you, Eisha and Ismael," Becky said. "Is the recipe for the biryani in here?"

"Yes, and lots of Gera's other recipes," Eisha said. "She wrote it."

Becky had not taken notice of who the author of the cookbook was. Now she looked at the cover more closely. Gera Hagarson was the author. And below her name it said "with Eisha Hagarson."

"You!" Becky exclaimed. "And Gera. The two of you wrote a cookbook together."

"The recipes were all Gera's," Eisha said. "I just helped her compile and edit them. Plus, add a few comments in the introduction to the book."

"I'm amazed," Becky said, looking at the book with more intense interest. "And impressed. The two of you did such a good job on this. This is really professional quality."

"We had a lot of help and encouragement," Eisha said. "Gera's boyfriend, Rafi, the one she was in the car with when she died—when they both died—was a restauranteur. He had a couple of Bangladeshi restaurants in New York City. They met at a Bangladeshi food event, and he was so impressed with Gera's recipes that he started using them in his restaurants. And he suggested she put them together in a book. Which she—that is, we—did. Then he helped promote it. He knew Gera would be a great persona to promote both the books and his restaurants. He was right. Gera is master of that mysterious quality called 'presence.'"

"My mother would've started a restaurant of her own," Ismael added. "But as you might imagine, there's not much of a market for Bangladeshi food here in August Valley. She wasn't about to pick up and move to a big city. She'd made a life here and had her career managing the hotels."

"How interesting," Ike said, taking the book and looking it over. "Has the book done well?"

"It was a big hit in the Bangladeshi community in New York. There are over fifty thousand Bengalis there. I think every one of them bought a cookbook," Eisha said with a laugh. "Otherwise we couldn't have reached the sales we have."

"New York has by far the largest concentration of Bangladeshi immigrants," Ismael added. A smattering of others here and there, New Jersey, Detroit, North Carolina—where Eisha and I went to university and met. But the borough of Queens, New York—that's what you have to see. There's this area, Bangladesh Plaza, where you'd think you were in downtown Dhaka. All restaurants and shops are Bengali, and there's always one of our cultural events going on. Eisha and I go there on vacation frequently. That brings us to the second part of our gift. Eisha and I want to take you with us this fall to New York City. To see and experience it and take you to the restaurant that serves Gera's recipes."

"You mean the restaurant's still there?" Ike asked. "Even though Rafi is dead?"

"His family kept the restaurants going," Ismael said. "They're still doing quite well. Even without Rafi and Gera. Their presence lives on through the food, you might say."

"Wow, thank you so much," Becky said. "I can't wait. A chance to really be immersed in my half brother-in-law's culture."

"Yes, thank you," Ike added. "We need to get the dates you have in mind for doing this and put it on our calendar."

"The weekend of October seventh," Ismael said. "There's a big festival then."

"I think we can work that out," Ike said, looking at Becky, who nodded in assent.

"Eisha, I could use some help in the kitchen," Becky said. "Our fare is going to be pretty plain compared to Bangladeshi dishes. Just plain old American-style beef stew. Cooking is just not my forte."

"I'm sure it will be wonderful," Eisha said. "Ismael and I like most American food also. We just stay away from the barbecue and pork chops," she added with a grin.

"Of course, no pork," Becky said, as they were walking out of the room. "We'll always be very careful about that when we have you over. Pork isn't healthy anyway."

"Ismael, when are they going to allow you to return to work?" Ike asked.

"Monday," Ismael said. "Got word today from the department head. I'm looking forward to things getting back to normal."

"And your pay for these past eight weeks?" Ike asked.

"I've still been getting paid. It was considered a leave of absence with pay."

"Good," Ike said. "What will you say to your students? I'm sure they'll have questions."

"I'll make some joke about finally being absolved of being a terrorist and move on. Though I'll also warn them that they might want the charges reinstated when they get their next exam."

"Cute," Ike said. "Sounds like a good way to deal with the issue and get it out of the way. What about things with you and the Muslim community?"

"That's going to be a more difficult matter," Ismael said. "Some of them are still reluctant to associate with me. Maybe it just needs time. Can you believe this, Ike? Some of them still say the murder accusation was all my fault because I lost my temper over the sale of Street's property."

"You weren't being meek and submissive," Ike said. "That's so easy for them to say in retrospect. You were standing up for the right to be treated fairly. Standing up for the rights of all Muslims to be treated like anyone else. And this is the thanks you get."

"I'm not going to make a big deal of it," Ismael said. "With time, it'll blow over. But the whole experience, the reaction of the Muslim community—my friends—has made me a little more circumspect."

"What do you mean?" Ike asked.

"I don't look at being a Muslim the same," Ismael said. "Before this, before my arrest, I took being a Muslim as a given. As a part of my identity. With that, I took for granted that I'd always have the support of my community. Being a Muslim, following Islam, was being a part of something larger than myself. I didn't question things about Islam too much. There wasn't much need to. There was my life as a Muslim, and then there was the world outside of Islam where I lived in American society and had my career. For the most part, I was left alone to do those things without me being a Muslim interfering. This incident has forced me to do exactly the opposite. To examine the extent to which the Muslim community allows me to be an American citizen and a political scientist. To ask questions. To be me. And it's not that the community didn't allow me. They did. But there was resistance. Before the arrest, I could just ignore the Muslim tendency toward mindless submission. But the events of the past two months forced me to take a deeper look at how my community functions and what I believe.

"The truth is not as simple as my community makes it out to be," Ismael continued. "The truth is complex. It requires us to question, to use our faculties of reason. To sometimes dissent and even get angry. In Islam, it's called *ijtihad*. It actually comes from the same root word, *jihad*, 'to struggle.' But ijtihad is not like jihad, like the violent struggle of war; instead, it's the struggle to understand ourselves and the world by being reflective, by using our faculties of reason and common sense.

"It makes most Muslims uncomfortable, but it's something our community has got to do if we are going to live civilly and peaceably in the world of the twenty-first century.

"Maybe I'm losing my faith. Maybe I'm no longer a true follower of Islam. I don't know. Some in my community will say I'm not, if I continue to talk like this. All I know is I can't go back to the way things were. Always accepting at face value what the imams say and what the tradition says. I can't do that anymore."

"You're growing up, Ismael," Ike said. "Spiritually, I mean. You're taking some courageous steps that have to be taken in any faith tradition to develop and become a more complete spiritual being. You're now willing to suffer the pain of challenge by examining the givens of your religion. That's always risky. Many people will resist that. God knows I've experienced my share of such resistance from the church of my upbringing, of my father and mother. But that hasn't made me unfaithful. On the contrary, because I've had the courage to ask questions, I've been strengthened in my convictions and in my faith. I hear the same thing happening to you, from what you're telling me. In your desire for truth, real truth, truth that can be real for you in the real world, you've dared to question Islam. I suspect this makes you a better Muslim, not a lesser one."

"What you're saying makes a lot of sense," Ismael said. "I've never thought about it in quite that way. But I'm beginning to see the need to. Not only for my sake, but for the sake of all Muslims."

"For the sake of all people, regardless of their religion," Ike said. "Regardless even if they don't have a religion."

"Thinking in this way puts all people everywhere sort of in the same boat," Ismael said. "Everybody needs to believe in something, some religion or something greater than themselves to guide their lives. But at the same time, everyone needs to be able to think critically about it. Question it. Not just be at the mercy of the human leadership of our religious institutions."

"Exactly," Ike said.

Then, after a pause, Ike changed the subject. "Ismael, I want to tell you something. Now might not be the best time, but then again, it's probably as good a time as any. I talked with Street. Patterson Street, that is, the brother of Lee, the one who now controls the fate of the store down on Main Street. He says he's willing to sell it to you. And I have good reason to believe the city council won't give you any more trouble. You still interested?"

"Ike, what have you been up to?" Ismael asked, as he gazed at Ike with impressive regard. "Patterson Street is a formidable man. Not easily persuaded by anyone or anything. How'd you manage to get such a concession from him?"

"Let's just say I was privy to some information about his brother's death," Ike said, rather deviously. "That's how I got his ear. But selling the property is strictly a business decision. He has no use for it. And you do. Your community does. Simply business from Street's perspective."

"And how do you know the city council won't continue to make it difficult for us?" Ismael asked.

"Because Street won't put up with their shenanigans," Ike said. "As you just said, Patterson Street is a formidable man. The council can't push him around the way they did Lee. If Patterson wants the deal done, then it'll get done."

"Okay," Ismael said. "I'll pass the word to the board at the masjid. They will probably still be interested."

"But you're not going to be a part of it?" Ike asked.

"I don't think anyone can fault me for bowing out," Ismael said. "Considering."

"I guess not," Ike said. "But you did all the heavy lifting. Surely they'll recognize that, won't they?"

"Maybe," Ismael said. "I don't need any pats on the back. I would like to see it happen, though. It's only right. Inshallah. God willing, it will happen."

At this point the women reentered the room.

"Dinner is served," Becky said.

Chapter 46

November 2016

"So, you and Ismael are half brothers?" Harbuck asked, as he fussed with the insulating sleeve on his Starbucks coffee cup.

"Yep," Ike said, pausing to take a sip of his cappuccino. "We began getting clues when Ismael was in jail. That was when he told me about his mother coming here as a refugee and being welcomed to this country by my parents. Then both of us started digging through our parents' stuff, letters and things, and figured out that my father must have had an affair with his mother, Gera. Ismael and I totally convinced ourselves of this based on the evidence we uncovered. But our wives weren't convinced. Eisha and Becky kept on prodding us, so we finally sent our DNA samples off and had them tested. And sure enough, we share half our genes."

"Good thing no one knew this when Ismael was arrested," Harbuck said. "If they had, everyone would've thought you just made up that story about Street and the homosexuality and his guilt just so you could get your brother off the hook."

"Yeah, it's funny how everything turned out," Ike said. "Think about this. If Ismael hadn't been indicted for murder, we'd probably never have discovered we were brothers. Or that we actually like one another."

"You're brothers that actually get along," Harbuck said. "That's pretty amazing too."

"Well, we have so far. Ismael, me, and our wives went to New York City together last month. There's this little Bangladesh community right there in Queens. We had a great time together. It's been fun learning about this sibling of mine and getting immersed in his exotic culture. I'm also learning a lot about his religion."

"And getting pretty involved with it too, I understand," Harbuck said. "I hear the mosque project is back on track."

"The Islamic community closed on the property last week," Ike said. "They hope to have the renovations done by next spring."

"Patterson Street agreed to sell it to them," Harbuck said. "Never thought that would happen."

"Street wasn't so hard to persuade," Ike said mischievously. "Just a matter of using an approach he could understand."

"From what I hear, you had a hand in that persuasion, too," Harbuck said with a grin. "Tell me, how'd you go from the top of Patterson Street's hit list to being his best buddy?"

"Patterson's a great fellow," Ike said. "He just wanted to do what was right. For the community and for the Muslims."

"I'm going have to call bullshit on that one," Harbuck said. "Patterson Street hasn't got an altruistic bone in his body. You want to try that again, sport?"

"Okay, okay," Ike yielded to Harbuck's protest. "I learned what the 'good reason to believe they know about us now' was that Lee Street mentioned in his suicide note and what pushed Lee over the edge and onto the end of a rope. Patterson became a little kindlier disposed toward me once I shared that information with him. Oh, and I suggested to him that selling the property might infuriate the city council. For some reason, he seemed to take to that suggestion."

Harbuck chuckled. "You played ol' Patterson pretty well, I'd say. That is, if your ultimate goal was to see the mosque built."

"Once Ismael and I got to be friends, supporting his cause was a no-brainer," Ike said. "Even though I'm a Unitarian and support the cause of religious freedom, initially that was a tough one for me. I didn't think I could ever be supportive of a Muslim after losing a good friend named Josh in 9/11. But becoming friends with a Muslim made the difference. A huge difference. Supporting a mosque here in August Valley now is just an extension of supporting my friend. And my brother.

"You know, Jim, Islam was no more responsible for Josh's death than it was for Lee Street's. Josh was killed by Islamic extremism—Islamic fundamentalism. Street was killed by Christian fundamentalism. Those bigoted Christian fundamentalists that expend all their energies sifting through the Bible so they can find ways to condemn people who are different, like gays, and totally ignore the spirit of the great commandment to love others as self. That's been my one great lesson from this whole miserable ordeal. Fundamentalism kills. Fundamentalism of any kind. Narrow-minded, simplistic thinking that allows no room for honoring and respecting the life experiences of others."

"I can't disagree with that verdict," Harbuck said. "In spirit, anyway, Street might have killed himself. But his community and his church put the noose around his neck. It's a pretty sad state of affairs."

"Change comes slowly when it comes to changing the way people think," Ike said. "But there's hope. After all, Patterson Street came around. And this town is getting a mosque. Who knows, we may even get Patterson to come to the dedication ceremony."

Harbuck whistled and said, "May the saints preserve us."

Chapter 47

March 2017

The weather cooperated perfectly. A cloudless spring day greeted those who came to town for the masjid dedication. Spring came early this year, and, as if on cue, the azaleas proudly displayed their pastels of red and purple. There was only the slightest hint of winter in the late March breeze upsetting the white blossoms of the dogwood trees that lined Main Street.

After completing the sale of the property, Street had let certain people in influential positions of city government know of his support for the masjid project. Ike had no way of knowing if that was why the Islamic community had pulled off the permitting and building process with so few hitches. No reports ever surfaced in the local news to suggest Street had ever played the ace he had up his sleeve to persuade Jerry Jones and the city council to go along.

For Ismael's part, he passed on Ike's news about the property being on the market again to the board of trustees of the masjid. It surprised Ike to learn that the imam was not included in the decision-making process about the property or the building project. As Ismael explained the governance of the American masjid, the board makes all the administrative decisions. Imams are only religious leaders. They lead prayers and teach. The board does the heavy lifting when it comes to executive decisions and running the financial affairs.

Ismael had also followed through on what he told Ike in deciding not to take any part in the sale of the property. But he did remain as chairman of the masjid project committee. In that role, he pushed for some structural modifications that would give the women equal space in the facility, as well as their own entrance and equal access. These initiatives met with stiff resistance, but in the end they were accepted, in large measure due to his leadership. When Ismael explained his part in the process to Ike, and his determination to see that these things became a part of the project, he justified his actions with a quote from the Quran: "God does not change the condition of a people until they change what is inside themselves." Ismael said he wanted, in some small way, for his community to show God that they were reflective about their actions in the world and were willing to be agents for change. For equal treatment and inclusivity.

Ismael got his inspiration for this inclusive stance from the story of Asra Nomani. She was one of four Muslim women who recently staged a pray-in at the Islamic Center in Washington, DC, by praying in the men's section of the mosque. The police had to be summoned by mosque officials to remove the women. Nomani considered the segregation of women in mosques a symptom of a much larger problem—the subjugation and marginalization of women. The problem, in her estimation, is one of interpretation of the tradition, and she took her protest into the prayer hall of the mosque. She considered the segregation of women in prayer as symptom of a much larger problem, a harbinger..."A harbinger of practices that enable honor killings, suicide bombings, and violence." Risking ostracism and arrest, she took a stand to preserve her integrity as a both a Muslim and a woman.

The architect hired by the masjid project committee made some fortuitous choices that contributed to the city's acceptance of the project. He suggested only minor alterations to the exterior facade of the building. The glass front was replaced with solid walls. But other than the gold gilding on the trim work and the arabesque patterns embossed on the panels of the entrance way, there was little else to suggest what the building was now housing.

The inside of the building was a different story. Having the large, open, rectangular shell of a former department store to work with gave the architect complete freedom to lay out the interior much the same as a traditional mosque. In the center was the large prayer hall. The entrance area was partitioned from the prayer hall, and the walls were lined with shoe bins. Entering worshippers next encountered the ablution area and bathrooms used for the ritual washing before offering prayers. Situated along the other three outside walls of the large rectangular structure were the service areas, which were divided into smaller classrooms, a library, a kitchen, and a nursery. A common feature to all mosques is something called the *mihrab*, which is a niche in a wall where the direction to Mecca is indicated. Muslims align their bodies in the *quibla*, the geographic direction toward Mecca, when they pray.

The Islamic community wanted to honor Ike for the role he had played in proving Ismael's innocence and in facilitating the renewal of the masjid project. They asked him to take part in the dedication ceremony. This was a first for Ike, and he was, as might be expected, nervous about what he should say. He researched mosque dedications and, to his surprise, discovered that President Eisenhower took part in the dedication ceremony for the Islamic Center in Washington in 1957. The speech Eisenhower gave on that occasion is a marvelous paean to the American ideals of equality and religious tolerance. Ike studied the speech given by his namesake and used it as an outline in crafting some of his own remarks:

Board members of the Islamic Center, distinguished guests of the larger Islamic community, citizens of August Valley, brothers and sisters.

I am indeed honored and humbled by this opportunity to stand before you on this day, a day filled with promise for the Muslim citizens of August Valley and filled with hope for a brighter, healthier future for the larger community of August Valley. The writer Carlos Fuentes said, "People that live in isolation perish and it's only people that give things to one another that thrive, that live. I think having an identity means that you can accept challenges and influences from everywhere." The people of August Valley accepted the challenge to overcome the isolation that religious institutions sometimes create and claim their identity as a people of goodwill and as a people with the foresight and determination to lay a lasting foundation for cooperation and peace.

The structure and the institution we are here to dedicate for the use of and service to our community today is quintessentially American. The idea that people in this country are free to worship as they choose is what makes us who we are as a nation, and this structure stands as a testament that those ideals are still alive and well. While we are here today to dedicate and celebrate this wonderful edifice and honor the hard work and determination of those who turned a vision into reality, let us also honor the values and ideals that made its construction possible. The courage to transcend our individual differences is what advanced citizenship in the United States is about. Today we are witnesses to the fruit borne by the vision and courage of the leaders both of the Islamic community and of our great city.

I consider it a great honor to take part in the opening of this Islamic Center, and I wish peace and blessings on all who enter here.

Ismael and the imam were among the others who spoke at the dedication. The mayor of August Valley was also invited three months in advance but declined due to a "previous engagement."

At the reception following the ceremony, Ismael and Eisha conversed with Ike and Becky.

"You got it done," Ike said to Ismael. "Congrats. The mosque is beautiful."

"With the help of Allah," Ismael said. "And Patterson Street," he added with a wink. "There's no way this would've happened if it had been left up to me and the means at my disposal."

"I hear what you're saying, Ismael," Ike said. "In the Christian tradition, there's a saying, 'God moves in mysterious ways, his wonders to perform.' Everything that's happened in the past year has been part of a great mystery. A mystery that is larger than we are."

"That's a beautiful saying," Eisha said.

"Yes, that's lovely," Becky agreed.

"I'm thinking what Gera wrote on that little piece of paper forty-five years ago is just as timely today as it was then," Ike said. "'God has heard our affliction.' Ismael, you were named appropriately. This community really needed someone like you to come along and for this to somehow, mysteriously, be made to happen."

Chapter 48

Ike found the new stone with his mother's name. Sarah Street Benheart. A few weeds had sprung up around his father's, missed by the perpetual care staff of the cemetery. Ike resolved to start being more attentive to the plots. He thought for a moment about how to work periodic visits to the graves into his schedule, some kind of routine like his visits to his mother when she was at the nursing home.

"Mom, life's been eventful since you died. I found out that I have a brother. Ismael, Gera's son, was fathered by your husband, Abe. My father.

"I know there's no love lost between you and Gera because of this. You made your feelings about Gera perfectly clear. You're justified in your feelings. Dad was unfaithful to you. You have every reason to be angry about that.

"Now that all three of you are gone, there's no way for those of us who remain in this world to know exactly what happened way back when. What led to the affair. The pregnancy. But we're the ones that have to pick up the pieces now. The three of you unconsciously formed some unspoken pact to keep this information from your children. Keep this great secret.

"I do know this. It's no good that way. Ismael and I, our wives, our children, have to live with your actions, your decisions, and the guilt that was silently transferred to us in a thousand tiny ways. You might have been the innocent victim forty-six years ago, Mom, but you chose never to tell me, even when I became an adult. So, that makes you guilty, too. You were an unwitting accomplice in this conspiracy of silence.

"Your family has to find some way forward. I will tell Jake everything I know about his grandfather and grandmother when I think he is old enough to understand. I'll do this not because I'm proud of this, or ashamed, or guilty. I'll do it just because it is a part of our family history. Whether we talk about it or not, it's still a part of who we are. At least if we acknowledge it openly, it gives us a chance to own it.

"To the best of my ability, I've forgiven Dad, and I've forgiven Gera. Maybe forgiveness is not exactly the right word, because no matter what wounds they inflicted on our family, their affair produced a wonderful human being. I can't feel sorry for that. If there is any sort of afterlife, or life beyond time, I hope you can find it in your heart to forgive Gera too. She suffered in unspeakable ways from the war. If any human being deserves an extra extension of grace, it's her.

"Jake now knows that he has an uncle. He was already friends with Bai, Ismael's son, his cousin, even before we discovered this great secret. And Jake is developing a good relationship with Ismael. It's a good thing, Mom. They're good for each other. Ismael is quite the amateur astronomer. Jake has a budding interest in the stars. He's often at their house late when it's not a school night.

"The next generation will be a little less estranged from each other. East can meet West. The people of God are all one family. Literally, that is, in our case. I've no idea how all this would have worked out had we known of our kinship growing up. But for now, living our lives in light of this knowledge has been a good thing.

"Your cousins, Patterson, Gordon, and Lee, have also made my life interesting in the past few weeks. Even though they sort of disowned me when I went astray religiously in their eyes, there's some hopeful signs I may one day be welcomed back into the fold. At least with Patterson I think I'm getting there.

"But Lee is dead. He was gay, Mom, and the church heaped so much guilt on him he couldn't take it anymore. Took his own life. Well, he's at peace now. But what a terrible way to find relief. I'm wondering if the church will ever learn to love the way Jesus loved? We can only hope, I suppose.

"I love you, Mom."

Acknowledgments

I want to thank Gary Moss and Fatina Bisat for reading early drafts of this manuscript and making many constructive suggestions.

Author Biography

Fred Howard is the minister of the Unitarian Church of Valdosta, Georgia. He has also published *Transforming Faith: Stories of Change from a Lifelong Spiritual Seeker*, which won the Nautilus Book Award.

Howard was born and raised in Macon, Georgia. He studied at Valdosta State College and the Medical College of Georgia and spent twenty years practicing medicine. Howard then chose a new calling and graduated from the Candler School of Theology at Emory University in 2006. He spent a year in the clinical pastoral education program at Emory Hospital and was ordained by the Christian Universalist Association.

Howard lives with his wife, Kathy, in Valdosta. They have three children, Mandy, Misty, and Dustin, and seven grandchildren.

The author welcomes feedback on the story. He can be contacted through the book's website at www.childrenofcovenant.weebly.com.

CPSIA information can be obtained
at www.ICGtesting.com
Printed in the USA
LVHW111521011119
636084LV00002B/381/P